The Wayward Path

by

Mark Love

The Wayward Path

Cover Art by *Debbie Taylor*

The Wild Rose Press, Inc.
PO Box 708
Adams Basin, NY 14410-0708
Visit us at www.thewildrosepress.com

Publishing History
First Edition, 2022
Trade Paperback ISBN 978-1-5092-4219-1
Digital ISBN 978-1-5092-4220-7

Published in the United States of America

My left arm felt funny. A glance at my weapon confirmed it was empty. I pulled the fresh clip from the shoulder holster and managed to load it. I fumbled my left hand in place and racked the slide, sending a fresh shell into the pipe. Bringing the gun up, I pushed off the tree and got to my feet.

The gunslinger was slowly advancing in my direction. With the angle he was taking, the tree wouldn't do me any good. He lowered his left hand and shoved the gun into a pocket of his jacket. An evil grin crossed his face.

"Don't need that one anymore. Now it's just down to you and me. You're screwed. You are just so stupid that you don't realize it yet."

My gun was pointed at his core. He was only fifteen feet away. "Doubt I could miss from here."

He rapped knuckles against his chest. "Body armor."

I didn't move.

"Latest and greatest, so they say. Can stop a shot from an elephant gun."

"You're assuming I'll shoot for center mass."

"Of course. That's what they teach you Boy Scouts." He started to bring his right hand up to bear on me. "This shit is state of the art. There's nothing…"

Tilting my weapon slightly, I fired twice, striking him in the forehead. He flopped backward on the ground. I walked over and kicked his gun underneath the Pontiac's rear wheels.

"Never was a Boy Scout."

Dedication

For Kim

Acknowledgments

One of my favorite parts about writing stories such as this is the opportunity to connect with people who have expertise in various fields. As Bill Nye (the Science Guy) said, "Everyone you will ever meet knows something you don't."

I keep that in mind because you never can tell when that connection may present itself and give me the opportunity to take the story in a new direction. Most people are willing to share some information about a topic they are knowledgeable or passionate about. Some may do it in the hopes that once I have answers to those questions, I will leave them alone.

So this is my chance to express a note of thanks for your help.

Susan Stejskal from Cimex Detector Canine Services who graciously shared the details for a human remains dog and handler.

Eric Berger, a true Civil War expert, who provided tales of reenactments, equipment and battles.

And to Kim Love, Helene Love Snell, Mary Morehouse, Olivia Sholtis and Jerry Sorn, who read earlier drafts of this book. Their input was essential to helping me craft a better story.

Any mistakes are mine.

Other Wild Rose Press Titles by Mark Love

Why 319? – A Jefferson Chene Mystery, Book 1
Your Turn to Die – A Jefferson Chene Mystery, Book 2

Chapter One

Olivia Sholtis focused her gaze on the camera as she spoke into the stick microphone. "Blighted houses are the bumper crops of a distressed city. Over the years more and more abandoned homes have dotted Detroit neighborhoods that had once been prosperous, well-maintained dwellings filled with families of all sizes. The exodus started in the 1950s when white residents began moving to the suburbs for improved living conditions, quality schools and better public services. Three decades later, the middle-class blacks followed in their footsteps.

"Rental houses in these areas remained unwanted. Squatters would come and go. Crack houses sprang up, driving property values down in a nasty, rapid spiral. There was always talk about the city developing a plan to address the problem. Too many neighborhoods fell victim to the situation to accommodate an easy fix." Olivia waited while Myles, the cameraman, finished panning the block of desolate homes.

"Now the mayor has been able to obtain funding from the federal government. Working on one quadrant at a time, blighted houses that had long been abandoned or taken over by squatters are scheduled to be torn down. The intent is to clear out these eyesores, haul away the crap and clutter and let the rebuilding begin. Hopefully, the funding would sustain it and draw people back to the city, bringing energy, enthusiasm, and their money," Olivia said.

She paused while Myles turned his attention to a cluster of police cars. The producer's voice sounded softly in the earbud. Olivia resumed her comments for the voiceover. "Channel Four is exclusively covering today's activity. Representatives from several law enforcement agencies and fire departments will be utilizing this abandoned neighborhood for training purposes. Cadets from local fire academies will also have the opportunity to gain firsthand experience as two designated structures are scheduled to be burned down."

Olivia described the scene. Two Detroit Police Department squad cars blocked the access from the main road. Four uniformed officers manned the barricade, making sure only those with authorization were getting close to the activities. Three weeks ago, no car could have navigated this road. It had been a dumping ground. Battered furniture and torn mattresses overflowed from the scrub lawns into the street. Rusty appliances, their panels dotted with bullet holes, leaned precariously against lampposts and tree trunks. Bald tires, some with the wheels still intact, clogged the rainwater from reaching the sewer grates.

Heavy equipment was brought in to remove it all. Local contractors were anxious to start the demolition work. Scavengers had already removed anything of value from the buildings. The utilities had long been disconnected.

In the middle of the block was a small gathering. Sheriff deputies, uniformed officers and detectives were clustered around a short woman with a dog on a leash.

The dog sat calmly beside her. She wore heavy boots and the brown uniform of a county sheriff's deputy. The name tag read Scanlon. Olivia managed to become part of the group.

"What kind of dog is that?" a lieutenant asked.

"Springer spaniel. His name is Buzz." The dog perked up when she spoke. Scanlon reached down to scratch between his ears.

"So, he's a cadaver dog?" another cop asked.

The woman bristled. "It's really human remains detection. Sometimes there isn't a cadaver, but trace elements are found."

"No offense." The cop gave her a thin smile. "I've never worked with a dog before. So do you just let him run?"

"No, I keep Buzz on a leash. We'll work the buildings together."

"Anything we need to do?" Lieutenant Chalmers asked.

Scanlon considered it. "There are twelve houses on each side of the block. If you want everyone to see Buzz in action, you could coordinate the groups."

The detective took charge and soon clusters of people had gathered. He sent each group to wait in front of a building. Olivia hung back, chatting with a group. Myles followed behind, still recording as Scanlon gave Buzz a command and guided him toward the first house. Half a dozen people followed. They watched without comment while the dog scouted the overgrown yard and the first floor of the building. It took time for him to check each room, hesitating on occasion near the remnants of a mouse or bird. Thirty minutes later he cleared the house.

The process was repeated with another set of spectators. Olivia drifted between groups. Slowly the dog worked his way along the block. Behind him, crews were starting the demolition work. Gas-powered saws added to the noise. Buzz was able to ignore the distractions and continue. Scanlon followed him into the third house. That's when his behavior changed.

It was subtle. But they had worked together long enough for Scanlon to recognize it. She waited patiently while the dog moved close to a wall near a narrow staircase. Chunks of drywall were missing from the wall, a result of weather, abuse, and an infinite number of brawls. Buzz went back and forth twice before assuming the position of alert. Scanlon turned to Chalmers, who had been watching the dog's performance at each house.

"I think he's found something."

"Is that a good or a bad thing?" Chalmers asked.

She gave him a wry smile. "Good. Somewhere behind that wall you'll find evidence of human remains."

"Like a body?"

"Possibly. Or that a body was kept there." She pointed at two of the holes, which were about four feet off the ground.

"So, what do we do now, boost the dog up?"

Scanlon scowled at him. "Maybe one of the departments has a hand saw. Or one of the demolition contractors. We just have to remove it carefully."

Chalmers paused to confer with a couple of other uniforms. Within minutes two men from one of the demolition companies returned with a heavy box. One guy pulled a tablet computer from a case and powered it up. The other guy drew a long cable from the box, attached a small device on the end and began to feed it through the closest hole in the wall. He glanced up at the small group clustered around him. Nobody noticed that Myles was in a corner, still recording. He whispered Olivia's name. In a flash, she appeared beside him.

"Optics will let us see what's back there before we start cutting. We use this on some renovation projects, making sure we're not cutting into any electrical or plumbing that was part of the original construction but became obsolete over the years. This gadget has paid for itself several times over."

Chalmers and Scanlon flanked the guy, staring over his shoulder at the computer screen. Within minutes, the cable was fed through the holes and down to the floor close to where Buzz sat patiently, awaiting his next instruction.

"Hold it!" the demo guy said to his helper. Tapping a few buttons on the tablet, he was able to magnify the picture. In her peripheral vision, Scanlon saw the guy swallow hard a couple of times.

"Kind of looks like a body," Chalmers said.

"Small one," Scanlon agreed. "Maybe wrapped in plastic."

Chalmers clapped the computer guy on the arm. "You can bring that back out. Guess we're gonna need a saw."

The guy nodded and motioned for his colleague to retrieve the cable. The lieutenant instructed the others to clear the room. He shifted his gaze back to Scanlon. "Looks like Buzz just earned his pay."

"Several times over."

He pointed at the news crew. "Think it's time for you two to step outside. And turn that freaking camera off."

They did as he instructed. Myles ducked his head so he could whisper in Olivia's ear. "Is this what they mean by 'breaking news'?"

"Oh yeah, baby. And we're the only station on the scene."

****

Before proceeding, Chalmers called the coroner's office and asked for instructions. They were told to wait until a crew was dispatched. Meanwhile Scanlon and Buzz searched the rest of the house, then continued up the block. Rumors were already circulating about the find.

A battered white van bearing the coroner's logo crawled slowly past the barricade and rolled to a stop at the end of the block. Two men wearing worn blue coveralls emerged. Chalmers motioned them inside. The heavyset black man in the lead dropped a heavy case and extended a hand.

"I'm Doctor Osborn." He inclined his head toward the younger black man who had an equipment box in each hand. "That's Monroe, my assistant."

Chalmers introduced himself and recapped the situation. Osborn studied the computer tablet that still bore the image inside the wall.

"Need a saw?" Chalmers asked.

"We'll start with pictures and video, get as much detail as we can. Measurements, sketches, and whatnot. How long has this place been vacant?"

The detective checked his notebook. He'd called in for a background and title search on the property when the body was found. "Last official owner was 2014. It was one of several buildings purchased for next to nothing on the street here. Some hotshot developer was gonna fix them up and flip them."

"Obviously, somebody neglected to conduct their due diligence," Dr. Osborn said with a grin. "It would take a major overhaul of more than just this street to bring people back to live here."

Chalmers found a relatively clean section of the wall to lean against. He watched the pair take measurements and pictures of the room. Only after the doctor was satisfied did he request the saw. A construction worker came in and carefully cut through an entire section of the wall. More pictures were taken. The coroner measured the body, rattling off details into a small microphone that was part of a headset hooked around his ear. When he was satisfied that all the pertinent information had been listed, they moved the body out onto the floor.

It was a small figure, wrapped in thick plastic and secured by duct tape. Osborn wiped the dust away with a gloved hand. Chalmers stepped over to get a better look.

"Female, probably early teens," Osborn said.

Chalmers shot him a surprised look. "It's a skeleton, Doc. How the hell can you tell that?"

"Clothes are mostly intact. That's the skirt from a private school uniform. Of course, we'll confirm that back at the morgue. May be able to get cause of death as well as an idea of how long she's been dead. No sense removing the plastic here."

He sent Monroe out to fetch the gurney.

"Anything else you can tell me?" Chalmers asked.

"She may not have been killed here. Chances are that she wasn't. It's entirely possible that once she was interned in that wall, she's been undisturbed. The plastic was thick enough to keep the odors within, which kept any wildlife or predators away. With the heat, humidity, and temperature swings, that could have expedited the mummification."

"This strike you as unusual, Doctor? The extra care in wrapping the body. Not removing the uniform, which may help identify her? Makes me think someone wasn't worried about her being identified."

"That's very possible. This area isn't far from that section upriver that became something of a dumping ground. Bodies were found there frequently, tossed aside like last night's garbage."

Chalmers nodded slowly. "You got any good news?"

"I'm afraid not. But a case like this will capture the attention of the public. No doubt the mayor is going to be involved, which could help expedite any additional testing."

"My lucky day."

****

The rest of the demolition project had gone without incident. Within an hour of the body's discovery, two detectives from the Fifth Precinct's homicide squad appeared on the scene. Chalmers showed them where the body was found and answered their questions. It was a hell of a way to start the week.

Detective Tim Malloy was accustomed to working with dead bodies. It was a routine part of his day to arrive on the scene, get a look at the dearly departed victim and absorb all the details he could. There was no spray of blood along the wall, no fragrance of gun powder or fecal matter. Any recent activity in this house probably had absolutely nothing to do with the homicide. Malloy looked around the place. All the plumbing fixtures were gone. Chunks of walls were missing, allowing access to copper pipes that may have fetched a high dollar. Windows were shattered, the glass ground to a fine dust beneath the tread of countless shoes and boots. Cardboard squares filled a few window frames. The house itself had died a long time ago.

His partner, Elise Tucker, joined him. "Is there any point in sticking around here? Chalmers will send us the report, along with statements from everyone who was on the scene when they discovered the body."

"You work with him before?" Malloy kept his eyes on the hole in the wall where the remains had been found.

"A couple of cases. It was before I transferred to the Fifth." She read the hesitation in her partner's eyes. "He's thorough. I'm sure he'll deliver."

Malloy could see no other benefit to remaining on the scene. Chances are the coroner may have taken a quick look at the remains, more out of curiosity than anything else. A complete autopsy would take time. He knew the medical examiner's office often had a backlog of work. But paying them a visit may help to generate some ideas. He led Tucker back into the street.

"Think this will get a lot of press?" she asked.

"This whole demolition project is part of the mayor's program to revitalize the neighborhoods. I'm surprised the media isn't already swarming."

As they climbed into the unmarked police car, they

noticed a white van with a roof antenna and the Channel Four logo parked down the street. Malloy shot a glance at his partner.

"You just had to mention the media."

Tucker shrugged. "They're like seagulls. There is no escaping them."

"Seagulls are prone to pick through the garbage, looking for a treat."

She shrugged again. "Like I said. Seagulls."

****

Malloy and Tucker entered one of the autopsy suites. They stood back for a moment until Dr. Osborn motioned them forward. The heavy plastic that had covered the girl was already removed and set aside. It would be dusted for any possible fingerprints.

"Been a while, Tim," Osborn said quietly. In the background, noises from tools and bone saws at work could be heard from adjacent rooms.

"Took a little vacation, Doc. Went fishing up near Traverse City."

"Have any luck?"

"The only thing I caught was a hotel bill. But the kids had fun."

Osborn glanced up and grinned. "Nothing wrong with that."

"Any light you can shed on our victim?" Tucker asked.

The medical examiner tipped his head toward an array of evidence containers. He stepped away from the remains and joined them, using the tip of a clean scalpel as a pointer.

"White cotton panties. No signs of any residue, but the lab will test them for seminal fluid. What was between her knees was a bit of a surprise."

Tucker glanced up. "A good surprise or a bad one?"

"Guess it all depends on your perspective. It looks like a business card, or at least, a large portion of one."

Malloy leaned close, reading it over her shoulder. It was faded but most of the details were legible.

"I'll have the lab check that as well. It's possible they can fill in the missing pieces. And it appears there are most of the phone numbers on it. So that could prove to be helpful," Osborn said. "And then there's this little goody."

A clear plastic envelope was on the counter. Inside was what looked like a linen handkerchief.

"Where was this?" Malloy asked.

"The edge of it was under her skirt. As if someone had tried to clean up after a little misbehavior."

Tucker glanced back at the remains. "That's not the sign of a little misbehavior, Doc. That's a whole shitload."

"Agreed."

"Any idea as to cause of death yet?" Malloy asked. "I realize you've only had her for a few hours, but there's always hope."

Osborn chuckled. "We handle three thousand cases a year. Some of them are as easy as grandma's sugar cookies. Others are more…challenging. My preliminary thoughts are that she was strangled. The hyoid bone is fractured. That would be enough to kill her. But I'm not putting that in writing until I complete the autopsy."

"Understood," Tucker said. "Any idea how long she's been dead?"

"If you want a guess, I'd say at least seven years,"

Osborn said. "She was petite. Maybe five foot two or three at best. We'll be able to get DNA from her teeth. I'll be sending one to the lab right now. I've also got complete dental x-rays, which can help confirm identification."

Tucker looked up from the evidence bags. "We could start with missing person's files. Meanwhile, we've got a couple of more recent cases that could use our attention. You know, cases we could actually solve."

"Might as well."

Osborn promised to send the report as soon as it was completed. The two cops walked out into the fresh air of summer, leaving the dank fetid odors of the morgue behind.

****

Four days later, Malloy and Tucker were in the detective squad room at the Fifth Precinct. Malloy was trying to figure out when he could schedule his next vacation. The fishing trip up north had been a great experience. The kids were already clamoring to spend more time together. Malloy had been staring blankly at his computer monitor when Tucker hung up the phone and cleared her throat.

"Bad coffee?" Malloy asked, glancing up.

She waved a finger at him. "That was the lab. Remember that business card that was found with our Jane Doe?"

"The mummy. Yeah, Doc Osborn said some of it was faded."

Elise leaned closer. Their workstations were side by side. She looked around to see if anyone was listening. "Joyce was able to get enough to raise a phone number. She called it, but the number is no longer in service."

"No big surprise there. That girl's been dead a long time. People move on."

"Naturally. But most numbers get recycled after a while and entered in the system for the next customer. Same routine with landlines and cell phones. She tried variations of the number, just in case. No luck."

"What's got you wound up?" Malloy rolled back in his chair and faced her. "You act like this girl is going to walk right in and say hello."

"Joyce said they also got a positive ID from the dental records. The victim's name is Charity Gray. She's on that missing persons list we checked the other day. She disappeared fifteen years ago."

Malloy shifted to his computer and punched in the details. This was a suburban girl from Oakland County. He scrolled through the details while sending the file to the printer.

"A little more than fifteen years since she vanished," Tucker said, reading over his shoulder. "The dentals were perfect. Only one filling and…"

"Tucker. Malloy. My office." The captain in charge of the detectives scowled at them. This was not a good sign.

They hustled into his office. Two men in suits were already in the small room. One sat in a visitor's chair. The other lounged against a file cabinet.

"These are Special Agents Sedlak and MacGregor with the FBI. They have an interest in that Jane Doe case you caught," the captain said.

"A vested interest," Sedlak said. "So much so that we're going to take that case off your hands. This has now fallen under the jurisdiction of the Federal Bureau of Investigation."

Malloy and Tucker exchanged a glance. "I didn't realize the FBI was involved in homicides," Elise Tucker said.

"We are now," Sedlak said. "We appreciate your efforts on this case. The captain has assured us that copies of your notes and files will be provided. The coroner's office has already been so informed. All records are now federal property." He motioned to MacGregor. The two agents moved toward the door.

"She's not Jane Doe anymore," Malloy said. "The coroner's office just notified us. Her name was Charity Gray. Fifteen years old, she's been missing for fifteen years since late April." He extended a copy of the file to the captain. Sedlak intercepted it.

"Our case now. We appreciate your efforts."

"Wait a minute!" Elise Tucker said. "How in the hell did the discovery of a teenage girl's body even come to the attention of the feds?"

Sedlak paused at the door. "That business card. He's someone we've been after for a very long time."

Chapter Two

The quiet, upper-class neighborhoods of Grosse Pointe Shores were rarely disturbed by police presence. Even the squad cars that routinely patrolled the residential areas were subdued. The lush streets, bordered by exquisite landscaping, could easily have been transported to any suburb that was home to millionaires, successful entrepreneurs, politicians, professional athletes, musicians, and entertainers.

So, it was unusual when a small convoy of black SUVs appeared, rounding the corner from Lakeshore Drive in tight formation at seven o'clock on a Monday morning. The center unit eased into the half-moon driveway. The other vehicles rolled to a stop, successfully barricading the two exits. Six agents dismounted. Each was dressed in a black or dark blue business suit. Even the two female agents' attire was cut from the same cloth. All eyes checked the street and the surrounding homes. Satisfied, they looked to the agent in charge. He nodded once to the team. Executing a turn with military precision, he approached the front door, rang the bell, and knocked twice.

A tall young woman appeared. She was dressed in a T-shirt and loose-fitting canvas shorts. Thick blonde hair was pulled back in a ponytail. Her eyes flicked over the scene. But she didn't cower. Her hand firmly gripped the door.

"Can I help you?" Her voice was clear and calm.

"I'd like to see Leo Agonasti."

There was a flicker of humor in her eyes. "And I'd like to win the mega-million lottery drawing so I can buy a new Porsche. I've got my eye on that 911 model. Think we're both gonna be disappointed."

He hesitated. "I'm serious."

"Nice to meet you. I'm Diana."

From the inside pocket of his suit, he withdrew some papers. "I have a warrant." Extending it, he made to enter the house. Diana didn't move, even when he crowded her personal space.

"Listen, Serious…"

"Special Agent Sedlak."

"Okay, listen, Special Agent Sedlak, there's no one else here but me. If you'd like to leave the paperwork, I'll make sure Mr. Agonasti sees it when he returns. Whenever that may be." Diana smiled sweetly and extended her free hand.

Sedlak hesitated. He could hear no one else in the house. In the background, classical music was playing softly. Reluctantly he gave her the warrant. Quickly she scanned the content, folded it, and tucked the papers in her back pocket. Sedlak took another step forward. Diana gave her head a slow, negative shake.

"This is an arrest warrant, not a search warrant. I've already told you that Mr. Agonasti is not here. If he's not visible, which he isn't, you need a search warrant to enter the property. Or my permission."

Her comments surprised Sedlak. He was about to bluff his way inside, but her awareness of the law stopped him. "That's pretty savvy for a maid."

"Never said I was the maid."

"You didn't say what your relationship with Mr. Agonasti is," he said.

"That's right. Are we done, Special Agent Sedlak?"

He tried to see beyond the foyer, but it was no use. "I'll be back with that search warrant."

"Better make it good," Diana said. Smiling sweetly, she closed the door.

Sedlak turned to the agent beside him. "Tomlin, call the office. We need a search warrant for this address."

"On what grounds?"

"Harboring a suspect in a homicide investigation. Tell them to make it quick. We'll need a copy here. Meanwhile, we wait."

Inside, Diana retreated to an office at the rear of the house. She checked the security monitors and made sure the system was recording the events outside. Satisfied that everything was working properly, she pulled out her cell phone and speed-dialed the primary number. A deep voice answered before it completed the first ring.

"We have a problem."

****

"I can't remember the last time you actually went on vacation, Pappy," I said. "Nice to know you're confident in our abilities to keep things going."

"Y'all okay, Chene. But keepin' an eye on them young'uns will keep ya busy. Suarez is still gettin' used to the way we do business."

"I'll work with Suarez."

It was early Monday evening. We were in Captain Pappy Cantrell's office at the state police post. From the open casement window behind him, I could hear the ebb and flow of traffic racing along Gratiot Avenue. For many people, the workday was over, which meant rush hour was winding down. In Motown, rush hour can last for two hours on either end of the usual nine-to-five. The rest of the squad was gone. Cantrell and I were reviewing pending investigations. A month ago, we'd wrapped up a complicated homicide that uncovered almost half a million dollars in precious gems, multiple extramarital affairs and involved more than a hundred suspects. But that's the kind of major case this team of detectives handles. Now we were looking at a string of home invasion robberies, a series of luxury car thefts and an extortion case with a local surgeon who may have been indiscreet a time or two.

"Don't need the whole squad on any of 'em," Cantrell muttered in his Southern drawl. "Y'all probably crack the blackmail afore the weekend."

"We can have Kozlowski and Atwater run the home invasions. I'll take Suarez with me on the extortion."

"Y'all droppin' the girlie on the cars?"

I shook my head. "Spears can review the files and look for a pattern. She did well with that on the serial killer. If there's a system in play, she'll find it. Then I'll take her and Suarez to follow it up."

Pappy grunted his approval. A tilt of his head preceded a plume of cigarette smoke. It drifted out the window. Smoking wasn't allowed in public buildings in the state. Pappy torched the memo. If he stepped outside every time the nicotine urge hit, his office would have to be a lean-to in the parking lot.

"Bet you're looking forward to that vacation," I

said.

"Yup. Leavin' Friday. Two weeks in the Blue Ridge Mountains. No Yankees allowed. Y'all on yer own. Think you can handle anythin' pops up?"

"We got it covered."

"Lot can happen inna few days."

A knock on the doorframe interrupted my response. The desk sergeant poked his head in the room. "Sorry to bother you, Captain. Chene has a very impatient visitor."

"Expectin' someone?"

I shook my head. "You get a name, Burnley?"

The sergeant nodded. "Not sure I believe it. Maximo Aurelio."

I'd been slumped in the chair, legs out and crossed at the ankles. Before I could move, Cantrell was at his computer, clicking buttons and pulling up the security camera that focused on the lobby. "Fuck me hard," he muttered.

Maximo Aurelio was standing three feet from the reception desk. His hands were out, palms up and empty. He was looking right up at the camera.

"Hope y'all ain't got a date, Chene."

I pushed out of the chair. "I'll go see what he wants."

Pappy was right beside me. "We go together."

Max greeted me with a bone-crushing handshake and a brief attempt at a grin. He and Cantrell exchanged nods. We led him to the conference room and got settled around the table. This was no social call. Just the idea of Max being inside a state police post was enough to put me on edge. No doubt he was as well.

Maximo Aurelio was a reputed lieutenant for one

of the Detroit area's largest organized crime families. There was a history of violence that many had tried to attribute to him over the years, without success. Ten years ago, Max, who was also known as Maxie A, had gone into retirement. The Mob had changed a lot in the twenty-first century. Max was supposedly living a quiet life, spending a great deal of his free time with Leo Agonasti, a childhood friend. If Max was a lieutenant, then Leo was a captain. Our paths had crossed occasionally since I became a cop.

Pappy took his usual spot at the head of the conference table. He turned his full attention on Max. The idea of him sitting calmly in the middle of a state police post was surreal. Cantrell wagged a finger back and forth, his variation of "get on with it." Max understood the unspoken message.

"The FBI has an arrest warrant out on Leo for murder," Max said slowly, his gravelly voice reaching even lower on the register than normal.

"Why come to us?" I asked.

"Leo's instructions. When he heard the charges, he told his lawyer two words. 'Get Chene.' Far as I know, he's not saying anything else. The lawyer called me. Guess she didn't know you."

"Where's Leo at?"

"Doing his impersonation of Harry Houdini," Max said.

"Who dat?"

Max swiveled slightly to face Cantrell. "He disappeared. I think he's still in the area but can't even begin to guess where he's at. Chances are he's going to keep moving."

"Will Agonasti try to leave the country?" I asked.

"The FBI may be watching the airports. TSA could have an alert already."

"I don't think he's running. Leo's never been the type to run away from trouble. But he's no murderer, Chene. You gotta believe that."

Pappy squinted at Max. "We ain't gotta believe nuthin'. We're talkin' 'bout criminal activity. Y'all ain't exactly a couple a Girl Scouts sellin' cookies."

"Say whatever you want, but Leo was a background guy. He's not violent. Never was. He couldn't murder someone."

"He had y'all for that?"

Max clenched his jaw before swinging to face me. "This isn't about me. It's about Leo. He needs your help. Can you at least check into the warrant?"

My gaze flicked to Cantrell. He gave me a minuscule nod in response. "The FBI does not normally handle homicide investigations. Are you sure the information you got is accurate?"

Max slid a business card across the table to me. It bore the FBI logo and contact information for the Detroit office. I turned it so Pappy could see it. His stare was burning through me. Getting involved in an ongoing federal investigation was contrary to the way Cantrell operated. There would be the question of jurisdiction. The feds were rarely inclined to play nice with other local agencies. But I didn't think walking away was an option.

"I'm going down there."

Pappy shook his head. "Un nuh. We goin'."

Max raised his palms. "I'm not stepping foot in that building. Surprised they're not looking for me right now."

"Give 'em time," Cantrell growled. "Day ain't over yet."

Despite the traffic, we made it downtown in half an hour. Cantrell took his own wheels. We parked in a lot near the McNamara Federal Building and walked inside. They knew we were coming. I'd made a call on the way, speaking to one of the guys I'd worked with in the past. We got waved through security and escorted up to the proper floor.

Half a dozen agents were gathered around a cluster of desks. Nobody was talking. They were all staring expectantly at the closed door of a conference room. Pappy hung back a step. I approached the group. A short, burly guy pointed a finger at me and dropped his thumb as if it were imitating a toy gun.

"Been a while, Chene."

"That it has." I turned and gestured at Pappy. "Scott MacGregor, this is Captain Cantrell. He runs the squad."

They shook hands. MacGregor waved toward the others, calling off their names. Rayburn, Lee, Tomlin, Klein, and Banks. They were all in FBI business suits. Lee and Banks were female. Rayburn was the only African American in the group. Pappy nodded to the others. I did the same.

"What do you have?" I asked.

"Pretty solid case, from the looks of it. What confuses me and the rest of the group is your connection. You're too much of a choirboy to be under the influence of organized crime. Care to fill in the blanks?"

Pappy caught my eye and gave me that minuscule nod of approval. So I told them the abbreviated version.

Years ago while working on patrol, I happened upon a parked car with a young couple making out inside. Approaching the car, I learned that the young lady was not a willing participant. The guy had been trying to get lucky, plying her with booze and refusing to take no for an answer. Upon learning her name, I cuffed the guy and radioed for another unit. Then I took the girl home. She was Agonasti's youngest daughter.

"What did he do?" MacGregor asked.

"Offered me a sizable reward for my efforts. I declined. Offered even more to give him the name of the kid involved. Declined that too. Offered me a job. Explained that I already had one. He didn't like my answers. Told me to name my price, along with the name of the kid. Finally told him I wouldn't take the money, but a reward would be his word not to harm the guy if he ever found out who he was. Eventually, Agonasti agreed."

MacGregor slowly shook his head. "You're one crazy bastard, Chene."

"Goes with the territory."

I explained that since then, Agonasti would occasionally reach out. He followed our investigations and had been a source of information more than once. I didn't go into specifics.

"Do you really have enough to charge him with a crime?"

"Yeah. The US Attorney's office reviewed the case and took it to court. The judge approved a warrant for his arrest. ASAC Sedlak tried to serve it this morning at his residence, but he wasn't there." MacGregor's gaze went around the circle of agents and came back to me. "We were checking all known locations. Then you called."

"MacGregor mentioned he's worked with Chene but didn't understand why you were interested," Agent Banks said. She was one of the two female agents. Honey-colored hair brushed the top of her shoulders. She was about five foot eight, just a couple inches shorter than me. An athletic build gave me the sense that she could hold her own in any kind of skirmish. "The background information explains a lot. Except how you even know about the warrants."

"So y'all don't know where's he at?" Pappy interjected.

MacGregor gestured a thumb at the conference room door. "Not for lack of trying. ASAC Sedlak is in with the lawyer. Not your typical picture of a consigliere, but hey, it's the new millennium. Stereotypes are meant to be broken."

My gaze fell upon Cantrell. His eyes burned into me. I'd been subjected to that glare for years and knew the meaning without a word being spoken. I nodded to MacGregor. "Let's join the party."

The others remained in a loose circle. MacGregor escorted us to the conference room, knocked twice and opened the door. Standing at the end of the rectangular table was a tall, blonde woman. She was pacing by the window. Seated at the table was another agent in a dark suit. He had a stack of files before him. His dark hair needed a trim. I noticed his tie was snugged up tight against his Adam's apple, as if to hold it in place. There was a pair of wire-rimmed glasses perched on top of the files.

He shot a disgusted look at the interruption. "What?"

MacGregor hooked a thumb in my direction. "State cops have arrived. This is Sergeant Chene and Captain Cantrell. They are…familiar with Leo Agonasti."

Pappy pushed MacGregor aside as he entered the room and dropped into a chair. "Y'all need us."

Sedlak threw his pen down on the table in disgust. It skittered across the surface and was headed for the edge when Pappy stopped it with a fingertip.

"Y'all know where Agonasti is?"

Sedlak went rigid. "We'll find him, Captain Cornpone. We don't require any assistance from the locals."

"So, you do need us." I slid into the seat beside Cantrell.

"That's bullshit."

The blonde had been watching this exchange with interest. She cleared her throat and took a step in our direction. "Your name is Chene?"

"That's me. And you are?"

"Diana Trevino." She sat beside me. "I represent Mr. Agonasti. He's mentioned you occasionally in the past."

Sedlak's gaze was flicking across the three of us. He settled it briefly on Pappy. I thought there was a glimmer of recognition, but it may have been my imagination. Cantrell is definitely memorable.

"Why don'tcha take Miz Trevino outside and lemme have a minute with Mr. Sedlak. Mebbe we can speed things along."

MacGregor was still standing in the doorway. He looked at his boss but got no signal that I could see. I stood and extended a hand to the lady. She took it lightly and grabbed her purse off the table as we exited the room. MacGregor followed and closed the door behind us. He waved at the group clustered around the desks. Banks came forward and escorted Diana Trevino to the restrooms.

"What the hell was that about?" he asked quietly.

"Looks like old home week. Give them a few minutes."

"You think they know each other?"

I leaned against the wall. "How long has Sedlak been the assistant special agent in charge in Detroit?"

"Three years, maybe four. Why?"

"You think he and Pappy haven't crossed paths before, between meetings, conferences and task forces?"

Mac shrugged. "Hadn't really thought about it."

"If Pappy didn't know him, he would have shot him for that cornpone wisecrack. They were just playing for the audience. Chances are Pappy reached out to him while we were driving downtown."

That brought a grin from MacGregor. "Well, that's a twist."

I watched Banks bring Diana Trevino back into the office area. She guided her over to the coffee urn.

"How soon can you give me a copy of the case file you have on this homicide investigation?"

Mac scoffed. "Seriously? What makes you think we're going to share?"

"Pappy isn't trading recipes for chicken fried steak. You don't know where Agonasti is. His attorney wouldn't share that information anyway, even if she knew. So I'd expect this to become a joint investigation within the next ten minutes. Might as well get me a copy. And don't bother redacting it. I want the whole thing."

"Damn, you're cocky."

I grinned. "There's a difference between confidence and cocky. You should learn how to tell them apart."

"Fuck you, Chene," he said with disgust.

"That's not very original. You need someone to write some fresh material."

The conference room door opened and Sedlak waved us in. Pappy was rolling a cigarette slowly between his first two fingers. It wasn't lit, which I took to be a courtesy on his part. If we were at the post, it would already be trailing smoke toward the ceiling.

"Agent MacGregor will provide you with a copy of our files on this investigation," Sedlak said. "Probably easiest to give them a flash drive."

"Make it two," Pappy said. "May as well git started tonight."

"You will keep us informed of any discoveries you make," Sedlak said.

Pappy gave him a curt nod. "Course."

"And if you learn the whereabouts of Leo Agonasti?"

"Y'all be second to know."

MacGregor trotted off to make the copies. Pappy and Sedlak continued to stare at each other. I waited in the silence. Five minutes later, Mac returned and handed me a pair of flash drives. I passed one to Cantrell. He tucked it in his shirt pocket and pushed out of his chair.

"Chene, give Miz Trevino a ride home. Ah believe she be done here."

Sedlak adjusted the knot in his tie. "Yeah, we're done. For now."

"Copy that," I said.

Chapter Three

We were in my Pontiac, heading east on I-94 toward Grosse Pointe. Diana was quiet until we got out of the downtown area. I had a feeling that Max was somewhere nearby but didn't see him when we came out of the McNamara Federal Building. I'd noticed before that she wasn't dressed like a typical lawyer. Diana was wearing tailored linen slacks and a turquoise silk blouse, with a pair of modest heels. The blouse was open at the throat and left a lot of tanned forearms visible. It also emphasized her shoulders and toned upper arms. Maybe she swam competitively or played a lot of beach volleyball. Apparently, the feds had been insistent that she accompany them downtown for questioning after they served the warrants and searched the property.

"Mr. Agonasti speaks highly of you," she said.

"We've had our moments. Known him long?"

"Most of my life. He paid for my college education."

"You're really an attorney?"

She flashed a quick smile and dug a pair of sunglasses out of her purse. "Yes, I passed the bar and everything. Practiced for a couple of years with a big firm downtown, mostly doing employment law."

"Did you enjoy it?"

Diana scowled and shook her head. "It was boring.

After a while I felt like every case was the same. But it was good experience."

"Still practicing?"

"Yes. I moved to a boutique firm. We have several specialized areas. There is no desire to get with criminal activities. None of the attorneys want to interact with crooks or murderers."

"Interesting choice of words."

She shifted in her seat to look directly at me. I hit the exit for Eight Mile Road and eased up the ramp from the freeway.

"Mr. Agonasti is not a client of the firm. We have an…understanding."

"Did you successfully explain that to the FBI?"

"Special Agent Sedlak is very narrow-minded."

I considered that to be a requirement for federal agents but kept the comment to myself. We rolled to a stop at the light on Mack Avenue.

"Where should I take you?"

"I'm living at Leo's house in the Shores." She rattled off the address in case I didn't already know it. I'd never been there, but Max told me it was where the feds had appeared. Apparently, it was Leo's address on record.

"That part of the understanding?"

Diana scowled at me. "Are you being crude?"

"Just asking questions. There's a lot about Leo I don't know."

She gnawed the inside of her lower lip. Conversation ended until I pulled into the half-circle driveway. A dark green Mini Cooper was parked close to the garage. I shut down the Pontiac and looked at her. After a moment she inclined her head toward the house and got out. I followed.

Inside, Diana switched off the alarm and led me to a gorgeous kitchen. Stainless steel appliances gleamed as if they were fresh from the showroom floor. She pointed at a stool next to a high counter. I settled in. Deftly she removed a bottle of Chardonnay from the refrigerator and several packages of cheese, meat, fruit, and vegetables. I watched as she quickly put together a platter of food. With a chef's knife dangling from her fingers, Diana gestured at the cupboard to my right. I grabbed two long-stemmed glasses and poured the Chardonnay. She slid a container of hummus between the two stools and centered the food so it was within easy reach.

"My stomach was grumbling so loudly it could have drowned out the traffic noise on the freeway," she said.

The charcuterie platter was artistically arranged in neat wedges, not thrown randomly on the plate. I didn't know if it was for my benefit or the way she always did things. Could be a quirk in her personality. There was a basket of crackers as well. There were no individual plates. We just grabbed bites of food. Neither of us spoke as we worked on dinner.

After a while, Diana settled back and released a pent-up breath. I got the impression she'd been holding it in for some time.

"You must have more questions," she said quietly.

"That's an understatement. But I'm not sure how much information you can share without violating the attorney-client privilege."

Diana topped off our wineglasses and swiveled her stool to look directly at me. We'd put a significant dent in the food, but she wasn't done. She dragged a cracker through the red pepper hummus and popped it into her mouth. I sipped the wine.

"Go ahead and ask. If I can't answer, I'll say so."

I nodded. "Fair enough. Let's start with why Leo would pay for your college education."

"My dad had a restaurant for years. Best barbecue ribs in town. They won a lot of awards. The restaurant always seemed to be doing well. Dad was the heart and soul of the place. Did the cooking, ran the kitchen and dining room, had pictures on the walls of all the local celebrities who'd stop in to eat. Leo was a regular customer. Always a generous tipper." She wiped her fingers on a paper towel then took a gulp of wine.

"What happened?"

Diana rolled her shoulders, as if trying to loosen a knot in the muscles. "Dad died. Heart attack. He didn't like doctors unless they were customers. One day he's in the kitchen, shutting things down with the cooks and the crew after a long day. He sat on his favorite chair, had a glass with three fingers of Jack. Took one sip, set the glass down firmly on the table and he was gone."

"Sorry for your loss," I said quietly.

Diana gave me a tired smile. "Thanks. It's been almost ten years now."

"So how did Leo come into the picture?"

"He was at the funeral. Squeezed my hands, gave me a little kiss on the cheek. Same with my mother. Expressed his condolences. A week later he stopped by the restaurant. It was after the lunch rush. Mom was trying to keep things going, but there was so much she didn't know."

Diana explained that Agonasti would often have a

meal at the restaurant when she was working. He was always very cordial, asked about her studies, about her plans after high school. She was eighteen when her father died, finishing her senior year. Agonasti said her father was extremely proud of her. Years back, he had given Leo some money to invest for her education.

"Leo said he oversaw the funds and there was enough to pay for my full tuition, including graduate school if I chose to go. I was shocked. Dad never mentioned anything about college. I'd been saving what I could all through high school, but it wasn't adding up to much."

"Was there a catch?"

"Not at all. He gave me a card for an investment banker, along with an account number. Leo told me to check it out. The money was earmarked for college, so I couldn't just cash it out and become a gypsy riding the trains through Europe or something like that."

"Interesting." I mulled the situation over.

"Tell me about it. Leo was this nice guy and suddenly I've got a bucket of money sitting in the bank for my education. And it was just the start."

"How's that?"

Diana hefted the bottle. There was only about two inches of wine left. She raised her eyebrows at me quizzically. I gave my head a negative shake. She poured the last of it in her glass, then waved me from the counter. I followed her to the rear of the house where there were skylights above us and double-paned windows overlooking a manicured yard. Diana settled on thick cushions at the end of a sofa. I chose a maple rocking chair. She took another sip of wine then placed it gently on a marble-topped table.

"Leo brought in an attorney to represent my mom. She didn't know enough about the restaurant to keep it going. The attorney spent hours with her, going over the books, hiring a kitchen manager, getting everything back on track. One night she had a long talk with Leo. He asked what she really wanted to do." Diana gave her head a slow shake at the memory.

"Did Leo buy the restaurant?" I asked.

"No, but he did offer. He helped Mom list her options. Sell the place, keep it, stay involved with it, trust the attorney and the managers to properly run it." She shrugged. "I'm sure there may have been other options. But he told her she should do two things."

"What was that?"

"Take as much time as she wanted. And talk it over with me."

"Not exactly a strong-arm approach," I said.

"Hardly. And by that time, I was already enrolled in classes at Wayne State. I wanted to stay local, so I could see Mom frequently."

"Only child?"

"Is it that obvious?"

I smiled. "Lucky guess."

Diana told me that when she first found out about the college fund, she was skeptical. So she met with the financial adviser and he showed her the records. The account had been started with a modest amount years before. Some automotive and tech stocks, a lot of high yield targets. It was an aggressive approach, but it had accumulated enough to cover everything. Her father, or Leo, had been adding capital periodically each year.

"Maybe Leo was just helping out a friend," I said.

"It does make you wonder. Every week I went by

the restaurant. Things were very prosperous. The managers and the attorney were keeping a close watch on the operation. A couple of years passed. Mom was still involved, mostly there in the evenings to talk with the regulars." Diana gave her shoulders a little shrug. "She didn't have much else to keep her busy."

"And then?"

"The year I finished my undergrad studies, she sold out. Took the cash and had the same guys invest it who had worked on my college program. Mom got tired of winters up here. She moved down to Arizona. Four years later, she passed away. Traffic accident. They said she fell asleep at the wheel."

I kept quiet. Diana let her head loll back on the sofa cushions.

"That's about the time I quit working at the big firm downtown. Leo attended that memorial service too. I'd seen him every few months or so, keeping in touch. He asked if I was happy. I couldn't honestly answer that."

"So eventually you took him up on his offer," I said.

"Yes, but it's not what you think."

I was skeptical but kept a straight face. "Tell me what it is then."

"Leo put up the funding for the boutique firm. It's low-key, no pressure, no big courtroom dramas, or criminal litigation. He'd started it years ago. We have one person who handles family law, one attorney does real estate, another focuses on estate work. One specializes in entertainment, another patents. We all support each other. I came in as a partner.

"In addition to my work, Leo offered me the use of

this house. He doesn't live here. The arrangement is that I live here, making sure the grounds are taken care of, the property is maintained. I've been here two years. Leo's come by half a dozen times, just to visit. We'll have dinner and catch up. That's it. No sex, no games, just a comfortable arrangement."

"Why you?" I asked.

Diana flashed a quick smile. "Why not me? Leo wanted someone he could trust to maintain the residence. I get a beautiful place to live in for free. There's a checkbook in the office to pay the bills. There is a security system in place."

"You think Leo has other properties like this around town?"

She nodded. "I'd count on it. Over the years, he's told me repeatedly that he's retired. His family is no longer in the area. After his wife died, his kids drifted away, following their own careers, starting their own families. Leo is…restless. He may be here some days when I'm at work, but that's just a guess."

I didn't say anything, just kept turning it over in my head, trying to see all the angles. She picked up her wine and drained the last of it.

"So that's the arrangement," Diana said.

"Any restrictions on you, or the house?"

Diana gave me a throaty chuckle. "I can date whoever I want. And if I bring them home, that's my business."

I couldn't argue with that. But this didn't solve any parts of the Agonasti puzzle. If he had multiple residents around the area, he could be anywhere.

"Tell me what happened when the feds showed up."

Diana described the initial approach by Sedlak and the brief delay while they obtained a search warrant. Diana had watched them fidget out front on the security monitors. Apparently, they'd been hoping to bluff their way inside.

"Who did you call?"

She flashed a brief smile again. "Mr. Agonasti. It was an emergency number that he'd given me once I moved in. Never used it before." She shrugged. "I tried it again when they gave me the search warrant. It was disconnected."

"Probably a disposable phone. After you called, I expect he pulled the battery. Maybe even crushed the SIM card."

"Seriously?"

I nodded. "That's what I would have done. Maybe even dumped the actual phone. That could have given a location as to where he was."

"Leo may not be an angel, but I can't picture him killing this girl. Or anyone really." She gave a little shudder. "So what are you going to do?"

"We're going to look into the case. Best way to clear Leo is to figure out who did it." I stood up. "Thanks for dinner. And the conversation."

Diana walked me back to the kitchen. She pulled an expensive leather case from her purse and handed me a glossy business card. "Let me know if there's anything I can do to help. Leo always said you were good at catching killers."

"Thanks."

Back in the car, I couldn't help but wonder if her last statement was something Agonasti was counting on.

Chapter Four

Elusive. That was the word Leo Agonasti thought always described him the best. Elusive. He learned a great deal during more than forty years with organized crime. There were enough interesting characters whose paths he crossed that were always willing to share some of their trade secrets. Leo was a willing student. While he learned about economics, supply and demand and financial matters in college, that was only the tip of the iceberg of his education.

And he was still learning.

There's an expression he'd come to live by. "Hope for the best. Expect the worst." Or words to that effect. Agonasti first heard it years ago and took it to heart. In his case, he was fond of saying, "Always have a backup plan." Leo took that one to the next level. He had backup plans for his backup plans. Contingency plans were the essential key to his freedom.

He'd bought the luxurious house in Grosse Pointe Shores when his wife was still alive. It was her dream home. A place not far from the lake, where she could step outside, draw a deep breath, and taste the fresh water in the air. A deck on the second level faced the lake and was screened from below by a row of arborvitae. His wife had worked with a decorator, setting the mood for each room. She was frugal, despite his encouragement. After she died, he rarely set foot in the house.

But Leo was a long way from homeless.

There were five other residences scattered across Wayne, Oakland, and Macomb Counties. Each had a caretaker, just like Diana. The neighbors all believed it was the caretakers who owned the properties, which is exactly what Agonasti intended.

In every location, there was an isolated bedroom secured for his purposes only. The lock on the door included a numeric keypad, which he had programmed with a series of numbers that were never written down. Sporadically during the summer, he had also been staying aboard his yacht. But there was no discernible pattern to his movements. Leo would never be predictable.

Now he entered the loft apartment in the old Detroit Free Press Building. He was within blocks of the McNamara Federal Building, a fact that caused him to smile, albeit briefly. Agonasti knew they were searching everywhere for him. But he had taken great care setting up the purchase of these residences, creating a series of small corporations for each acquisition.

This apartment was without a caretaker. It was his latest purchase. Leo liked the ambience of downtown, being so close to the sports venues, the nightlife, and the resurgence of businesses that were bringing so many people back into the area. It was easy for him to blend into the crowds moving about their days. At one point this evening, he'd been enjoying a leisurely dinner at a new restaurant. The meal was good, but he was there for the view. Out the window, he watched the activity near the federal building. He couldn't help but smile watching Chene leaving with Diana Trevino. No matter what else may develop, he sensed that Chene would not let him down.

Agonasti secured the door and set the alarm system. In the master suite, he approached an oil painting, a scene depicting a young redheaded woman, kneeling beside a black Labrador retriever. He thumbed a tiny catch on the lower left. There was a soft click that allowed him to move the painting on its hinges. Behind it was a small safe. Deftly he keyed in the numbers and opened the box. Inside were two thick stacks of fifty-dollar bills, an inexpensive cell phone with a charger and an envelope. Leo left the cash and took the rest. He moved to the window and gazed down at Lafayette Street. As the phone booted up, he slit the flap of the envelope with his thumbnail. Inside was a driver's license and two credit cards. Agonasti noted that the license was enhanced, which allowed for passage between the US and Canada without the need for any other documents.

When the phone was ready, he keyed in a number and waited. It was answered on the second ring.

"Yeah?" a deep, guttural voice responded.

"I'm safe. You?"

"Sharks are circling, but they ain't in the neighborhood."

Leo pondered the response briefly. "Is our friend going to help?"

"Him and the boss. Caretaker filled me in just a minute ago."

"Understood."

"Anything you need?"

"Stay in the shadows," Leo said.

"Gotcha. Twenty-four?"

"If not sooner."

He ended the call and immediately removed the battery and the SIM card. Leo had no doubt that Max was doing the same thing. They had prepared for situations like this for years. Each had half a dozen phones hidden around the city. They would only be active when needed and used sporadically. Leo preferred to use these only once. He glanced down at the phone. Thoughts of his friendship with Max flashed in his mind, going back to his youth.

Leonardo Agonasti was the youngest child in a family of three boys. Folks used to say he was the "late baby" since there were almost ten years between him and the middle brother. This was in the early 1950s. The Agonasti family resided on the eastern edge of Dearborn, close to the Detroit border. It was a rough-and-tumble blue-collar neighborhood, filled with factory workers and immigrants. The houses were mostly bungalows, jammed tightly together on narrow plots of land. You could practically reach out the window and shake hands with people living next door. Or pat them on the ass if that was more appropriate.

Agonasti's early childhood was uneventful. He was a better-than-average student and one who got along well with almost everyone. Leo excelled at sports, particularly baseball and football. He wasn't a star, but he was steady. Before he reached high school, both of his brothers were out of the house. At times, his parents looked at him as if he were a stranger, wondering where this boy had come from. His mother withdrew into a small circle of friends, other women in the area of Italian and European descent.

His teenage years were a trial. When Leo was fifteen, Mario, the middle brother, joined the army. He was sent to a base in a foreign land and never returned. A year later, his father was fatally injured in a car accident. It had been his practice to stop at a nearby bar after a hard day's work on the Ford assembly line. It was a night like so many others. The bar was dark and smoky. Beer mugs and shot glasses lined the scarred wooden counter. Men came in to drink and wash away the aches of a day's labor.

This night wasn't very different. It was payday. The senior Agonasti chased his troubles down with half a dozen boilermakers. The years of heavy manual labor were taking their toll. When he staggered out to his battered Ford Fairlane, it started to rain. Agonasti didn't even notice. He swung the car onto Michigan Avenue. Mistaking the accelerator for the brake, he jammed it toward the floor. The big motor roared. He looked down, trying to find the switch to clear the windshield. He never saw the flatbed truck, loaded with steel. He never saw the small red flag dangling off the back. Chances are, he never felt the impact.

Young Leo was now the man of the house. There was a little insurance money and a tiny savings account. His oldest brother, Antonio, had left home a dozen years ago. No one knew where he was. There was no trace of him. Now it was just Leo and Carmela, his grieving mother.

Sixteen years old. Leo didn't want to drop out of school. But he needed to find a job. There was nothing he knew how to do. Yet he was desperate.

Leo turned to Max, one of his childhood friends. Max was the opposite of Leo. He wasn't an athlete. He wasn't tall with broad shoulders. He mostly kept to himself. Max was an average student, while Leo earned As and Bs. But Max had a job. And Leo needed one.

Max worked on a loading dock near the railroad yard. Steel shipping containers from all over the world came in daily. While a lot of the freight would be hauled directly to its final destination, many cargo containers needed more attention. These would be backed up to the docks and the cases of goods inside had to be stacked on square wooden pallets. The palletized products would then be transferred to another truck for easier handling. Max's job was to unload the containers and assemble the goods in a proper order.

He'd been doing it for almost a year. Despite his short stature, the manual labor had resulted in solid muscles throughout his frame. Now he dragged Leo onto the dock to meet the boss.

Max had already told the foreman about his friend and the circumstances. The foreman was a squat Polish man with a twisted lump of a nose and an ever-present cigar stub in the corner of his mouth. His name was Stanislaw, but everyone called him Sticks. The old man gave Leo a quick glance, nodded and pointed a bent finger at a twenty-foot cargo container that was packed from the floor to ceiling with cases of wine. "Go," was all he said.

Leo learned quickly. Max showed him the ropes, how to stack boxes in a pattern and how to run a length of heavy twine around the top stack of cartons on a pallet to keep them secure. It was rough, physically demanding work.

Sticks noticed how well the boys worked together. From his stool on the loading dock, he watched Leo determine the number of boxes on each skid and log the information. Math apparently came easily to him. His mental calculations were done in a flash. Sticks gave up checking his efforts after the first week.

Leo and Max worked every day after school and all-day Saturday. When summer arrived, they were at the freight yard as the sun was coming up. Leo forgot about baseball and football. Work was more important. Putting food on the table mattered. Keeping his mother happy mattered. For more than a year, that became his life.

One evening in late October, Sticks waved the boys over.

"Got a little job for you." He slid the cigar stub from one side of his mouth to the other. "You up for somethin' different?"

Leo didn't know how to react. But his friend did. "Sure. Just tell us what we need to do," Max said.

"Go with Vince." He pointed at a heavyset man leaning against the closed door to a semi-trailer. "He'll fill you in."

Leo and Max did as they were instructed. Vince jumped off the dock and headed for the cab of the semi. The guys followed, scrambling through the passenger's door as he fired up the engine.

"Where are we going?" Max asked.

"It don't matter," Vince replied. His voice was raspy, little more than a guttural growl.

Leo glanced at Max. He shrugged. They bounced along in silence. Half an hour later, Vince swung the big rig into a large yard filled with other trailers. There was no one else in sight. Vince maneuvered the rig until it was close to the rear of another trailer. He lifted a pry bar from the floor and handed it to Max.

"Break the lock. Then open the doors on both trailers."

Max and Leo jumped from the cab.

"What the hell are we doing?" Leo glanced back over his shoulder.

"Whatever it is, we'd better not ask any questions."

With the trailer doors opened, Vince backed up the rig until it banged against the bumper of the other trailer. He shut down the truck and joined the boys.

"Here's the story." He pointed at the truck they arrived in. "There's pallets in my trailer. Some rope too. The boss wants about half the merchandise. Stack them waist-high. Get busy. I'll keep a lookout."

Max scrambled up into the empty trailer. Leo followed. Vince handed them two lantern-style flashlights before marching away. With the lanterns, they could see the jumble of wooden pallets. Max grabbed two and dragged them up to the nose of the trailer. Leo turned, looking at the cargo they were supposed to unload. He focused the lantern on the white cardboard carton with the cursive logo.

"You're not going to believe this," he whispered.

Max appeared beside him. "Whiskey. Wonder if they'll give us some?"

Leo punched him in the arm. "This isn't funny."

"Yeah, but something tells me we won't be laughing if we don't do as this Vince guy said. Let's get started."

For the next four hours, they carried cases of Canadian Club whiskey into their trailer. Stacked waist-high on the pallets, they lashed them together with lengths of rope. Leo was carrying the last two cases for a pallet when Vince appeared beside them.

"You guys done good. But we're outta time. We'll leave the rest."

Exhausted, the two teens jumped out of the trailer. Vince pulled the rig forward. Leo and Max secured the doors on both trailers and climbed back into the cab. Vince didn't say anything else, just drove off into the night. Half an hour later, he stopped outside the freight yards where they worked.

"The boss will be pleased. Sticks will take care of ya. Be ready for next time." Vince pointed out the window at the darkened street.

Leo slipped from the cab. But Max hesitated. Vince looked at him closely in the dim glow of the dashboard lights.

"If there's a next time, bring a two-wheeled dolly. We could have moved all those boxes with some equipment." Max thrust his hand out to Vince. Surprised, he hesitated for a moment then he shook hands.

"You all right, kid."

"Thanks. Don't want to disappoint the boss."

Max climbed down to the street and joined Leo. Together they watched Vince put the truck in gear and roll it away.

"What the hell just happened?" Leo asked.

Max looked at him and shrugged. "We moved some freight. Same as any other day. Let's go home."

****

The next afternoon, Sticks waved them over with one grimy finger. After making sure no one was paying attention to them, he pushed a letter-size envelope of cash at each one. The boys were skeptical. It wasn't payday.

"Put them in your pockets. Don't say nothing to nobody."

They did as they were instructed. Sticks told them to go sweep out the containers at the end of the docks.

And so it began.

Over the next six months, they worked with Vince about once a week. It got to the point where they didn't even wait for instructions from Sticks. If Vince showed up on the docks, the boys would follow him out to the cab and drive off into the night. Sometimes it was electronic gear, console televisions and stereo systems. Other times it was clothing. Furs were popular. One night it was cases of ammunition and weapons that were destined for the military. Neither guy asked questions. They simply provided the muscle to move the freight from one trailer to another. After the first night, Vince kept a two-wheeled dolly strapped behind the cab of his truck. The next day they would receive a thick envelope from Sticks.

It was the end of May. Leo and Max were due to graduate from high school in a couple of weeks. More than once, Max had considered dropping out. But he'd made a promise to his ailing mother years ago that he would finish school. Max was a man of his word. It was a trait that would serve him well the rest of his life.

They arrived at work on a hot Friday afternoon. As they approached Stick's stool, he inclined his head to the left. Vince was leaning against a support pillar. But there was no truck at the dock. Max and Leo walked over to him.

"Boss wants to see ya," Vince muttered.

Leo cast his eyes back toward Sticks.

Vince chuckled. "He ain't the boss. C'mon, we're going for a ride." He turned and jumped off the dock. Parked in front of the row of trailers was a large Mercury sedan. Max climbed into the shotgun seat. Leo slid in the back behind his friend. The radio was tuned to a broadcast of the Tiger's game. All three listened to Ernie Harwell describe the action.

Vince cruised the big Merc along Michigan Avenue, heading out into West Dearborn. Randomly he turned suddenly, switching onto side streets before cutting back to the main road. Leo reached up and tapped Max on the shoulder. His friend glanced back, raised his shoulders in a silent shrug, and turned his attention toward the windshield.

At length, Vince weaved his way deep into a residential neighborhood. The homes here were large and spacious. The lots were bigger. More distance between neighbors. Lawns were manicured. Trimmed shrubs lined the cement and stone paths leading from the driveways to the front doors. The Merc rolled to a stop behind a black Lincoln Continental and parked in the street.

"End of the line," Vince muttered, shutting down the V8 motor.

"You do realize that can be taken more than one way," Leo said as he cautiously opened his door.

Vince laughed. "Geez! Take it easy, kid."

In the driveway was another black Lincoln. This one was being washed by a burly man wearing a wifebeater T-shirt and dark slacks. Thick curly hair was visible across his chest, shoulders, and arms. He pulled a soapy sponge from a bucket and worked it in wide circles across the hood.

"Looking good, Bruno," Vince said as he led the boys past.

"Thanks. Gotta do it right. Boss is going out later."

Vince led them in the front door of the house without knocking. The floors were a glossy marble. The hallway extended straight back to the rear of the house. Leo slowed his pace, glancing into the archways on either side of the corridor. Living room, sitting room, dining room and kitchen flanked the hall. Vince went out the rear door and turned right. Here was a cement patio. A circular table with a large umbrella was in the center of the slab. Four chairs ringed the table. Seated with his back to the house was a handsome man with wavy black hair. A copy of the *Detroit News* afternoon edition was on the table before him. The man's attention was focused on an article in the business section.

"Here they are, boss." Vince stood across from him. Max was on his left, Leo on the right.

The man glanced up and nodded. He folded the paper and neatly added it to the other sections. For a moment, he didn't speak. He studied the two boys before him. Then a wide smile split his face and he spread his arms wide.

"Have a seat. Vince, there's a pitcher of iced tea in the kitchen. Talking can be thirsty work. And we have a lot to talk about."

"Yes, sir." Vince disappeared back into the house.

Max slid quickly into the chair. Leo hesitated.

"Relax, Mr. Agonasti. You're among friends here. Please, sit down."

"How do you know my name?"

The man waved his fingers at the chair.

49

Reluctantly, Leo took his seat. Max shifted and cracked his knuckles.

"Much better. It's high time we met. Our business arrangements have been very…lucrative for us all. Wouldn't you agree, Max?"

"A lot of sweat and sore muscles on our side. But the extra pay sure buys a shitload of liniment."

The man burst out laughing. "Well said, my young friend. Very well said."

Vince appeared with a tray of heavy glasses and a jug of iced tea. Large circles of lemon floated in the center of the crystal pitcher. Leo noticed there were only three glasses. Vince placed the tray in front of the boss. The man poured the amber liquid into each glass and passed one to Leo and another to Max. Then he raised his own high in a toast.

"To our continued successes."

He clinked the glass against the boys' and waited while each took a sip. Settling his own back on the table, he dabbed the moisture from his lips with the pad of his thumb. Dark eyes flicked between the two boys. With a shake of the head, he leaned back in his chair.

"I'm Romeo Giacalone."

Romeo knew he had their attention. While his own name may not be well known, the surname was recognizable in the Detroit area in the sixties. Giacalones were a significant part of the organized crime family. Anthony 'Tony Jack' Giacalone was a leader whose name would frequently appear in the local papers or newscasts. The reach of the Mob was growing. While they stayed away from drugs, there was big money to be made in so many other avenues. Gambling, sports betting, trucking, laundry services, construction and prostitution were very productive. Romeo was a distant cousin to Tony Jack, a recent addition to the family's operations. He explained this quietly between sips of tea. His audience barely blinked.

"We make good money. Lots of it." He rested his heavy glass squarely on the table before him.

"So, we've been helping with that?" Max asked.

Romeo nodded slowly. "I'm very grateful for your efforts. I appreciate your aching muscles. But one of my assignments is of a different nature. And that's where you two come into the equation."

Max and Leo exchanged a glance, then shifted their attention back to their host. Romeo took the opportunity to refill their glasses.

"I understand that you're quite adept with mathematics, Leo," he said, again dabbing his lip with the ball of his thumb.

"I do all right."

"Have you given any consideration to college?"

Leo shook his head. "I can't afford it. Even with the…extra money we make doing special jobs for you, it's still a struggle to pay our bills. Mom can't work, so it's up to me."

Romeo nodded sagely. "And you, Max? Any interest in furthering your education?"

"I'll be lucky to graduate high school."

"Never let school stand in the way of your education," Romeo said quietly.

A confused look passed between the two boys. Giacalone caught it and smiled widely.

"Let's discuss this individually. Leo, what would you say to a…scholarship that would pay for your books and tuition?"

Leo didn't hesitate. "I'd be surprised. That kind of thing goes to people way smarter than I am."

"Let's assume such a thing was possible. What would you study?"

"I'm not much for science. Probably accounting or something like that."

Romeo sipped his tea. "How about business management? That would allow a mixture of different subjects, such as accounting and marketing."

"I guess that would be good."

"You're a better-than-average student. Higher education should appeal to you. A chance to do better than your father. Or do you see yourself doing manual labor your whole life?"

Leo shrugged. "I haven't thought about it much. But my mom won't let me work on the assembly line."

"A wise woman." Romeo shifted the stack of newspapers and removed a book. "This is a course catalog for Henry Ford Community College. You have an appointment Tuesday afternoon with Benny Crenshaw. He's a guidance counselor. He will help you enroll for the fall semester. You will attend full time." He slid the book to Leo.

"I have no money for college." Leo left the book on the table between them.

Romeo wagged a forefinger back and forth. "Remember the scholarship. Here's my offer. You will work this summer on the docks, just like last year. If Vince needs your services, you will assist. Come September, you will begin classes. Full time. Crenshaw will set you up. He will give you an invoice for the semester. Bring that to me. I will write a check for the school."

"But I've got to work," Leo said nervously.

"You will be working."

Little did he know that would be the next step in his career track.

Chapter Five

After spending most of the evening reading over the various parts of the case file, I knew sleep would be elusive. I built a tall gin and tonic and drifted out to the dock, where I could dangle my feet in the water. The fiberglass speedboat that rocked gently against the pilings wasn't mine, but I did have unlimited access to it. Gazing out toward the lake and the sky above, I wondered if there were answers hidden in the stars.

If they could find him, Agonasti would be arraigned on a murder charge. As if that wasn't bad enough, this was a cold case, where the victim had been dead for over fifteen years. She was a fifteen-year-old girl. A pretty girl, just on the cusp of adulthood. Her body was tiny. Just a touch over five feet tall, with jet-black hair. At the time of her disappearance, Charity Gray weighed a hundred and two pounds. She had been to the doctors the month before for a sports physical. Charity was going to play softball.

I had a difficult time picturing Agonasti killing this child. In the ten years that I've known him, a penchant for violence was never evident. Leo was a devout family man. I could picture him lashing out at someone who threatened him or his loved ones, but that's no different from most people. Could he have killed this girl? How did they meet? What action could have possibly resulted in her death?

When our paths first crossed, I did some digging on Agonasti. There were some shady operations back then, but he wasn't at the center of it. If anything, he was deep in the background. He kept a low profile, managing several diverse businesses. At one stage, Agonasti was like a venture capitalist, identifying new opportunities that the Mob could get behind to clean their money. There were always several degrees of separation from the actual business to organized crime. He was a history buff. He'd learned well from the mistakes of others.

The gin was gone. Clouds scuttled across the sky, blocking out the moon and the stars. It was well past midnight when I gave up and went back inside.

****

Tuesday morning there was a car parked across the bottom of my driveway. Not a sleek, suburban hotrod but a large dark sedan. It should have had a label across the doors reading 'Feds' or something along those lines. It had been out there since six. The driver's door opened as I approached. Banks, one of the female agents I met yesterday, slipped out from behind the wheel.

"Morning, Chene."

"Uh-huh. What brings you by?"

She checked her watch. It was one of those multi-function athletic things that probably doubled as a phone while checking her heart rate and counting how many steps she took. Maybe it monitored her biorhythms too. Or her aura. She held up a finger and appeared to be counting down. At precisely seven o'clock, the phone buzzed in my pocket.

"That will be MacGregor," she said.

"What's the deal?" I asked, clicking on the phone.

"And good morning to you, Chene. SAC's orders. You and Cantrell can dig, but we tag along. That way we're already up to speed if you find something."

"Who's riding with Pappy?" I tried unsuccessfully to fight back a grin.

"I am. We're just about to sit down to breakfast."

"Enjoy your grits." I switched off and tucked the phone back in my pocket. My eyes went to Banks. "I am not riding in that. You can either follow or get in my car."

She hesitated. "If I follow, do you promise not to try and lose me?"

"I can't be held responsible for rush hour traffic."

"MacGregor said you were a bit of a smart ass."

I shrugged. "Your call."

Banks ducked behind the wheel, started the heavy car, and rolled it back ten feet. Then she grabbed a thick file from the front seat, climbed out and locked up.

"So where are we headed?" Banks asked.

"Going to talk to a source. Make some connections."

She shifted and looked right at me. "You've had the case files less than twelve hours and you already have a source?"

"Sometimes it works that way."

I could have made this drive with my eyes closed. The Pontiac seemed to know exactly where to go. I pulled into the lot beside the old building. There was plenty of room to park.

Banks gave me an incredulous look. "We're going to church?"

"Like I said, meeting a source."

"You trying to tell me that your source attends early morning religious services on a Tuesday?"

I bit back a grin. "Something like that."

We headed to the rear doors. Inside the large cathedral there was a small gathering, about thirty people, scattered among the pews closer to the altar. We ducked into a row near the back of the church and watched the priest and an altar boy distribute communion. There was a blessing, followed by a brief prayer and a hymn. The altar boy collected a crucifix on a long pole and led the priest to the back of the church as the song faded. The priest's hands were pressed together in prayer as he drew close. I caught the nod and the wink he threw.

We waited while the faithful trickled out the various doors. Banks raised her palms and shot me a quizzical look. Only when I heard his footsteps behind us did I get to my feet.

"Hello, Jefferson. It's been a long time."

"That it has, Father Dovensky. You're looking well."

He scoffed and patted his protruding stomach beneath the vestments. "Maybe I will take up jogging. Or tennis."

"Start with a long walk. Ease into it."

"Should I assume your appearance today is related more to your profession than mine?"

"That's a safe bet." I gestured to the woman beside me. "This is Special Agent Banks with the FBI. We're working on a case together."

Dovensky turned his full attention on her and extended his hand. Banks gave him a firm shake, but the old man didn't let go. Instead, he took her hand in both of his and stared intently into her eyes.

"I'm a humble priest, but it's always been my habit to address others by their given name. What do your parents call you, my dear?"

Banks hesitated. I noticed a flush of color creeping up her neck as she responded. "Robin."

"Robin?"

She nodded. The color rose to her cheeks as a smile tugged at her lips.

"Robin Banks?" Dovensky was unable to keep from roaring out a laugh. "And you're an agent with the Federal Bureau of Investigation! Your parents obviously had a sense of humor."

"It's a long story."

Dovensky was still chuckling. "Those are the best kind. Jefferson, why don't you escort Robin to my office while I finish up. I'm sure you remember the way."

"Of course, Father. C'mon, Banks."

I led her up a side aisle as the priest walked to the altar. In my peripheral vision, he was still laughing, shaking his head.

Ten minutes later, Dovensky entered the office. He was in casual mode, khaki pants with a white golf shirt. A leather lanyard with a small wooden cross dangled down to his chest. I couldn't recall ever seeing him this way. Right behind him was one of the housekeepers for the rectory. She was bearing a tray with a decanter of coffee, mugs, and a plate of oatmeal chocolate chip cookies. Dovensky settled behind his desk and waved two fingers at me. I poured a mug for each of us, passing them around. The cookies were in the middle. Banks demurely took one and set it on a napkin beside her mug. The housekeeper was an excellent baker. I took two for starters.

"Let's hear the story," the priest prompted.

She sipped her coffee and nibbled the cookie. Dovensky made a steeple with his fingers in front of his chest and waited. I didn't say anything.

Banks explained that her original last name was Morris. Her parents divorced when she was five. Two years later, her mother began dating. It was a long, slow courtship. His name was Nathan Banks. He knew it was a package deal: mother and daughter. Morris had moved away and rarely saw his daughter. On almost all the dates with her mother, Robin was included. When Nathan proposed, he included her. They both said yes. A few months after they were married, Banks wanted to make it official and adopt her.

"I don't remember much about my biological father," she said. "It's been years since I've seen him. When Nathan adopted me and I took his last name, I never thought much about it. I was no longer Robin Morris. I became Robin Banks. At work I go by my initials. R.A. Robin Ann. I took some ribbing while going through the academy, but it's rare that it comes up nowadays."

Dovensky sipped his coffee. "Doesn't the FBI investigate bank robberies?"

"We do. But I've been working different task forces over the years."

"Robin Banks." He grabbed a cookie and chuckled again. Then his eyes shifted to me. "Now I suppose you'd like to get back to the matter that brought you and Robin here."

"I'd appreciate that."

Banks and I took turns describing the cold case. Dovensky's humor faded quickly as we talked about the disappearance of Charity Gray fifteen years ago and the recent discovery of her body. We didn't get into the arrest warrant for Leo Agonasti. I'd told Banks before that our focus with the priest would be on the girl's life. Father Dovensky leaned back in his chair, the mechanisms creaking under his weight. His coffee remained ignored on the desk blotter.

"The poor child. But what assistance do you think I can provide?"

"Charity attended St. Bartholomew's Catholic School. I thought you may know the principal there, maybe even the nuns who taught her classes."

Dovensky steepled his fingers again, propping his wrists on his stomach. "It's possible some of the staff may still be affiliated with the school. But it's August. School is not in session. It's not uncommon for the sisters to go on sabbatical during the summer months, or perhaps traveling to other areas and continuing their work. There are many parochial schools in the Detroit area. We're not exactly Facebook friends."

"I'm open to suggestions, Father."

With a sigh, he turned to the computer on the edge of his desk. A few keystrokes later, the priest found what he was looking for. The printer behind me hummed to life. Dovensky pointed over my shoulder.

"Contact information of the principal. Sister Augusta. A good person. I expect you to treat her and her role with dignity and respect."

"Of course, Father D."

He made a noise that could easily have been a scoff of disbelief.

Banks and I stood. Dovensky hesitated, as if he had something to add. He shook it off, then moved from behind the desk. I grabbed the sheet from the printer as he escorted us out. He took Banks by the hands and beamed a smile. "Robin Banks. Even under these difficult circumstances, it was a pleasure to meet you."

"Thank you, Father Dovensky. Same here."

"I'd like a minute with Jefferson," he said.

"Of course." She glanced at me. "I'll meet you at the car."

We watched her walk down the sidewalk. "What's on your mind, Father?"

"This old case. A young girl taken like this is very sad. You really think someone at the school can help you with the investigation?"

"I need background information. The more I know, the better chance there is of figuring out who killed her and why."

He nodded and extended his hand. "Be careful, Jeff."

"Always. And thanks, Father."

"You're welcome here anytime." A wide smile crossed his face. "Not only when you're chasing the bad guys."

"I'll keep that in mind."

I was three strides down the walk when he called after me. "Be polite with the fair sisters. I understand they still swat knuckles with rulers."

****

It was a flashback to my youth. In the fifteen years since Charity Gray disappeared, St. Bartholomew's Catholic School remained a constant in the community. Like my own educational experience, this one was staffed by a mixture of lay teachers and nuns. Arriving at the administration office, we were quickly ushered into a bright, sunny room.

Behind the desk was a woman in her fifties. Her curly brown hair was streaked with gray and curled across the top of her shoulders. She wore a simple blue dress with short sleeves. A chain dangled from her throat, adorned with a Gaelic cross. As we entered, she bounced to her feet, a warm smile on her lips. When I was in school, most of the nuns still wore the full black-and-white habits, where only their face and hands were visible. Times change.

"I'm Sister Augusta. What can I do for you today?" Her voice was friendly and sincere.

Banks introduced us. The good sister grasped our hands with both of hers, like a politician at a rally. She guided us toward a little cluster of upholstered chairs surrounding a low table. There was a twinkle in her eye as she settled in across from me.

"Father Dovensky called you?"

Her smile widened. "He did. We're old friends. He also suggested I keep a ruler close to hand."

"Nice to see you share his sense of humor," I said.

"Many believe it's a necessary skill required for the job."

I shrugged. "Never thought of it that way. Did he tell you why we were coming by?"

She gave her curls a slow shake. "Police business is all he said."

Banks and I took turns explaining the case as we had done with Dovensky. Sister Augusta folded her hands in her lap and gave us her undivided attention.

"I know it's been a long time, but we were hoping

someone here might remember Charity Gray. Perhaps one of the faculty or someone from the administration office," I said.

"I've only been here eight years. But several of our lay teachers have been with the school more than twice that long. And a couple of the sisters may be able to help as well." She went back behind the desk. A moment later her secretary came in with a notepad. Banks and I sat quietly while Sister Augusta gave her instructions. She requested the complete schedule of classes Charity would have taken that year, as well as a list of all faculty and staff during that time. Then she picked up the phone.

"I'm checking the convent. If Sister Mary Margaret is around, she just might remember Charity."

Banks fidgeted. Maybe she was having flashbacks of her own time in the principal's office. I watched Sister Augusta go through several people on the phone before having a very animated conversation. She ended the call and grinned at me.

"You're in luck. Sister Mary Margaret will be joining us shortly."

"We appreciate the assistance."

The secretary came in with a sheaf of documents. Several pages clipped together made up the class schedule. There was a list of faculty members, which included addresses and telephone numbers. There was also a small photo, probably from their school ID card. It was apparent that Sister Augusta ran a very efficient office. As the secretary was leaving, a short, stocky woman in jeans and Detroit Tigers T-shirt entered. There was sweat and dirt on her face and on the knees of her jeans. She was scrubbing grime off her hands with a rag.

Sister Augusta clucked in dismay. "Really, Margaret, you could have taken a few minutes to clean up."

"I was working in the garden. And there is still plenty of work to do. I saw no need to waste the water, particularly when you said it was important." The woman had an East Coast accent, possibly Brooklyn or New Jersey. Only now did she realize we were in the room. I got to my feet. Banks did as well. She didn't hesitate, just stuck out a grimy hand. "I'm Sister Mary Margaret."

I took the hand and introduced myself. There was mischief in her expression that went along with the firm grip. She looked Banks up and down as she shook hands.

"It's too nice a day to be stuck inside," she said. "Come along."

Sister Augusta bit back a grin. She extended the paperwork to me and motioned that we should follow. Banks walked ahead with Sister Mary Margaret. Augusta fell into step beside me.

"She's a bit unorthodox, but the kids love her. Many of the staff do as well. And Mary Margaret has been here ever since she took her vows, twenty-three years ago."

Around the corner from the school was the convent, a large three-story stone structure that was probably built in the 1950s. In the yard behind the building was a gigantic maple tree that cast plenty of shade. Beneath it was an octagonal picnic table. On the far side was a garden, teeming with a variety of flowers. I recognized two shades of roses, red and white, mixed along with other types of flowers and plants. Roses are the only flowers I can identify. Deal with it.

Mary Margaret gestured toward the picnic table. We settled in. While Banks filled her in on the reason for our visit, I scanned the paperwork the principal had shared. The list for faculty who taught Charity Gray included up-to-date contact information. A couple were crossed out with a thin red line and the word 'deceased' neatly printed beside it. All together there were six teachers' names. I tucked them in my jacket pocket as Banks finished up.

"Charity Gray was an inquisitive child," Sister Mary Margaret said. "She wasn't satisfied with the standard answers. Charity always wanted to know more."

"You seem to remember a great deal about her, even after all this time," Banks said.

The nun gave us a sad little smile. "After taking my vows, I spent several years doing community service. It was my first-year teaching. Charity was a special student. Those are the ones that are always memorable. I teach math and religion. Charity was in both of my classes."

"Was she more interested in one subject than the other?" I asked.

"She was interested in everything," Margaret said.

"How much of the poor child's background do you already know?" Sister Augusta asked quietly.

I glanced at Banks. She shrugged. "Just what was in the report. Only child, parents doted on her. Seemed like she didn't have any family issues."

Augusta deferred to the other nun. Sister Mary Margaret elaborated. "Charity was what most people would consider a late baby. Her parents were in their forties when she was born. It was unexpected. I'm sure it was a huge adjustment for them, having their first child at that age."

Margaret described what she knew of the young girl. It wasn't just school that she was curious about. Nothing bored her. Charity was like a sponge, trying to absorb everything. She often had questions well beyond the scope of her studies.

"She was inquisitive," Sister Margaret said wistfully. "Charity loved the gardens back here. She could name every flower, every plant. She was always feeding her curiosity."

I wondered if that curious nature had created a problem.

Chapter Six

Rudy Fen is the coroner Squad Six uses religiously. He reminded me of a bantam weight fighter in size and in attitude. Fen is a Chinese American whose parents pushed, nudged, and prodded him to go to medical school. His mother was hoping he'd become an award-winning researcher. His father was thinking of something more practical, like discovering the cure for the common cold. What they didn't realize was Rudy had little interest in dealing with the living. Learning the secrets of the dead held much more appeal to him.

Fen was in the autopsy suite, standing at the head of the slightly elevated table. In front of him was the corpse of a stocky man, who appeared to be the victim of numerous blows to the head. Fen leaned forward and delicately scraped something from the victim's ear canal.

"Guy had a hygiene problem, Rudy?" I asked.

He raised his eyes to meet mine. "Even you should know there is a difference between ear wax and brain matter."

"Somehow I always get those two confused."

Fen placed the material in a specimen cup. His assistant made a notation and went off to the lab to have it analyzed.

"That a wood splinter in the sample?"

He graced me with a nod while removing his

gloves. "Good eyes, Chene. So, what brings you by? I don't recall seeing any bodies from your squad on today's docket."

"I wanted to get your thoughts on a case. Wayne County's coroner did the work. I sent you an email last night with the details."

Fen nodded and guided me out of the autopsy suite. Banks was standing by the wall, finishing up a call. I introduced them as we stepped into his office.

"Since when do you work with the FBI?" He dropped into his chair and reached for the computer mouse.

"Since this morning. Think of it as a joint investigation. Did you review the file yet?"

Fen gave me an exasperated look. "Chene, it may be difficult for you to believe, but I do have other cases. There is nothing about this one that would take precedence over any of the other investigations on my calendar."

"Pappy's taking the lead."

That got his attention. "Seriously?"

"He's riding with another fed as we speak. Surprised he hasn't called yet."

As if by magic, the desk phone rang. Fen snagged it and muttered his name. He listened intently and jotted some notes on a pad. He didn't get a chance to say anything else before the connection broke.

"That was Cantrell. He expects my opinion within the hour."

"Guess we'll leave you to it," I said, trying my best not to smirk.

Fen turned his attention to the computer as Banks and I headed out. She gave me a curious look as we got back in the car.

"If Captain Cantrell was going to call, why did we have to swing by here?"

"Think of it as a courtesy. I sent him the file so he could be prepared. Pappy's sending the remains. And this case will move to the top of his list."

I explained that Fen's reputation was legendary. On more than one occasion he had discovered something during the autopsy that other medical examiners had missed. While he primarily focused on Macomb County cases, it wasn't uncommon for him to get called in to assist or offer opinions from other jurisdictions. Pappy fully expected Fen could discover something from Charity's remains that the Wayne County medical examiner may have overlooked. And Rudy Fen knew better than to incur the wrath of Cantrell.

"Basically, the visit was a form of motivation," Banks said.

"You could look at it that way. Besides, one of the teachers on that list lives in Mt. Clemens. Since we were driving by, it was not a problem to stop in."

Angela Durfee lived in a condominium not far from Lake St. Clair, just south of downtown Mt. Clemens. According to the details provided by Sister Augusta, Ms. Durfee had been teaching at the school for twenty years. Charity Gray would have been in her homeroom. The photo showed a dark-haired woman with small round glasses. Banks pointed out the address as we pulled into the parking lot.

"Looks like her vehicle in the carport." I indicated a late model Ford sedan. There was a sticker on the bumper for St. Bartholomew.

"She could have more than one car."

"Not according to the Secretary of State. I sent the information to the post, and they ran names and details. Got a list of current vehicles. Ms. Durfee only has the one."

We approached the unit. Banks reached for her creds. I waved her off. "Some people get nervous when you start flashing badges. This is just a little old lady schoolteacher. Let's take it easy and see how she reacts."

I rapped a couple of knuckles on the thick wooden door. Footsteps could be heard in the entryway. The door swung open. I can't speak for Banks, but the person who stood before us was not the image of any female schoolteacher I'd ever met, old lady or otherwise. A quizzical expression and a smile were frozen on her face. She was a dark-haired, petite woman with a golden tan and a trim figure, wearing a skimpy purple bikini.

"Obviously, you are *not* the pizza guy," she said nervously.

"Nope. Ms. Durfee, I'm Sergeant Chene with the state police. This is Agent Banks with the FBI. We'd like to ask you a few questions."

Her eyes flicked across us. The badge was visible on my belt. I noticed her fingers tighten on the door.

"What's this about?"

Banks chimed in. "Perhaps we could step inside to keep the conversation private." She inclined her head across the courtyard. An old-timer was shuffling down the driveway, his eyes locked on the purple bikini.

Angela Durfee nodded and stepped back, opening the door all the way. "Let me put a few more clothes on. I'll be right back."

Bank clicked the door shut behind us. "That happen to you a lot? Sexy women in bikinis greeting you at the door?"

"On a daily basis. It's one of the requirements Cantrell insists on."

She grunted in disgust and moved toward the kitchen. I strolled into the living room. The furniture was high quality. I was impressed. This didn't look like the accommodation of a typical schoolteacher. At least not any I knew. But maybe Durfee came from money or had a successful ex-husband who paid out big bucks for the divorce. I stopped beside a walnut cabinet that was adorned with photographs in heavy silver frames. One at eye level caught my attention. I picked it up for a closer look. It showed four women in tight red evening gowns, flanking a local celebrity.

"Oh shit!" Angela Durfee appeared beside me. She was wearing blue shorts with a white tank top now. "That's just an old photo of some friends." She gently tried to take the frame back.

"You're an Ah Girl." I handed it over.

She held the picture close to her chest. "This isn't widely known."

"What's an Ah Girl?" Banks asked.

Despite the deep tan, I saw a flush of embarrassment creep up Angela Durfee's neck and onto her cheeks. "Nothing, really."

"The Ah Girls are a musical group. They perform at one of the casinos downtown, have a regular slot in one of the lounge shows," I said. "Four or five years running."

Angela set the frame on the shelf and pointed at the

plush sofa across the room. "Surely you're not here to discuss that."

"No," I said. "We're here to talk about Charity Gray."

Her eyes went to the floor. She took a deep breath, let it out slowly and then glanced up. "That poor girl. I saw a news item that they found her remains."

Banks explained our joint investigation and led her through the questions we'd asked back at the school.

"Charity was in my homeroom and English class. She was a bright student, quick to smile but a bit shy. At the start of the semester, she held back a little." The teacher slowly crossed her arms over her chest and shivered. "Her papers were always meticulous, well written. She had an excellent imagination. You could tell just by reading her assignments that Charity was talented."

"Charity must have been special if you remember her so clearly after all these years," Banks said.

Angela nodded. "You never forget the best students. Some will even stay in touch or drop by after graduation and college. That is so rewarding to see them grow. Makes me think maybe I had a little something to do with their academic success. Even if it was just a fraction."

"Can you remember anyone in particular that Charity associated with, any classmates or people from different aspects of the school?" I asked.

"It was so long ago. I only really saw her in the English class. Homeroom was just a quick appearance at the start of the day where we took attendance, announcements were read and then it was a mad dash to classes. I do remember encouraging her to write for the school paper. But I don't think she ever did."

I'd been recording the conversation, with Angela's permission. Now I clicked it off and tucked the device back in my coat. Banks started to rise, but I didn't move.

"Tell us about being an Ah Girl," I said quietly.

Angela Durfee shook her head slowly. "Not going away without that story, are you?"

"I'm a detective." I gave her an innocent shrug. "Information is everything."

"It's not pertinent to the case. The group's only been around for six years now." Angela crossed her legs. They were toned and shapely.

"No disrespect. I've seen the show a couple of times. Think of me as a fan."

Banks and I were still on the sofa. She leaned forward now, her notebook back in her jacket. "I'd like to hear this too."

Angela chuckled and sighed. "Fine. I'm one of the original members. There are eight girls now. Four of us were enjoying a ladies' night out. It was the end of the school year, and we were celebrating. We went to the casino. They were having a karaoke show." She shrugged, lost in the memory.

Angela described how the four women went on stage and sang a handful of Motown classics, including popular hits by Diana Ross and The Supremes, Marvin Gaye, and Aretha Franklin. When they came back to their seats, the audience was cheering. The lounge manager approached them about a regular gig. In addition to Angela, there was a Maria and one woman named Gabriella. The manager bought their drinks and dinner and came up with the "Ah Girls."

"We do two shows on Friday and three on Saturday. Every week. That's why we grew to eight members. Nobody wants to perform all the time, and we each have regular jobs. A couple of the women have kids now," Angela said. "It's a lot of work. But it's fun. The casino takes good care of us. We get to meet some celebrities and a lot of nice people."

Banks pointed at the furnishings. "Pay must be good too."

"You bet your ass. We must stay in shape and keep up appearances when we're on stage or at the casino. Like I said, it's a lot of work. And the school understands I have a second job, but I keep the two roles separate."

I nodded and pushed off the sofa. "You put on a great show. It's been quite a while, but I enjoyed it."

"Come back. We're always adding new material."

"If you think of anything else about Charity, no matter what it is, I'd appreciate a call." I handed her one of my business cards.

Angela studied it. Then a wide smile crossed her face. "Squad Six. Isn't that the major case squad?"

"That's right," I said hesitantly. Not many people refer to it that way.

"Then you probably know Detective Kozlowski?" Angela asked eagerly.

That fucking Koz. "Yeah, we work together most of the time."

"Would you tell him I said hello?" She was almost breathless now.

"I'll pass that along."

Angela ushered us to the door. Banks gave her a card as well, but she didn't even glance at it. As we headed out, an old car pulled into the courtyard with a sign on the roof from a local pizzeria. The kid who jumped from the seat would be slightly disappointed that the purple bikini was covered. That's life.

Banks and I headed out. "Who's this Kozlowski guy? Durfee looked like she was about to melt just at the mention of his name!"

"He's the state police's version of Casanova. You're probably the only attractive woman in three counties who doesn't know him. Or know about him."

That earned me a bawdy laugh. "Can't wait to meet him."

That fucking Kozlowski.

****

The morning had flown by, with one conversation after another. Not far from Durfee's place was a popular Jewish deli tucked back off the road. Banks was still chuckling about the way Angela reacted to Kozlowski's name when I swung into the lot and parked.

"Maybe she needed his help reaching a high note," Banks said with a giggle.

"Sonofabitch probably has trading cards like football or hockey players," I muttered in disgust.

"What a great idea! I'll bet there are some dating apps that would print those up. Women could trade them; make ratings on the guys they've dated. They could use one of those sites where the woman has to make the first move."

"Are you ready to get back to the case?" I asked, popping open my door.

She snorted. "C'mon, Chene. You gotta have a laugh occasionally to keep yourself from going crazy."

Banks looked around. "What are we doing here?"

"It's called lunch. Best deli on the east side."

We entered and took a table in the back. I prefer to sit facing the door, so I can see trouble if it's headed my way. Banks settled in across from me and picked up a laminated menu.

"What's good?"

"Everything. People will line up for the corned beef and not just on St. Patrick's Day. It's legendary."

She scanned the menu as the waitress appeared. I got a brief nod of recognition.

"Pastrami on rye, with deli mustard and iced tea," I said.

Banks looked up. "I'll try the turkey with swiss cheese and mayo, on white bread and a Diet Coke."

The waitress shook her head once in dismay. She hustled away to place the order.

"Turkey on white bread with mayonnaise. You sure know how to live on the wild side, Banks."

She shrugged. "I'm a WASP from Vermont. Deal with it."

"Wouldn't hurt you to expand those culinary horizons a little."

I pulled the list from Sister Augusta. Near the bottom was the name and contact information for Leon LaChance, a retired science teacher. Banks gave me a quizzical look as I circled the number.

"What happened to doing the interviews in person?"

"LaChance retired and moved away. From what Mary Margaret said, he lives up in the Traverse City area during the summer and Savannah, Georgia in the winter. So, unless you have access to the FBI corporate jet, we'll do a video conference call with him."

Banks nodded. "That jet is way above my paygrade. The video call makes sense." Her eyes went wide as the waitress returned with the sandwiches on two gigantic platters. "You have got to be shitting me!"

"You can always get a doggy bag."

I cut my sandwich into quarters and dug in. Banks hesitated, then copied my moves. Her eyes narrowed as she took a bite. The cookies and coffee we'd had with Father Dovensky was the closest I'd gotten to breakfast. Food was definitely needed. Banks tried to start a conversation at one point, but it was impossible to understand her around a mouthful of turkey. I took a slice of the pastrami and set it on her plate.

"Try it. Just take a bite."

She eyed me suspiciously and daintily wiped the corner of her mouth with the paper napkin.

"It won't kill you."

"Is this considered soul food?"

I almost choked on my iced tea. "It's made from a beef brisket. Just seasoned and sliced thin. You want soul food, that's in another part of town."

Banks speared it with her fork and took a tentative bite. She chewed it thoroughly, then set the rest on her plate. She reached across and snagged the quarter of the sandwich where the sample came from.

"You're right. A girl does need to expand her culinary horizons."

In short order, my lunch was finished. Banks offered part of her turkey sandwich, but I declined. White bread and mayonnaise. God help me. The last of the lunch crowd was long gone. We pushed the plates and cutlery to the side. I dialed the cell number for

LaChance. He answered on the second ring. Apparently, Mary Margaret had given him a heads-up.

"You one of the cops?"

"I am. Sergeant Chene with the MSP. Any way you can do a video call?"

LaChance chuckled. "Sure, if you don't mind a little background noise. I'm a ranger at a golf course. Which basically means I ride my ass around in a cart and keep the duffers going. Let me get away from this tee box."

"You do video calls often?" Banks asked me.

"Rarely. I prefer face-to-face conversations, but we'll make the best of it here." I motioned her around to my side of the table, so we could both see the retired teacher, and he could see us. I switched to video mode. His face appeared a second later. LaChance looked to be around sixty, dark blond hair with gray streaks at the temples. He was sporting a good tan, no doubt the result of so much time spent outdoors. His blue eyes burned right through the screen as I identified the two of us.

"You really with the feds?" he asked.

I hooked a thumb at Banks. She flashed her badge and ID card. That earned a nod of approval. Banks ran through the usual questions.

"I've been gone five years now. Charity was a sweet kid. I'd always hoped that she'd just run away," LaChance said quietly. "Makes me sad to learn she's been dead all this time."

"Which one of your classes was she in?" I asked.

"Chemistry, for the full year. She was bright. Inquisitive. And she was quick to help others. There were two girls who nearly fought to be her lab partner. Class was held in the lab, so the kids usually worked in pairs, sharing Bunsen burners, microscopes and the other equipment."

"Do you remember the names of the girls she partnered with, Mr. LaChance?" Banks asked.

"Call me Leon." He ran his free hand through his hair. "It was something unusual, like Rapunzel. I'll have to think about that a bit."

"Can you remember anything else about Charity?" I asked.

He took some time to consider it. "I've been kicking this around since Mary Margaret called me. Hard to believe how long it's been since she vanished. I taught everything related to science St. Bart's had to offer. Chemistry, geology, physics, even astronomy. That's a lot of classes and a lot of students. And I taught twenty-five years at St. Bart's after five in the public school system. That's a mountain of students."

"Anything else come to mind, Leon?" I asked. "No matter how insignificant it might be."

"Nah. But the yearbooks might give you a clue as to who she hung out with. Class pictures and clubs and all that kind of crap."

I glanced at Banks and saw her eyebrows jump up. Neither one of us had considered the school's yearbooks.

"Don't suppose you kept a set of books?" I asked.

Leon LaChance barked out a laugh. "Hell no. You ever heard of a tiny home? One of those compact numbers?"

"Sure, three or four hundred square feet of living space, or something like that," I said.

"I've never measured it, but that's what I've got. It's on a little trailer, which makes it easier to haul down to Georgia for the winter and back up to TC for the summer. Every square inch of storage belongs to something vital."

"And twenty-odd years of high school yearbooks aren't necessarily vital."

"Damn right," LaChance said. "Listen, I've gotta get back to work. It's a cushy job, but I still take it seriously."

I asked him to call if anything else came to mind. He agreed and broke the connection. Banks had returned to her side of the table and was already calling St. Bartholomew to get copies of the high school yearbooks. It was a long shot. But in this kind of case, it pays to cast a wide net.

Chapter Seven

The school only had one copy of the yearbook in the library. Sister Augusta pulled rank and gave permission for us to take it off the property. Wanting a quiet place to review it and immediate access to the state's resources, I headed for the post. As luck would have it, the other members of Squad Six were all out on various assignments. I commandeered the conference room. Banks had been poring over the photos on the way across town.

"Nobody named Rapunzel," Banks said glumly. "That would have been too easy. And neither Augusta nor Mary Margaret recognized that name. Maybe Leon was having a senior moment and his memory is on the fritz."

I shook my head in disagreement. "He was pretty sharp. And he said it was something like Rapunzel. Let's look at the other girls in the freshman class. Mary Margaret said that back then they kept the students separated by grade. Whoever it was, she must have been about the same age as Charity."

Slowly we went through the gallery of students. I was making a list on a pad of possibilities. We got to the end with no obvious candidates. Banks thumped the table with the heel of her left hand.

"We're spinning our wheels, Chene."

"It goes with the territory." I pulled the book over

and continued to slowly page through it.

"I've already looked at everything," Banks said. "On the off chance, I even looked at the other classes, just in case someone made an exception. No Rapunzel. Not even anything remotely close to that name. And there were no students absent on picture day."

Ignoring Banks was easy. My concentration was on the book. It was near the back, just before the various advertisements from local businesses that helped offset the cost of printing. There was a section under the heading of events. This included pep rallies, team games and award ceremonies. And there it was. Six full pages, a montage from various dances. There was one to start the school year, homecoming, the winter carnival, a junior-senior prom, and a couple of casual-themed events.

"Fuck me hard," I said quietly.

Banks' head snapped up. "Excuse me?"

"No offense. Just a favorite expression of Pappy's that we've all seem to have adopted. Often muttered when everything falls into place or we get a break."

"You're telling me we got a break?" It was obvious she didn't believe me.

I spun the book around and jabbed a forefinger at a picture. It was a Valentine's dance with a fairy tale theme. One photo showed a guy dressed up as Prince Charming, down on one knee before a young girl. She had on a blonde wig that extended beyond her feet and followed behind her like the train of a wedding dress. Beneath the picture was a caption identifying them both.

"Rapunzel." I tapped the book.

"Holy fuck," she whispered.

"Close enough."

Banks grabbed her phone and called the school. I hit the computer, searching for details on both students. Fifteen minutes later, we were out the door. Banks had tucked one of her business cards in the yearbook to mark the place.

"Chene, we're about to interview a character from a fairy tale."

"That's another one of Cantrell's requirements. Sexy women in bikinis, young maidens from fairy tales."

Banks was laughing as she gave her head a shake.

We parked in front of a house with a Cape Cod design in an upscale neighborhood in Troy. These were sprawling lots, with the houses set back from the road at the end of long driveways. A small cluster of toys covered the grass beside the garage. I counted three bikes, a couple of skateboards, baseball bats and gloves and other implements of play. The cement pad at the base of the drive displayed a rainbow of chalk and several stick figure drawings. The garage door was open. Inside was a large, late model SUV.

As we climbed out of the car, a black Labrador came loping around the corner of the house. It took one look at us and decided Banks was the less intimidating figure, so it bounded in her direction. The dog barked as it approached, but the tail was wagging nonstop.

"You're gorgeous!" Banks declared, scratching the top of the dog's head. He skidded to a stop and enjoyed the attention.

"Keep your new friend occupied. I'll check the house."

I knocked on the frame of the open front door.

There was a flurry of footsteps as if a race had started. Three blonde kids slid into view, two boys and a girl. The girl, who was probably the youngest, was in the middle. They hovered just inside the door.

"Is your mother home?"

"Uh-huh." This from a boy on the right.

"Can I talk to her?"

"Sure," he said. Then all three turned around and screamed "Mom!" at the top of their lungs.

Other footsteps sounded. At their approach, the kids scattered. An attractive young woman wearing shorts and a T-shirt came into view. Thick blonde hair, the same shade as the kids', hung in a ponytail below her shoulders. She flashed a smile as they scampered past her. Banks stepped up alongside me, the dog bumping its head against her leg.

"Can I help you?" the woman asked.

"We're looking for Nancielle Chandler," I said.

A puzzled expression crossed her face. "The only one who calls me Nancielle is my mother, usually when she's extremely pissed off or setting her sights on another grandchild. She refuses to believe that I'm done. Everyone else calls me Ellie."

I introduced us. Without a moment's hesitation, she unlocked the screen door and led us to a comfortable kitchen. Outside the back window we could see the kids playing on a swing set. We settled around the table, and Ellie poured out glasses of lemonade.

Banks explained the investigation and our efforts to learn more about Charity Gray. The smile on Ellie's face faded. Banks put the yearbook on the table and opened it to the photo. It was fifteen years ago, but there was no mistaking Ellie Chandler as Rapunzel.

Even after giving birth to three kids, I got the impression she could still fit into that costume.

"Charity and I were lab partners in chemistry. She was incredibly smart. The nuns hinted that she was gifted. It wouldn't have surprised me a bit." Ellie took a sip of lemonade and gathered her thoughts. "It was all so strange when she was gone. There were rumors, but nothing I took seriously."

"What kind of rumors?" I asked.

"She was kidnapped by white slavers. Her parents decided to join a cult and they all moved to Oregon. Charity got tired of life and ran away. She was selected to star on Broadway." Ellie tapped a nail on the table. "She moved to Australia and was writing paranormal romance novels. And my favorite, the CIA recruited her to run a cyber-intelligence unit."

"We know it's been a long time, but we're hoping you'd have some memories of her," I said.

Ellie sat back for a moment and closed her green eyes. I'd notice the same color on all three of the kids. I watched as she pressed her palms together and drew a deep breath. Banks nudged me with her elbow. I raised a hand. We waited quietly. Then Ellie pursed her lips and let the breath out slowly.

"Yoga?" I asked.

"Meditation," she said with a smile. "Helps to calm me, clear my thoughts. With three kids, I need to find peace of mind on a daily basis."

"Stir up any memories of Charity?" Banks asked.

She nodded. "Charity was a gentle soul. She would never say a harsh word to anyone. Everyone liked her. At first, a couple of girls teased her, but within a week of school starting, she'd won them over. Charity was smart but not a brainiac. She didn't flaunt it. And she had the greatest memory. Charity could read a chapter from the textbook and recite it almost verbatim. And details! She didn't miss much of anything!"

"Can you give me an example of that?" I asked.

Ellie blushed. Her eyes were dancing at the memory. "We had to wear uniforms to school. White blouses, plaid skirts, nothing fancy. No lipstick, eye shadow or makeup of any kind. If our ears were pierced, we could wear stud earrings. Black pumps, no heels. And tights in the winter. If we were cold, we could wear a sweater."

"Did Charity violate the dress code?" Banks asked.

The blush went a shade deeper. "No, but I did. And she helped me."

Ellie explained that she had been interested in David, a boy in several of her classes. On more than one occasion, he walked her home. It was fall and getting colder out. She came to school one morning. Her locker was in the same section as Charity's, and they would often chat before chemistry since that was their first hour. Ellie stated that Charity suddenly grabbed her arm and dragged her into the restroom. There she pulled Ellie's hair back, revealing a large hickey on the right side of her neck.

"Charity was wearing a sweater with a high collar. She loaned it to me to help cover it up. Otherwise I would have spent the afternoon in detention for 'moral misbehavior.' Fortunately, this was on a Friday, so I had the weekend to let it fade. But she never teased me about it."

"I'd have given that David guy some serious shit," Banks said with a grin.

"Trust me, he got an earful."

We sipped the lemonade. "When you heard about Charity's disappearance and the rumors started to flow, did you have a theory?" I asked.

"I met her mom a couple of times, at the house. She was nice. Charity was in school on that Friday, then didn't show up on Monday. She was never sick. I stopped by after classes, but no one was home. I never believed any of the rumors about the cult or her parents just deciding on the spur of the moment to move away. She did have a beautiful singing voice. I wanted to believe she was on Broadway or with some traveling theater company, performing. But after a week without any word from her, I was afraid she'd never come back."

"Did Charity have a best friend? Someone she was close to?" Banks asked.

"Yeah," Ellie said quietly. "Me. We were only in that one class, but we always ate lunch together, sat together at pep rallies and games and anything else at school. Neither one of us was from rich families, like most of the other kids. Charity and I just connected. That's why it was so hard to believe she'd leave without telling me."

I glanced at Banks. She shook her head. No other questions came to her mind. But I had one.

"Whatever happened with David?"

If you could measure the power of a smile, that one from Ellie was at least a thousand watts. Her eyes twinkled with delight. "Married him two years out of high school. He's as blonde as I am. The poor kids never had a chance. Twin boys and a little girl."

"Cute kids," I said.

"We named the boys after our grandfathers, Matthew and James."

"And the little girl?" I asked.

"Charity."

****

Pappy called just after we left Nancielle Chandler's place. It was almost six o'clock. He and MacGregor had been doing the bureaucratic tango most of the day. Somehow Cantrell wrangled a search warrant and had gone to the house Charity Gray lived in. Fortunately, the house had not undergone any major modifications. They'd searched the entire property, just on the odd chance that something would turn up. The people who lived there now bought the place from the Grays.

"Ah got a meeting in half hour. Meetcha at Nino's inna morning an' we'll catch up," Pappy said. "Y'all makin' progress?"

"Chasing leads. Think we'll make one more stop before we call it a day."

"Don't be keepin' that fed out late. They gonna bill me for overtime."

"Copy that. See you at Nino's."

Banks was trying not to show her displeasure. "One more interview? You have something that can't wait until morning?"

"You got a date? I can always drop you off. Or you can call for an Uber or something like that."

That earned me an outright scowl. "Where are we going?"

"According to the faculty list, there's another teacher who lives nearby. It's about halfway between Ellie's and my place. You could say we're not going out of our way, just making a little detour."

"That's so comforting," Banks said sarcastically.

She was silent as I cruised along. As a law enforcement officer, Banks would be well aware of the fact that no two days are the same. Nothing is predictable, and dinner plans or a date would have to be fluid. Shit happens in this job. If you wanted a nine-to-five routine, be a freaking accountant. Or a bank teller.

Obviously, Banks didn't know the territory. Otherwise, she would have realized I'd lied about this being on the way back to my place. I was headed north and east, working our way into Sterling Heights. Some of the subdivisions here were older, going back sixty years or more. These homes had more character and fully grown trees on the property. I found the address in the middle of the block. It was a sprawling brick ranch with a detached two-car garage.

"Who are we interviewing?" she asked as we stepped from the car.

"Alain Bissett. Teaches foreign language."

"Great," Banks grumbled. "Probably fucking Latin."

"Latin is the foundation for many dialects and languages."

That comment didn't earn me any points. We followed the path from the driveway to the front door. There was no screen door here, just a solid wood panel painted a dark shade of purple. It was complemented by white shutters around the two windows. A pair of pillars supported the overhanging roof. What looked like river rocks made up the base of the columns. Instrumental guitar music was audible as I knocked. Banks replaced the scowl with her version of a professional expression.

I was about to knock again when the door swung open. The music had muffled the sound of approaching footsteps. The guy standing there looked like something out of central casting for a Hollywood movie, or maybe one of those romance television channels. He was about five-eight with jet-black hair combed straight back. A few strands at the temples were flecked with gray. A couple days' stubble covered his chin. He was barefoot, wearing faded jeans and an old white dress shirt, spotted with flecks of red. It was too bright for blood.

"Yes?" he asked. There was just a trace of an accent.

"We're looking for Alain Bissett," I said.

"I am Alain."

Somewhere between the car and the door, Banks had lost her voice. I identified us. Seeing the skeptical look on Bissett's face, I showed him my credentials. He glanced at Banks, and a quick smile crossed his lips. I explained the reason for our visit. Bissett nodded, stepped aside, and invited us in.

"It is quite comfortable on the patio," Bissett said, "a good place to have a little conversation."

Banks merely nodded and followed close behind him. Four wrought iron chairs with thick cushions surrounded a glass table. A wide yellow umbrella offered plenty of shade. There was a gas grill on the edge of the patio. Small curls of smoke were issuing from the hood.

Bissett settled into a chair and gestured toward the grill. "I do hope this will not take too long. My wife is due home for dinner shortly."

"We'll try and make it quick," I said.

Banks found her voice and ran through our

questions. She had her notebook out, but she wasn't writing anything down. My recorder was on the table. Bissett gave her his undivided attention and considered each question carefully before responding.

"Charity was in my freshman French class. A brilliant student. If you have spoken with other teachers, I am certain you have heard this before. Charity was like a young hawk. She was…destined to soar."

"First time I've heard it put that way," I said.

Bissett flashed that quick smile again. "I dabble in poetry. Painting too." He gestured at the red splashes on his shirt. "Abstracts mostly. I cannot get features accurate to the point they would be recognizable."

"Anything else you can recall about Charity?" I asked.

He raised his palms slightly. "It has been a long time. When I saw the feature on the news recently, it stirred up a few recollections."

"Good or bad?" Banks asked.

"Perhaps you would say a little of both. Times were different then. Some people were less…accepting of others. Especially in a Catholic school."

"Are we talking about political or social beliefs?" I asked. "Or maybe different teaching methodologies?"

Bissett gave me a slow nod. "Let us just say many things. But as to Charity, I recall her intelligence, her grasp of details and her…curiosity."

"We've heard that a few times today," I said.

"Perhaps this is a situation that reflects the old children's saying," Bissett said. He turned his hands palm up again and raised them a little higher.

Banks was eyeing him closely. "What saying is

that?"

"Curiosity killed the cat. Perhaps her level of curiosity caused her such harm. That would be sad if it were true."

We spoke for a few more minutes about teaching at St. Bartholomew and the students in general. I ran out of questions. Banks had nothing to add. Bissett graciously led us to the front door.

"Will you apprehend whoever did this poor child such harm?"

"We're sure as hell going to try," I said.

"Then I wish you the very best of luck. Sadly, we will never know what levels that young hawk may have achieved. C'est la vie."

Bissett gently closed the door behind us. Banks was silent as we walked to the Pontiac that was parked across the street.

"Something wrong?" I asked. "You got unusually quiet back there."

Her eyes were on the sidewalk. "When you said the name, I thought it was a woman. Elaine. He was not what I expected. That man can't be a high school teacher. He belongs in the movies. With those looks and that little accent, he'd make women swoon. Or worse." Banks chuckled. "Or better maybe."

A small sedan pulled into Bissett's driveway. The guy behind the wheel tipped a two-fingered wave in our direction, then reached up and hit the button to open the garage door. Bissett's comments about the school and acceptance floated to mind. Banks caught my eye and slowly shook her head.

"Like the song says, 'goes to show you never can tell'." I put the Pontiac in gear. It was definitely time to call it a day.

Chapter Eight

The sun was beginning its descent when we got back to my place. Banks left a few minutes ago. After a long day of chasing leads, I was tired but knew sleep would be sporadic if it arrived at all. The late lunch was a distant memory. What I really wanted to do was clear my head and put this case on hold for a little while. Simone answered on the first ring.

"It must be telepathy. I was just thinking about you," she said.

"That's why I called."

Her soft laughter echoed in my ear. "Liar. I didn't expect to hear from you with this new investigation you're on."

We had talked briefly last night and, without getting into details, I'd told her there was a good chance I'd be tied up all week. But Cantrell would never object to a little downtime.

"I know it's short notice but thought you might want to grab a drink."

"Where are you?" she asked.

"My house. But I could be near your place in half an hour."

There was no hesitation. She named a bar in Madison Heights, which was about halfway between our respective homes. "Twenty minutes, Chene. And just one drink. I have an early meeting in the morning and need my beauty rest."

"See ya."

A suave, charming guy would have made some comment that Simone was so beautiful she could have skipped the whole night's sleep without it having a negative impact on her looks. But I'm a long way from charming. I jumped in the car and headed for the bar.

Simone was waiting in the parking lot when I arrived. She greeted me with a long hug and a slow, soft kiss. We went through the bar to a large wooden deck out back. The waitress appeared quickly. We both ordered glasses of wine, and Simone pointed at the menu. The pub was known for their nachos, with several types of meat and cheeses and enough veggies to satisfy a vegan. Out here, we were alone. There were many people inside, watching baseball games on the large screen monitors.

Our wine arrived as we talked. Within minutes, the nachos appeared as well. They were as good as advertised. I was pleased to see Simone eat her fair share after liberally pouring on some spicy salsa. With the food gone, we sat there quietly. Faintly in the background jazz was playing. I noticed speakers mounted on the overhang. Feeling restless, I got to my feet and leaned against the railing that circled the deck. Simone gave me a shy smile as she stood beside me.

"Do you realize in the time we've been dating, there are still so many things about you I don't know?" she said.

"I'm an open book."

That earned me a burst of laughter from her. "Yes, and I'm Venus de Milo."

"Nice to see you, Venus." It was impossible not to

smile with her, no matter how tired I was. "What do you want to know? Keep in mind we both have a very early morning."

She thought that over briefly. "How did you ever learn your way around town after being raised in an orphanage? I'm pretty good with the area, but you seem to know where everything is."

I motioned to her. "Raise your left hand."

She did, giving me a quizzical look.

"Welcome to Michigan. You know the lower peninsula is shaped like this."

"Of course."

"Let me have your right hand. It will be easier to show you this way."

Taking her by the wrist, I turned her palm so she could see it in the dim outdoor lights. "Down here, near the base of your thumb, is roughly where Detroit is." I slid two fingertips across her palm toward her index finger. Her skin was soft and warm. "This gets you near Dearborn and maybe a little bit toward Westland."

Her shoulders were swaying ever so slowly. Simone's gaze kept flicking from my fingers to my face.

"A little further this way, it gets closer to Romulus, Belleville and Ann Arbor." I continued in what would be a western direction, then moved up from the palm to the base of her first two fingers. "Livonia, Plymouth, Northville, Farmington, Novi and Wixom are this way."

Simone drew a deep breath and moved in front of me. She turned, pressing her back against my chest. Her hips were moving in rhythm with her shoulders. In the background, the jazz music seemed to grow louder. "Keep going," she whispered.

I dragged my fingertips back toward her thumb. "Southfield, Royal Oak, Clawson, Birmingham. Further east, you get Mt. Clemens and St. Clair Shores. A little lower, you have Grosse Pointe."

Without noticing it earlier, I was matching her movements, a slight sway of the shoulders and hips. She leaned back against me. My right hand still held hers. At some point my left hand found her hip. Movement at the doors of the saloon caught my attention as the waitress started to come check on us. She hesitated, flashed a smile, and ducked back inside.

"Chene." Her voice was little more than a whisper.

"Yes?"

"Either take me home, or I'm going to jump you in the parking lot."

"What about your early morning?"

"I'll be fine. The question is, will you be?"

I couldn't see her face but knew she was smiling.

"Without a doubt."

Simone turned around in my arms. "You'd better kiss me now so I don't lose interest."

"No man alive could resist that request." A long, slow kiss followed. Then she pushed me away, grabbed her purse and headed for the door. I threw cash on the table, nodded to the waitress and followed.

At her apartment, Simone returned to the comfort of my arms.

"You expect me to believe you know your way around town because of landmarks on your hand?"

I shrugged. "That, along with maps and a GPS."

****

Twilight was late descending on Motown. It was almost nine as Leo Agonasti pulled into the driveway in

97

the quiet neighborhood in the Oakland County village of Milford. This was about as far west as he could go and still be in the tri-county area. He drove an old pickup truck with a few dents and rust spots along the rear quarter panels. There was nothing about the vehicle that would stand out in anyone's mind.

Leo wore a simple pair of jeans, worn scuffed boots and a faded golf shirt. He looked like a guy who had spent his day working outside. A sweat-stained Tigers cap, complete with the Gothic D was tipped low over his forehead. Gray and black stubble covered his cheeks and chin. He parked the truck on a slab of concrete beside the garage.

The house was a 1960s ranch with an addition on the back. The detached garage was set at the rear of the property. Trees provided a natural divider between the neighbors. Leo climbed out, stretched, and entered the garage through a pedestrian door. The far wall was made up of pegboard. Tools of various shapes and sizes hung there. All the equipment had the look of being used yet well cared for. One window on the opposite wall provided just enough daylight. He went to the left side of the wall and lifted three screwdrivers of varying length from their pegs. Leo pressed a finger against the edge, and the entire panel popped free. A small box was mounted between the wall studs.

Leo opened the box and confirmed the alarm was set. He deactivated it. There was a lever beneath the control panel. When he pushed it, a hatch opened, revealing a narrow spiral staircase. As Leo descended the stairs, lights flickered on, leading the way. Behind him, the hatch automatically closed, and the pegboard panel slid back into place.

At the bottom of the stairs, he powered up today's cell phone. He had ten minutes to spare before Max called. Leo's gaze swept the room. There was a wooden wine rack, a refrigerator, stove, and microwave suitable for a studio apartment. He moved to the stereo. Soon Beethoven's Piano Sonata No. 1 began to play. Leo opened a bottle of cabernet sauvignon and let it breathe. He settled in a thick upholstered chair in the corner as the phone buzzed.

"Hey, boss," Max said. The tension in his voice was evident.

"Hi, honey. How was your day?"

Max chuckled. "Nice to know you still got your sense of humor."

"If I can't find something to laugh about, Max, you might as well just kill me now." Agonasti lowered the volume on the stereo a notch. "Any news?"

"Chene's investigating. So is the boss, Cantrell. And get this…"

"Yeah?"

"They each got a fed riding with them. Not much trust there."

Agonasti considered this. "Could be a token deal or a rare gesture of efficiency. If Chene uncovers the truth, the feds will not be able to ignore it. Have you been in touch or just observing?"

"Talked to him once. He's using this old saloonkeeper as a cutout."

"That would be Ted, from Sharkey's," Leo said.

"Yeah, that's the guy. Gave me his number. I told this Ted fella the number for my burner. If I have anything, I reach out to him and he's gonna relay it to Chene. And it goes the other way too."

Leo caught himself nodding as if Max was in the same room. "Smart move. Chene wants some separation between you and him just in case the FBI is monitoring his calls."

"You staying mobile?"

"I am indeed. Not residing in the same place two nights in a row. What about you, Max?"

His old friend chuckled. "Different day, different girlfriend. You trashing this phone?"

"Of course. Right after our call."

"Anything you need, boss? I can go anywhere, anytime."

Leo looked around his underground room and smiled. Max would never believe some of the properties he owned. "I'm fine. Stay in the shadows. Let's make it an hour later tomorrow."

"You got it."

Leo ended the call and quickly disabled the phone. He would dispose of it tomorrow while continuing his circuitous route. It had been a stroke of luck to discover this property. The original owner had been a conspiracy fanatic. He was certain that the Cold War was going to result in bombs being dropped on the Detroit area since manufacturing was so prevalent. After all, the automobile companies even shifted their efforts during World War II to make aircraft bombers or parts for the military. The idea of a foreign power targeting this area made perfect sense if you believed in conspiracies. That led the owner to build a fallout shelter in his backyard.

Tomorrow Leo would head east. He had a date that nothing was going to disrupt. It wasn't a matter of convenience. It was a matter of principle. Agonasti knew he was putting a great deal of faith in Chene and his ability to solve the old murder. There were other options. But he wasn't ready to consider them at this point. Right now, he was counting on the cops to find the real killer. But not just any cops.

His money was on Chene.

With Max monitoring the investigation, Leo had the luxury of sitting back and strategizing. Since it was his nature to have a backup plan, Leo began to mentally review several options. He could, in fact, get out of the country. Canada was just across the river. It would be child's play to slip across the border. He could drive over the Ambassador Bridge, use the tunnel that ran beneath the Detroit River, or just hop on a boat and sail over. Leo knew he could also cruise up to Port Huron and cross into Canada on the Blue Water Bridge.

Once in Canada, he could easily travel to Toronto or Montreal and connect on a flight to anywhere in the world. London, Rome, Zurich, Tokyo, and Hong Kong were all accessible with a nonstop flight.

Staying within the tri-county area was a game to him. For that matter, he could easily drift into the shadows and head west, to Ann Arbor, Lansing, Kalamazoo, or Grand Rapids. Each city was large enough that he could easily disappear among the population. Leo could get lost in the shuffle of mass transportation, quality hotels and upscale restaurants. The vault in each safe house had bundles of cash. And cash left no trail. He smiled at the thought of the identities connected to every property. There were half a dozen names he used. Some were borrowed from old mystery novels. Three of his aliases had current passports in addition to driver's licenses. If he really wanted to disappear, he could be gone in a day.

Max knew him well. Running was not in Leo's character.

Leo drank some more wine and opened a can of cashews. He was not particularly hungry. A spark of an idea crossed his mind. No, he wouldn't run.

Still, another backup plan would come in handy.

Chapter Nine

Pappy was at his usual table in the back of Lil Nino's at six thirty Wednesday morning. Steam was rising from his coffee cup. There was a stack of newspapers in front of him. Despite so much information available electronically, Pappy preferred paper when it came to his news. I slid into the chair across from him. One of the waitresses appeared with coffee. Cantrell raised a scruffy eyebrow in my direction but said nothing until she had taken my order and walked away.

"Y'all look like hell."

"And good morning to you too. How was your day with the fed?"

Pappy scoffed and took a draw on his coffee. "Annoying lil shit. They must grow 'em that way. You?"

"About the same. They're supposed to be here at seven."

"Y'all hear any more from the shooter?"

He was referring to Max. The old gangster had the reputation of being a hitman, but there was never any proof or charges filed. "No. But I wouldn't be surprised if he's nearby."

"Suppose Agonasti still in town?"

"Running would make Leo look guilty. Max swears he didn't do it."

Pappy snorted a laugh and tossed the newspaper on the table. "Honor among mobsters. That there a new concept for ya?"

"Maybe among some mobsters. There's a lot of history there. Crime families often had agreements about not pissing in each other's pool. Plenty of money out there for everyone." I sipped the coffee, letting the heat scorch my throat.

"Y'all don't think Agonasti could kill?"

"Not a teenaged girl. Maybe in self-defense or protecting his family. But not doing something nasty with a young girl."

Pappy's eyes narrowed. "That so?"

"Yeah, that's so. You know how we met. He couldn't stomach the idea of someone taking advantage of his daughter. The man was a cleaner, for Christ's sake. He washed the money. Hardly the kind of guy who turns to violence."

"Wouldn't be the first un what changed. Won't be the last."

Before I could respond, the waitress returned with our meals. Pappy was having steak and fried eggs. A western omelet filled my plate. We dug in.

"Y'all really think we can clear the mob boy?"

"Best way to do that is to figure out who actually killed that young woman. The feds aren't exactly tearing up the town, looking for the real murderer. But they've yet to talk about a motive or even opportunity. They haven't figured out how Leo Agonasti is connected to Charity Gray. Sedlak and his crew think Leo's their man. Now all they have to do is find him."

"Be nice iffen he had an alibi, one of them airtight numbers. Force 'em to look elsewhere."

I grabbed a couple of slices of rye toast off the platter in between us. "You remember exactly where you were fifteen years ago on a spring day?"

"Nope. But ah ain't be accused of murder. Ah'll bet you can't do it either!"

"Not a chance. I was eighteen."

"Ain't no girlies you was chasing back then? Cute lil cheerleader types?"

I shook my head and ignored the jab.

We finished breakfast quickly. The waitress had just cleared our dishes and brought a fresh pot of coffee when Banks and MacGregor arrived. They opted for coffee. Cantrell waited somewhat patiently until they were served.

We recapped the previous day's efforts. Pappy and MacGregor had retraced everything since the discovery of Charity Gray's remains. I had written a report summarizing our interviews yesterday when I got back home. No doubt Pappy read it before breakfast.

MacGregor poured enough sugar into his coffee to make the spoon stand up. "What ideas do you have for the day, Chene? Any chance you'll actually try to hunt down Agonasti?"

"If the great and powerful Federal Bureau of Investigation can't find one little old retiree, what makes you think I'd fare any better?"

Cantrell's eyes danced. He enjoyed taunting the feds as much as I did.

Banks lifted a piece of toast from the platter and smeared strawberry jelly on it. "So what direction are we running today?"

"I'm going to swing by the Cyber Unit and toss a couple of ideas around with Sergeant Yekovich. Then we have two more faculty members worth interviewing." I looked right at Pappy. "How would you feel about getting the media involved?"

MacGregor sat up straighter in his chair. Banks froze with the toast halfway to her mouth. Pappy rolled an unlit cigarette between his fingers, a smirk crossing his face.

"Whatcha got in mind?"

"There was a fair amount of coverage when Charity's remains were discovered, and only a bit when they were identified. It's possible some of the other students from the school remember her, but they're probably scattered. Thought I'd ask Olivia to do some pulling on the heartstrings. She was the reporter on the scene that day. We might get someone to come forward, someone who saw her that Friday. Maybe get a little more background on the girl, to help fill in the blanks. The more information we get, the better decisions we can make."

I've known Olivia Sholtis for a while now. She's got good instincts and, as a reporter with Channel Four, has some excellent contacts. We've successfully collaborated a few times in the past, most recently with the Morrissey homicide. Pappy gave me a nod of approval. MacGregor choked on his coffee.

"I'm not sure the bureau will agree with this," he said.

"Good thing I don't work for the bureau. We're just asking for information. Nobody will say the FBI is interested or involved. The more we know, the better our chances for solving this case," I said.

"We've already solved the case. We just need to locate Agonasti."

I couldn't keep my own smirk from showing. "Good luck with that."

****

I made the call as Banks climbed into the passenger seat. Olivia answered on the second ring, gasping and panting for breath.

"Chene! I've been meaning to call you about that exclusive interview you promised me."

"Am I interrupting a little mini-cardio workout?"

She giggled in response. "If you're imagining a horizontal bedroom activity, you'll be disappointed. Just out for a morning run. Got something sensational for me? I could use another local Emmy Award."

I persuaded her to meet at the television station at nine.

"That will give me time to finish my workout, get glamorous and be ready to interview you."

"Nice try. I'm working a cold case. Thought a little feature on the noon broadcast might draw some reactions."

Olivia agreed to contact her producer and see if she could get a five-minute segment on the board. We ended the call. I headed north on Gratiot to the Cyber Unit's building.

"You seem pretty friendly with that reporter," Banks said. "We use an agent who deals with the newsies directly. Keeps the rest of us off camera."

I shrugged. "We're selective with the media. Pappy usually handles any press conferences with our cases. But there are times when a connection like this will pay off. Olivia is good. We met a few years ago. She always does a thorough job with her assignments. It's worth a try."

"You still believe in this Agonasti guy's innocence?"

"There's no way I can picture him killing a young girl. No way."

I swung into the parking lot for the Cyber Unit. Banks followed me inside. Yekovich was just going into his office. After introducing her, I handed him the school's yearbook.

"What exactly do you have in mind, Chene?"

"Work your magic. Run all the names through your databases. See if anything criminal pops up. Get me current addresses and details on the freshman class, any faculty and staff."

Yekovich riffled the pages with his thumb. "You trying to get a date with the prom queen?"

"I'm looking for a line on a killer."

That got his attention. "Who's the victim?"

I flipped the book open and tapped Charity's picture. "That's her. Probably the last picture there is of her. Charity has been dead for more than a dozen years. Whoever killed her has been living on borrowed time."

"We're a bit backed up here. It might be a week or two before I can put anybody on this," Yekovich said.

"I can give you thirty-six hours."

He groaned in protest. "You guys don't normally have such a tight deadline. Maybe I should talk to Pappy."

"Be my guest. He's liable to tell you twenty-four hours. Or maybe twelve."

Yekovich stared down at Charity's photo for a minute. Then he nodded, gathered up the book, marked the page with his finger and headed out toward the workstations in the back where his team of tech wizards performed their electronic magic. Banks and I took that as our cue and left.

"Cantrell certainly knows how to intimidate his colleagues," Banks said. "Yesterday, it was the medical examiner. Today it's your technology guy."

"Pappy is not a patient man. He likes results."

"From what I saw of his track record, he gets them." Banks studied my profile as we headed downtown. "Is the whole squad like you? A bunch of gun-toting, badass macho men?"

"Being a badass is a requirement. And just so you know, there are two women on the squad."

"Huh."

Something flitted across my mind about this case, but I couldn't catch it. Some little detail wanted my attention. I focused on driving. We had plenty of time to get downtown to the television station. Not wanting to get caught up in the freeway traffic, I cut over to Jefferson Avenue and followed the shoreline for a while. There was a nice breeze coming off the lake. With the windows down, I could feel the crisp, clean air. Banks was quiet, lost in her own thoughts. As we got close to downtown, we cruised past the intersection I'm named after. It's always a reflex to look at the street signs in acknowledgment.

There was a security guard at the station's parking lot. He raised his eyebrows at our credentials before waving us into a spot near the door. Banks followed me inside. Olivia Sholtis was waiting at the reception desk. The guard must have alerted her. She leaned forward and brushed her cheek against mine. I introduced her to Banks.

"Let's use this conference room. Then you can tell

me all about what's got you working with the FBI."

"Hope I didn't drag you away from an important story," I said.

"Told my producer I've got a hot lead on an in-depth interview with a rogue cop and his sexy girlfriend." She fluttered her lashes at me.

"You know, I almost forgot about your wicked sense of humor."

"Someday, Chene, you're going to sit down and tell me everything. By the way, you still owe me for that spa treatment from last month."

"Send me a bill. I'm good for it."

There was a small square table in the conference room with four chairs at the corners. I ended up sitting between Banks and Olivia. On the wall across from me was a large screen showing the current program the station was broadcasting.

Banks explained the details of the case. Olivia jotted down notes in her journalistic version of shorthand. Using a tablet computer, she called up the videos on the discovery and subsequent identification of Charity Gray. There had been little follow-up since that story ran. It was a bit surreal to be sitting across the table from her while she appeared on the screen, reporting the news. We watched the reports together on the big screen. There was not much to begin with. After reviewing her notes, Olivia looked at me and fluttered her dark lashes.

"What do you have in mind, Chene?"

"A quick interview. Get the public thinking about this poor girl who suddenly vanished, and no one's been held accountable for her death yet."

A look of surprise crossed her face. "You're

willing to go on camera? The elusive Sergeant Chene, being interviewed live on the noon news?"

"Hell no. You want someone people can relate to. Kids she knew then would be in their thirties now. They're probably scattered to the four winds, but some may still be in the area. And someone may remember her."

"Well, if you're not going on camera, who is?"

Banks piped up. "You're thinking one of the sisters from the school."

"Damn right. The principal, Sister Augusta, wasn't there when Charity disappeared, but Sister Mary Margaret was. She was one of her teachers."

Liv was adding to her notes. "You think she'll do an interview?"

"Bet your cute little ass she will," I said.

Banks offered to call the school and arrange it.

Olivia leaned close and whispered, "You really think my ass is cute?"

I winked at her. "Yeah, but don't tell Charlie."

She patted the back of my hand. "That will be our little secret. And I won't mention it to your new girlfriend when I interview her."

"You keep dreaming, kid."

"Always. When you crack this case, what's in it for me? Do I get a nice, juicy exclusive?"

I had already considered that. "Some of it may have to be off the record, but I'll make sure you get solid information."

"Promises, promises. You can be such a sweet talker, Chene. Telling me exactly what I was hoping to hear," Olivia said with a smile.

Banks confirmed that Mary Margaret was at the

school and would do the television interview. Olivia called for her cameraman then escorted us out the building. She would have them add a banner with the number for the post to call in case anyone had information to share.

Before leaving the TV station, I checked the list of faculty members. There were two people we hadn't spoken to yet. Eric Metcalfe from Redford, about twenty miles west of downtown and Elizabeth Quick, who lived in Wixom, an Oakland County suburb on the western edge of the territory. Redford was on our way across town, so I decided to stop there first. According to the school's list, Quick retired just last year. Metcalfe was still teaching. As I drove, Banks reviewed the case file for the tenth time.

Many of the houses in Redford were built in the late thirties or early forties. Metcalfe's residence fit the mold. It was a nice brick bungalow with a detached garage. Walking up the driveway, I could hear classical music. The garage doors were rolled up. The music was coming from there. Someone was moving about. The front door of the house was open. A knock on the screen was answered by a curvaceous middle-aged woman with gray-streaked brown hair.

"We're looking for Eric Metcalfe," I said after identifying us.

She flashed a bright smile that set her eyes twinkling. "I'm Ruth Metcalfe. The colonel is in the garage, reviewing his strategy. He'd love the company. But a word of warning. He's bound to talk your ears off."

"The colonel?" Banks asked.

"It's easier if he explains," Ruth said with a laugh.

She waved us up the driveway and ducked back inside.

"The colonel?" Banks repeated.

"Maybe he was in the military. Let's go find out."

We stopped just outside the garage. It was big enough for two cars, with additional space on the side for lawn mowers, yard equipment and patio furniture, but none of those items were present. Instead, there was a large trestle table in front of a couple of windows. Above it was a brass light fixture appropriate for a pool hall, with three large metal shades over the bulbs. A stocky man wearing khaki shorts with cargo pockets and a T-shirt was bent over the table. His right hand was in motion as if he were conducting the musicians currently performing. Sensing our presence, he turned and flashed a grin that equaled his wife's.

"Don't just stand there gawking. Haul your narrow asses inside!" His voice was a deep bellow, laced with humor.

It was impossible not to smile at this greeting. "Sergeant Chene, MSP. This is FBI Agent Banks."

"I was wondering when you'd get around to me. Sister Mary Margaret called yesterday. She wanted to make sure I was available in case you had questions. I'm on the road a lot during the summer."

A glance at the table showed maps and drawings from various Civil War events. On a clothes rack bolted to the far wall was a wool uniform of the Union Army on a heavy wooden hanger. There was an equipment belt on the shelf, with pouches and what could have been a saber in a scabbard. Metcalfe noted my attention. A gun cabinet was next to the rack.

"Is that an actual rifle?" I asked.

"A replica of a Springfield musket from 1863.

113

Comes with a bayonet too. Don't worry. This garage has a better security system than the house does."

Metcalfe spent a few minutes showing us around. It was like walking into a time capsule from the 1860s. He led us out to a picnic table behind the house. Eric Metcalfe was a bear of a man with broad shoulders and chest. His legs looked like tree trunks. A full beard and a shaggy head of hair, both going gray, added to the image of a sizable guy. In his late fifties, he'd cultivated his love of history into a career that awarded him the opportunity to participate in many Civil War reenactments around the mid-west.

He explained that his grandfather claimed to be a descendant of Orlando Metcalfe Poe, an engineer who served in the Union Army. Poe commanded a Michigan infantry regiment through several campaigns. Following the war, he was named Chief Engineer by the Great Lakes Lighthouse District. During his tenure, he designed and oversaw the construction of multiple lighthouses in the area, many of which are still standing.

"Orlando Metcalfe Poe was the engineer who designed the Soo Locks in the Upper Peninsula," Eric said. "Grandpa loved to spin tales of Poe's efforts and successes, both during and after the war. As a kid, I got caught up in those stories. By the time I was in college, my research confirmed many of Grandpa Metcalfe's stories to be true."

"Are you involved in reenactments only during the summer?" I asked.

"That depends on my availability. I've gone to many schools in uniform, not just St. Bartholomew, to help teach kids about the war. I'm active in the 19th US

Infantry, Company B. Education and preservation are the primary objectives," Metcalfe said. His voice was deep yet enhanced with that humorous inflection.

"Is that the group down at the old fort?" I asked.

He nodded, a bit of mischief in his expression. "That's Fort Wayne to the likes of you. Right on the edge of the Detroit River. Some groups use the fort for practicing maneuvers, honing their everyday camp life impressions, and drilling to keep those skills from getting rusty. These gatherings can be for as little as a few hours on an evening to as much as a full weekend."

Banks brought up the reason for our visit. Eric Metcalfe laced his fingers together and focused his attention on her.

"Do you remember much about Charity?" Banks asked.

"Yes, although to be honest, I hadn't thought about her for years until we saw the news broadcasts about her remains being discovered. When Mary Margaret called, it immediately brought back a lot of memories. But I'm not sure what good that information will do either of you."

Banks nodded. "We understand that. It's part of our investigation to gather as many details as we can. Something may give us a link or a lead as to what happened to Charity."

"I read the accounts from the papers. Learning when she disappeared triggered a few thoughts," he said.

"Can you elaborate, Mr. Metcalfe?" I asked.

"Call me Eric. I've been teaching US history forever and a day. So, my lesson plans rarely vary from year to year, although I do try to incorporate current events. During that period in April, my freshman classes would have been studying the 1860s. We discuss specific events, the cause and effect of certain actions. It's much more than just the names and dates of battles and conflicts to memorize. I encourage them to consider other roles within the war."

Banks leaned forward. Her notebook was on the table, next to my digital recorder. She pushed the recorder a little closer to Metcalfe with her fingertip. "What other roles?"

He had her now. "Support, tactics, logistics, supplies, communications. And, of course, spies."

"There were spies in the Civil War?" she asked incredulously.

Metcalfe roared with laughter. "Don't tell me you thought spies only started with James Bond! Or perhaps Mata Hari! Dear girl, there have been spies since the Revolutionary War. And perhaps since the beginning of time."

The back door of the house swung open, and Ruth stepped out, carrying a tray with mugs and a decanter of coffee. She joined us, perching beside Eric, and pushed playfully at his shoulder.

"Once you get him started, he won't shut up for hours," Ruth said.

Banks took a mug of coffee and sat back a bit, contemplating his remarks. Eric Metcalfe now looked like a playful teddy bear, eyes dancing, waiting for a chance to share more about one of his passions.

"You were discussing spies the week that Charity disappeared," I said. "You may have piqued her interest."

He shrugged. "The girl was always curious. You

must have heard that by now. A good student, well prepared, quick to ask questions and seek clarification. I do whatever it takes to trigger the imagination. So that week I wore my uniform to school. Even had a couple of seniors dress up and pretend to be soldiers, reporting in, or messengers. There are usually a couple of kids from the drama department who love to play along."

"Any of those kids female?" I asked.

"And the sergeant wins a cigar." Eric shifted his full attention to me. "How did you know there was a female?"

"Stands to reason. I recall accounts about women spies during that time. We've learned that Charity was inquisitive. Stories about a woman spying during the war may have intrigued her."

Ruth shifted uncomfortably. "Maybe she saw something she wasn't supposed to."

That was entirely possible.

"If you've got a few minutes, I'd love to show you my library," Eric said. "Sounds like you might appreciate the scope of it."

Ruth snorted into her mug. "Scope of it! You've got over eight hundred volumes on the war. Scope of it! I'm surprised the second floor hasn't collapsed from the sheer weight of all that paper."

"I'm a collector," Eric said sheepishly.

"Too bad you don't collect rare gold coins," she muttered.

Obviously, this sounded like an old argument about to be rehashed. I took that as our cue. We thanked them both for their time.

"Come on down to the fort sometime," Eric said. "I think you'd enjoy that glimpse back into the past."

"I'll keep it in mind. But right now, the only glimpse into the past I want is the one that shows me who killed this girl."

He nodded solemnly. "May your efforts be successful."

Chapter Ten

After our conversations with Angela Durfee and Alain Bissett, I was revising my stereotype of teachers. Maybe Elizabeth Quick would surprise me yet again. I'm beginning to think any stereotype should be chucked out the car window while doing sixty miles per hour. Quick's house was in a new subdivision, a nice little bungalow with cedar shingles. A wide front porch ran the width of the house. Brightly colored flowers in large clay pots and neatly trimmed shrubs graced the yard. As I parked in the street, the screen door opened, and two women stepped out. They settled into comfortable chairs in the overhang's shade.

"Showtime," I said.

"Any bets on which one is Quick?"

We were too far away to compare either woman with the thumbnail photo the school provided. I shook my head and led the way.

Both women were slender. They wore shorts and loose tank tops. Barefoot with tanned faces and limbs. Obviously, they spent a lot of time outdoors. Neither wore sunglasses.

"We're looking for Elizabeth Quick," I said.

"What's this about?" asked the woman on the right. She had ash blonde hair worn loose to her shoulders.

"I'm Sergeant Chene with the Michigan State Police. This is FBI Agent Banks. We're investigating the death of Charity Gray."

The woman on the left had auburn hair pulled back in a ponytail. "Can you prove that?"

The blonde chuckled and shook her head. "Prove that they're cops or that they're investigating Charity's murder?"

"Either. Or both. Yes, both!"

I pulled back my jacket so they could see the badge clipped to my belt, then held up my ID. Banks handed them her creds. The two women studied them closely and compared the picture to Banks's face. Satisfied, they returned the credential's case and waved us to a pair of empty chairs. There was a round glass-topped table between us.

"I'm Beth Quick," said the lady with the ash blonde hair. "This is Samantha Crosley, former librarian, a certified know-it-all and a true pain in the ass."

"Of course, I know everything. It goes with the job," Crosley said.

Banks went through the standard questions. I took the opportunity to study the two women. Quick was nearly six feet tall, although she slouched to appear shorter. Crosley was about five-seven. Both looked athletic and comfortable with each other. Their chairs were close together.

"Do you remember anything about Charity being in your class?" Banks asked. "I know it was a long time ago."

Quick gave her head a slow shake. "After thirty-nine years of teaching, it all blurs together. I do recall the stories about her disappearing, but that was a very trying time for me. My personal life went to hell."

She explained that her husband had suffered a massive stroke earlier that same year. Beth was struggling to keep working and care for him. Her own children had gone off to college and started their own lives out of state. Beth reached over and squeezed Samantha's hand, then resumed the narrative.

Friends since college, the two women had stayed in touch. Samantha began helping care for the ailing Mr. Quick. The stroke had left him paralyzed, unable to speak, unable to move. For almost five years, they took care of him. Along the way, Samantha's own husband drifted out of the picture. Her divorce followed shortly after the Quick funeral.

"We focused on work. It was a relief to get back to what many would consider a normal life," Beth said. "But somewhere along the line, I changed."

"I did too," Samantha said quietly.

"Neither one of us had any interest in dating. No desire to meet new men or go on one of those god-awful websites designed for desperate people," Beth said. "We just gravitated toward each other. Time passed. Eventually, I was ready to retire, to focus on doing some of the more enjoyable things I'd always wanted to do but never had the time or the energy."

Samantha had continued working. By that point, the two women had grown even closer. Elizabeth Quick was ready for a change. She sold the family house, where she raised two kids and cared for her ailing husband. Quick wanted a fresh start. She pitched the idea of living with Samantha, having their own new place. They found the house in Wixom. Crosley retired as well.

Quick laced her fingers with Samantha's. "We're

together. I guess we've been drifting in that direction for quite some time."

"But what does that have to do with your investigation?" Samantha Crosley asked. "You can't be that curious about the relationship of two old women."

"We're talking to anyone and everyone who may have known Charity during that freshman year, leading up to the time she vanished," I said. "You may have seen something, heard something, or noticed something that didn't seem important way back then. But it could have a bearing on the case now."

"I worked for the Troy Public Library," she said. "Don't think I ever had any interactions with Charity."

"It was a long shot," Banks said.

"And I wasn't exactly involved in a lot of extracurricular activities with school that year. All I did was teach geography and hurry home to care for Marvin," Beth Quick said with a shrug.

There it was. Like a smack up the side of the head. A thin smile crossed my lips as I stared at her. Banks started to get up, then hesitated when she realized I wasn't moving.

Geography.

Pappy's favorite expression flashed in my mind, but I managed to hold back from uttering it, not sure how the ladies would react. Instead, I held up one finger and ran to the Pontiac. On the way, I recalled last night's conversation with Simone. Maybe that's when the idea began to form, drawing my fingers across the palm of her hand. Could it really be just that easy?

I spread the Oakland County map across the table on the porch. All four of us were gathered around.

"Okay, here's the school." Beth circled it with a

red pen.

"What was Charity's home address?" I asked Banks. She shrugged, then hurried to the car to bring in the file.

"Why does this matter?" Samantha asked.

"Everyone has told us that Charity was a curious girl. We know she attended school that Friday and never made it home. She might have been bored walking the same route every day. So maybe she decided to follow her curiosity and take a different route on a nice spring afternoon," I said.

Banks returned with the file and rattled off the address. Beth Quick leaned closer, studying the residential streets. Then she jabbed a manicured nail on the map. "Right about here. And there are a million side streets that she could have chosen to get between the two points."

"According to the school's schedule, yours was the last class Charity had that day. I know it's ancient history, but would there have been anything special you'd cover in the spring?"

Beth Quick leaned back in her chair. There was an energy in her eyes, a level of excitement, of discovery that I have seen many times before with intelligent people. I glanced over to Samantha Crosley. Her eyes mirrored her partner's.

"When the weather's nice, in the fall and the spring, I encourage the students to explore. Don't be a robot and just trudge the same streets every day. Get out there. Take a wayward path. Look at your surroundings. Learn about landmarks. Try and visualize what's just around the corner." Beth's voice was a little higher than before, her words triggering memories.

"You're a damn good teacher," I said. With a nod to Banks, I started folding the map up. She tucked the file under her arm.

"You got that right," Samantha said.

"Former teacher. I'm retired," Beth said.

"No disrespect intended, Ms. Quick, but that's bullshit. You're still sharing your knowledge, keeping others engaged. That's teaching."

A wide smile filled her face. "Such a sweet thing to say."

I gently shook both women's hands. "Thank you."

****

Geography.

Why the hell didn't I think of that before?

"That's a lot of territory to cover," Banks said.

"Time for a coordinated attack."

She looked confused.

Pappy answered on the first ring. He agreed to meet at the post.

"Think about this. Metcalfe was teaching about women spies during the Civil War. Quick was encouraging her students to observe, consider landmarks around them, make walking outside an adventure. We know curiosity was a significant part of Charity's life," I said.

"Maybe the girl wanted to be a modern spy, keep her eyes open and see what was just around the next corner," Banks said.

"She would have made a good cop."

"Or a federal agent."

By the time we got there, Cantrell had a segment of the Oakland County map blown up, with the focus on the school and Charity's home address. Together we plotted out the various ways she could have taken to get home. MacGregor was excited, despite his attitude toward the case. Pappy had one of the administrative staff run off several copies so we could set each one aside.

"That's a lot of options to cover, even if we split it up," Mac said.

Pappy canted his head in my direction. "Steal help iffen ya need it." He tapped a button on the desk phone and lifted the handset. There was a muttered three-word conversation, and he dropped the phone back in the cradle.

I knew the rest of the team was unavailable, working other cases. But Pappy's reach extends beyond Squad Six. It may not be official, but he has never been one to color inside the lines. There was a sharp knock on the conference door before it swung open. Sergeant Clay Naughton entered. He was ten years out of the military, where he trained on recognizing and disarming bombs. Naughton oversaw Squad Five, whose primary tasks involved handling and disposing of explosives. But he was always eager to assist with our cases. Recently he'd given up on the fading crewcut hairstyle and had taken to shaving his skull. He was built like a sturdy brick wall, with muscular arms and legs.

Cantrell had often utilized some or all of the five-man team to assist in our investigations. Pappy made quick introductions and spelled out the situation.

"We got lots to cover in a lil bit of time. Ah wanna borrow two of your people and have 'em take a part of this. Y'all need someone who knows how to ask questions and lissen." Cantrell took a stack of maps with the adjacent streets highlighted and handed them to Naughton.

"Preferably someone who looks official but not intimidating," I said. "We can work up a list of questions you can use. Any results, good or bad, you can run through me."

Naughton nodded thoughtfully. "I've got two guys off duty right now. They're slated for evening, what with all the fireworks and whatnot going off after dark. I can leave Giles to man the desk and take O'Connell. She's new but good."

"A male-female team would be ideal," I said. "You know how to tread lightly and get people talking."

Pappy and I explained the case. "We're looking for people who lived there fifteen years ago. In some situations, the current residents may not have been on the scene. But they may be able to give you details about someone who was."

"Seems like a longshot to find anyone who not only lived there back then but also saw something," Naughton said.

"The approach to this whole case of yours is nothing but a longshot," MacGregor said. "But we're going to keep at it."

Neither Pappy nor I mentioned Leo Agonasti. It was easier to just have Naughton believe that we were assisting the FBI in an old homicide case. Pappy and MacGregor took the stack of maps that covered the eastern side of the grid and left. I would work the center with Banks. Naughton and O'Connell would have the western edge, which was the smallest quadrant. Pappy was respectful of their other duties, especially since our involvement in the investigation was unofficial.

Naughton called back to O'Connell's desk and

instructed her to change into civilian clothes. He would switch out of his black bomb squad threads before heading out. Working with Banks, we put together a list of questions that could be used. Naughton looked it over, made a couple of suggestions, then printed out several copies.

And just like that, our case was moving in a new direction.

Chapter Eleven

During late afternoon, Fen emailed me the forensic report. I read it while we grabbed burgers from a Woodward Avenue diner. He confirmed that Charity Gray had been strangled. It may not have taken much pressure since she was such a petite girl. Beyond that, there was not much information that was useful.

Several of the houses we'd visited earlier had been empty. Regular people working regular jobs. We were going to swing back through them after five, just in case. There are times when you get nothing. As Pappy was fond of saying, 'Sumtimes y'all is good. And sumtimes y'all gets lucky. And sumtimes it's a lil bit of both'. I was hoping this was one of those times.

Banks surprised me. She'd gotten a clerk at the bureau to pull up details on all the names of the residents in our area, going back to the date of the murder. If the people had moved, I was hoping we could get their current addresses. Somewhere, somehow, someone had seen something. Young girls don't just disappear in the middle of a spring afternoon without a trace.

The sun was setting. Banks covered her mouth with the back of her hand, smothering a yawn. Pappy and MacGregor were nearby, still working their territory. Naughton and O'Connell had finished an hour ago. We were down to the last name, an older couple named

Griffith. The house was on the corner of a residential side street.

Banks popped her door as I rolled to a stop at the curb. Stretching as I got out, there was a flicker of movement from between two houses across the street that caught my eye. At the same instant, I heard a dull snick that was too familiar by far. Banks moved forward, letting the door slam behind her.

"Down!" Instinctively I dove across the hood on my stomach and tackled her as the first shot rang out. What followed sounded like an open session at a firing range. Several guns were involved. The windows of the Pontiac imploded.

"What the hell!" she screamed.

"Stay low. Keep the engine block in front of you!"

Banks had her weapon drawn. Crawling toward the rear, I drew my gun. Risking a peek through the shattered windows, I saw three guys spread out across the street. Two had assault rifles of some sort. They were on the ends. The guy on the left was tall and lanky. The one on the right was short and stocky. The man in the middle had a revolver in each hand like a character from an old Western. He was the shortest of the three, wearing a suit and tie. He was methodically firing, first one gun, then the other, taking his time with his shots.

I squirmed low, sliding off the curb and under the Pontiac. If they blew the tires, I wouldn't have much time to get out before the car settled on its rims. But the element of surprise might be in my favor. Quickly I lined up the guy to the right. I couldn't see much. Hopefully, it would be enough.

A squeeze of the trigger sent three rounds at his

legs. He danced when hit, still firing his assault weapon. Bullets sprayed the air. Without hesitation, I swung to the left and got off three more shots. One was close. But then the rear tire exploded with a bang. I wiggled backward, not wanting to push my luck.

Banks was kneeling by the front wheel. She was pumping rounds at the guy on the right. As I glanced through what remained of the windows, she nailed him in the face. He dropped immediately in a heap. One down.

I slid closer to the trunk and aimed at the guy with the rifle. He staggered to his left. Someone was screaming in the distance. I could only hope it wasn't an innocent bystander caught in the crossfire. Banks was beside me now. She slumped against the rear door. Her face was ashen. There wasn't enough light remaining to see much else of her.

"You hit?"

"In the side. Don't know if it was a round or shrapnel." She gritted her teeth. "Hurts like hell. But I got that fucker when you shot him in the legs."

"Two guys left."

She nodded. "You got a plan?"

"Wait until they're out of ammunition or reinforcements arrive."

"That's not a plan!"

"The rifle's gotta run out soon. When he goes to switch the clip, that's when we move."

"You're fucking crazy!"

"I've heard that before."

"Cover me. I'm going for that tree to get a better angle," I said.

There was a chatter as more rounds slammed

against the Pontiac. Banks raised up enough to put the barrel of her gun where the backseat window used to be. She risked a glance at me and nodded. I got to my feet and ran. Beyond the driveway was a sizable oak tree. I was hoping it was solid enough to give me some protection. Banks fired. I swung my arm to the right and squeezed off several more shots at the rifleman. Something tugged my arm. I dove for the grass behind the tree and rolled to my knees.

A metallic clatter sounded across the street. I peeked around the tree's trunk. The rifleman was down. But so was Banks. The gunslinger stood in the middle of the street, one arm pointed in my direction, the other where Banks had been crouching. My left arm felt funny. A glance at my weapon confirmed it was empty. I pulled the fresh clip from the shoulder holster and managed to load it. I fumbled my left hand in place and racked the slide, sending a fresh shell into the pipe. Bringing the gun up, I pushed off the tree and got to my feet.

The gunslinger was slowly advancing in my direction. With the angle he was taking, the tree wouldn't do me any good. He lowered his left hand and shoved the gun into a pocket of his jacket. An evil grin crossed his face.

"Don't need that one anymore. Now it's just down to you and me. You're screwed. You are just so stupid that you don't realize it yet."

My gun was pointed at his core. He was only fifteen feet away. "Doubt I could miss from here."

He rapped knuckles against his chest. "Body armor."

I didn't move.

"Latest and greatest, so they say. Can stop a shot from an elephant gun."

"You're assuming I'll shoot for center mass."

"Of course. That's what they teach you Boy Scouts." He started to bring his right hand up to bear on me. "This shit is state of the art. There's nothing…"

Tilting my weapon slightly, I fired twice, striking him in the forehead. He flopped backward on the ground. I walked over and kicked his gun underneath the Pontiac's rear wheels.

"Never was a Boy Scout."

****

Sirens and flashing lights filled the night. Squad cars, fire trucks and an ambulance blocked the residential street and the surrounding neighborhood. Above the squawk of activity, I heard a distinctive voice snarl at one of the uniformed cops manning a barricade. Moments later, Cantrell appeared beside me. I was sitting on the inside step of the ambulance. A paramedic was cutting away my jacket and shirt.

"Fuck me hard," he muttered.

"Damn right."

He pointed over my shoulder at Banks, who was strapped to a gurney. "How's the girlie doin'?"

"Still alive. She got hit in the side. Something grazed her forehead too. Don't know if it was shrapnel or a piece of glass."

"You?"

I nodded toward the paramedic. He looked up from his efforts, pressing a gauze pad to my shoulder.

"He took a round. No exit wound, so whatever it is, it's still in there."

Cantrell shifted his gaze to me. "Don't y'all die on

me. It'll ruin muh vacation plans."

"I'll keep that in mind. Where's MacGregor?"

"Raisin' holy hell with the locals. He be along."

The paramedic was shining a light in my eyes. "We need to get rolling. You want to wait for another ambulance?"

"How far to the hospital?"

"Less than ten minutes with Naomi driving. She's hell on wheels."

"Let's roll."

Pappy helped me climb into the rig and slammed the doors. A squad car led the way, lights and sirens blaring.

The medic wasn't kidding. I'd swear Naomi took some of the turns on two wheels. Adrenaline must have been rocketing through her veins.

"You're gonna get us killed on the way to the hospital," the paramedic yelled over the squeal of the sirens.

"Don't be such a damn pussy," Naomi shouted back. "I haven't killed anyone tonight. Yet."

That was not a statement I could make.

At the hospital, the paramedic ran alongside the gurney as they hustled Banks inside. Naomi came around the back of the rig and looked me up and down. She had dark hair clipped short and a lanky body, almost as tall as me.

"Want a wheelchair?"

"I can walk."

Naomi glanced around to see if anyone was paying attention. "Let's make it look good for the cameras." She grabbed my right arm and slung it over her shoulder. Her left arm went around my waist, pulling me close.

"You gonna buy me dinner first?"

That earned me a bawdy laugh. "You know what you get when you say my name backward?"

Nothing came to mind, so I tried unsuccessfully to shrug.

"I moan." She gave me a sinful grin. "If you can't handle the cognitive part, the physical activity could put you in intensive care. Think you've had enough fun for one night."

"I appreciate your concern for my health and well-being."

Inside she started to pause by the main desk. I kept going, following the hustle of activity where they had taken Banks. Naomi ducked inside the curtained area and got an update.

"They're taking her up to surgery now."

"Prognosis?"

She shrugged. "Should be good. Some blood loss, but this is a top crew. They'll patch her up. Give her a sexy scar."

"Scars are sexy?"

Naomi wiggled her eyebrows at me. "Sexier than tattoos. And much better stories. Hey, I think that doctor is looking for you."

A doctor and nurse hurried over. Next thing I knew they had me on a gurney up on my right side. After pushing, probing, and consulting, they rolled me gently onto my back.

"You'll be going up to surgery," the doctor said calmly. "There is the possibility of some nerve damage."

"Any good news?"

"I'll leave that to the surgeons. You'll be in good hands." She swabbed my arm and jabbed a needle in a vein. I thought it was antibiotics, but shortly after that, I was gone.

Chapter Twelve

The car was a new Mercedes coupe, a gleaming silver beauty. It rolled up the blacktopped driveway to the country club, whisper quiet. A young man wearing khaki slacks and a white golf shirt with the club's logo above the heart popped the door as the German auto rolled to a stop. He stepped out smoothly, took the ticket stub the valet offered and tucked it into his shirt pocket. Eyes hidden behind dark sunglasses, Leo Agonasti scanned the property once before heading inside. On the way up the stairs, he shot his cuffs, adjusting the cut of his dove-gray suit.

The exclusive club was in northern Oakland County. Leo didn't play golf, didn't understand the rules or the game itself and couldn't care less. But he was happy to pay the exorbitant fees as a member under one of his aliases. Even Max knew nothing about this place.

"Good evening, Mr. Castle." An attractive brunette greeted him with a wide smile. "Your table is ready."

"Thank you, Gretchen. It's nice to see you."

"And you, sir. Your guest arrived a few minutes ago."

"Excellent."

Gretchen guided him into the dining room. Through the large picture windows, it was obvious that sunset was still a couple of hours away. Electric carts zipped along the path around the course. Agonasti moved between the linen-covered tables, responding to the occasional greeting with a nod and a quick smile. Gretchen stopped at a table near the windows, overlooking the water hazard for the eighteenth green.

"Enjoy your meal." She gave him a little bow.

"Thank you. Are the seats for the performance reserved?"

"Yes, sir. The concert will begin promptly at eight."

"Very good."

Agonasti waited until she was out of earshot before turning to his dinner companion. She was a petite woman in her early thirties with jet-black hair and an elfin figure. She wore a turquoise dress with black high heels. He leaned down and buzzed a kiss on her cheek. "Good evening, Valerie."

"Hello, Mr. Castle."

"Please, call me Marcus."

The young woman gave him a sweet smile. "Marcus. Thank you so much for inviting me. I've never been in a country club before."

They chatted for a few minutes while perusing the menu. After ordering dinner and cocktails, he let his eyes drift to the window. A flock of geese that had been idling on the pond took flight as an errant shot landed with a volcanic splash in their midst. Agonasti sensed a little discomfort in his dinner date. Turning his attention on her, he softened his features, portraying a sense of calm.

"Be assured, Valerie, that I didn't invite you here with an ulterior motive. This is simply an opportunity to have a nice meal, perhaps learn more about each other and enjoy a little music." He watched her draw a deep breath and slowly release it. Then she lifted her wine glass as if to toast him and took a sip.

"I wasn't sure what to expect. First you offer me a job *and* a place to live. Then a call to join you for dinner. It's a bit of a surprise," she said. "But then again, everything about this situation has been a surprise. Like how you even found me in the first place."

Leo Agonasti shrugged. "I'm a businessman. As such, I have crossed paths with many entrepreneurs over the years. Including your...former employer."

"Kyle Morrissey was a good man. He treated me well." Valerie Mann's eyes went to the tablecloth. She made elongated figure eights with a manicured nail. "It's hard to believe he's gone."

"I am always intrigued with the events that take place in our community. As such, I am familiar with the details about what happened to the late Mr. Morrissey," Agonasti said quietly. He sipped pinot noir from his glass.

"Which still makes me wonder why you'd make me such an offer. The job and the home? It's not like we knew each other before."

Leo gave it a moment when their salads arrived. "From my perspective, we mutually benefit from this arrangement. You have a new place to live, far from any former friends and coworkers who, for whatever reason, would look upon you in an unkind light. I have someone who is thoroughly capable of managing the property for me."

Kyle Morrissey, her former employer, had recently been murdered. While she was not directly involved in the crime, the outcome was enough to make Valerie resign from her job. She was suddenly single, unemployed, and unable to afford the hefty mortgage payments on her house. Three days after she quit, Agonasti approached her with an opportunity. He owned a small condominium complex, with two dozen units in Rochester Hills. The last unit would be converted from a display model into her living quarters. As the manager, she would see to any tenant issues, regularly scheduled maintenance and coordinate the work with outside contractors. She could also show any vacant properties as they occurred. Valerie had been on the job less than a month. This was her first social outing with the man she knew as Marcus Castle.

"I can't tell you how much I appreciate everything you've done for me," Valerie said. "It's truly a fresh start." Tentatively, she lifted her hand from the tablecloth and rested her fingers on the back of Agonasti's wrist. "How can I ever properly thank you?"

Agonasti gave her a soft smile, turned his hand, and gently squeezed her fingers. "Do a good job. Keep the tenants happy, the grounds immaculate, and the units full. That's all the thanks I want. Or need."

"I'll do my best, Marcus."

"That's exactly what I'm hoping for."

Casual conversation followed with dinner. If Valerie was disappointed by the rebuff, she didn't show it. Over coffee she regaled him with a tale about the need to replace three shrubs and repair a sprinkler head. Apparently, the man operating the commercial lawnmower was distracted by one of the resident's teenage daughters who was sunbathing in the buff. The man's initial reaction wiped out one shrub, but the greater damage was done when the girl stood up and waved to him. They were both laughing when the hostess appeared.

"The concert will begin in five minutes, Mr. Castle, if you'd like to freshen up before taking your seats."

"Thank you, Gretchen." He rose and slid back Valerie's chair. She put her hand on his arm as they followed the hostess out of the dining room.

"Who's performing tonight?" she asked.

"A quartet, three instruments and a vocalist. They're developing quite a following." He guided Valerie into a large banquet room that was dimly lit. Small tables and chairs were scattered about the room, giving it the feel of an old jazz or blues club. There were red globes on each table with a votive candle burning inside. Gretchen stopped beside a table on the right side of the room, about halfway back, with a clear view of the stage. Two snifters of top-shelf brandy magically appeared.

A minute later, the lights in the room dimmed, and the audience chatter subsided. From behind a curtain, a clear male voice announced, "Good evening, ladies and gentlemen. It is our pleasure this evening to introduce Orion's Belt."

From stage left entered a guitarist and a pianist, both men in their early forties. Entering from stage right was a male saxophone player and a young woman with long, sandy brown tresses.

For the next ninety minutes, the music flowed. While the musicians were talented, it was obvious that the star was the young woman. She had excellent range. Agonasti sat back, enthralled by the performance. The catalog of songs extended from the big band era to more contemporary tunes. The trio performed well. The audience response was so encouraging they did two encores.

Leo took Valerie's arm as they were leaving. He handed the valet his ticket and glanced at the young woman.

"I had one of those car services bring me here. I didn't know how late it would be or if I might have too much to drink. No sense taking chances. The last thing I need right now is a DUI," she said with a smile. "I'll give them a call."

"Nonsense. I'll drop you off."

He opened the passenger door for her, tipped the valet handsomely and drove out onto the main road.

"Did you enjoy the evening?" he asked.

"Yes! It was wonderful. A lovely meal. And the entertainment! That young lady, Katrina, has the voice of an angel."

He nodded in agreement. "Yes, I expect this is only the beginning of her musical career."

They were quiet for the short ride back to the condominium complex. Agonasti parked in front of her unit. He came around, opened her door, and escorted her to the condo's entrance.

Valerie cleared her throat. "It was a lovely evening, Marcus. I hope you'll forgive my clumsiness earlier."

"I've already forgotten it. It pleases me that you had an enjoyable time. Thank you for being my companion this evening."

She flashed him a wide smile. Agonasti leaned in and buzzed her cheek again. Valerie Mann had the feeling this guy would never have a problem escorting any lady any time he wanted.

"Good night, Valerie. Perhaps we can do this again next month."

"I'd like that. Good night, Marcus."

He watched her step inside and close the door. Back in the Mercedes, Agonasti drove to the far end of the complex. He touched a button on the dash and a garage door opened. Parking inside, he switched off the car and closed the overhead door. Entering the unit, he deactivated the alarm. Leo Agonasti left the lights off and moved into the master bedroom. Heavy drapes covered the windows, giving the room the atmosphere of a tomb. He turned on one lamp. After removing his jacket and tie, Leo entered the master bath. There were twin sinks here with a spacious ceramic counter. Three mirrored panels offered his reflection. The one on the left concealed a medicine cabinet. The one on the right held bottles of lotions and bath beads. The center one was secured with a hidden catch. He opened this panel, revealing a small safe. Leo entered the combination, and the door popped open. Inside there was a burner phone and a glossy leather wallet. He exchanged it for the one with the Marcus Castle identification and credit cards.

Agonasti reflected on the musical performance. No one would ever know that Katrina was his niece, the child of his in-laws. It had been more than twenty years since he'd seen the family. Leo discreetly followed her efforts. This was the second time in the past year when he was able to watch her from the audience.

He removed the cell phone and powered it up. The voice mail icon lit the screen immediately. Max with a report. It only contained four words.

—There's been a shooting!—

Leo punched in the number. Max seemed to answer before it even rang.

"Talk to me."

"Three guys went after Chene and that female agent. I was a few blocks away, keeping a loose tail on them. By the time I got on scene, it was over. Chene and the woman were the only ones breathing. Injured but alive."

Leo Agonasti listened without comment. His mind was spinning with possibilities. Obviously, this shooting was triggered by Chene's investigation. But who? Only an idiot would believe a firefight with the police was a resolution.

"Where are you, Max?"

"At the hospital, hovering in the shadows. They're both going up for surgery. I've got a nurse, providing information."

"Keep me informed. Use this line."

"Soon as I know something, so will you."

"What about Cantrell, the boss?"

"The man's prowling the halls. Looks like he's bringing in the giant and the rest of that team."

Agonasti considered that. It came as no surprise. Cantrell's squad was a tight-knit group. No doubt it was one of the reasons they worked so well together and solved such a high percentage of cases. "Proceed with caution, Max. Having Cantrell and that group on our side is the best way to clear my name. Call me in an hour with whatever information you have."

"Will do."

Agonasti ended the call. He turned the phone off and pulled the battery out of habit. He would replace it in an hour when Max was due to call. His friend would do the same to minimize the possibility of anyone connecting the calls with their locations.

Leo Agonasti went into the kitchen to brew a mug of coffee. He was wide awake now. Thoughts and effects of the evening had rapidly faded away. Leo gazed out the window at the dark landscaped area of the condominium complex.

Who would be stupid enough to take a run at Chene? The question intrigued him. Was there any one of the current families who would benefit from Leo being charged with murder? There may be concern from one or two syndicates that Agonasti would cut a deal in exchange for a reduced sentence. But why go after Chene? If there were true concerns about Leo Agonasti's loyalty, why wouldn't they come after him?

Of course, Giacalone would quash any action. Tony Jack's descendants knew Agonasti was an honorable man. Even during retirement, he still occasionally offered advice on projects.

"Who?" he asked his reflection. "Who would be so careless? So stupid?"

There were no answers.

Chapter Thirteen

There was a quiet mumbling of voices as I came around. It took a moment for my eyes to focus. I was in a private room, sitting up partway in a bed. My left shoulder was wrapped in heavy bandages. An intravenous port was tucked into the back of my left hand. There were wires running beneath the hospital gown, feeding the monitor above my head. Someone was squeezing my right hand. My neck creaked as I turned in that direction.

"Hey," Simone said gently. There were tears in the corner of her eyes. A few had fallen and streaked her cheeks.

"Hey." My voice sounded creaky. "How did you get here?"

She tilted her head toward the door. Pappy was leaning against the wall. He had been talking quietly with Laura.

"Ah pulled her number from yer phone. Thought y'all would want her here."

"How's Banks?"

"She gonna be fine." His eyes flicked to Simone. "Ah need to talk with Chene for a bit."

Laura moved toward Simone. "Why don't you come with me to the cafeteria? Maybe we can find something besides coffee."

She hesitated, then released my hand. Simone

walked slowly over to Laura but kept her eyes on me. "I'll be right back."

"Take your time. Something tells me I'm not going anywhere."

They stepped out and closed the door behind them.

"You shouldn't have called her, Pappy."

From his shirt pocket, Cantrell dug out a piece of paper that had been folded and creased many times. Without a word, he came to the bed and passed it to me. Flipping it over, I saw a picture of me and Simone. It must have been taken last night when we'd met for a drink. Above me, the machine began to beep faster. Probably monitoring my blood pressure. For some reason, it was a little difficult to take a deep breath.

"Found that on one of them shooters."

"You think she's at risk?"

He shrugged. "Ain't takin' no chances. Them going after family is way over the line."

I knew what he meant. It was one thing to go shoot at a cop. But would they risk endangering a girlfriend?

"So, what's our next move?" I asked.

Before he could respond, the door swung open. A doctor in scrubs and a nurse entered. The doctor did a quick check of the monitor. He looked closely in my eyes, then reached down and took my left hand with his.

"Squeeze it," he said. I did. He gave a quick nod of satisfaction. "You were lucky. That bullet must have bounced off something else before it hit you, so it didn't have full velocity. Mainly tore the supraspinatus muscle in your shoulder. Not too deep, but deep enough."

"When do I get out of here?"

He winked at the nurse. "That's another ten you owe me." Back to me, he said, "We'll keep you overnight. Give the antibiotics and pain meds a chance to work. I'm also prescribing something for sleep. Eight hours of rest will do you wonders." He made a note on the computer that was positioned on a cart near the bed. "See you in the morning."

I thanked him. Simone and Laura came back in. Pappy updated them. The picture was laying on my lap. Simone saw it and her eyes went wide.

"Who took this?" she whispered.

"Don't know," Pappy said, "but them shooters had it on 'em."

Her voice was still low. "What does it mean?"

"We don't know," Laura said. "But we want to be careful."

"Laura an' one of the others will take ya to a hotel. Keep a watch on you tonight an'—"

"No!"

Pappy stared at her. He was unaccustomed to being interrupted.

"No!" Simone repeated. Her arms were crossed defensively over her chest. "I said no. You can order them around, but not me. If he's staying, so am I."

I was chewing the inside of my lip. Pappy doesn't back down from anybody. But now he was hesitating.

"You're going to have one of the other detectives standing guard outside, aren't you?" she asked.

"Kozlowski isn't likely to leave while you're here," Laura said.

"That's the big guy?" Simone asked.

Cantrell nodded. "Yep. But what about tomorrow? Once Chene's released, I want someone with y'all.

Unnerstand?"

"Deal. But I'm not leaving tonight."

Pappy looked at me. I tried to shrug but only one shoulder moved.

"Got a plan for tomorrow?" I asked.

"Working on it. Gonna steal some help."

The nurse came back in with a syringe. "Regular visiting hours ended a long time ago."

This was not going to be Pappy's night. He made a fist and thumped me on the leg. Laura waved and followed him out. The nurse glanced at Simone. She settled into the chair beside the bed. The nurse nodded at her. She injected the syringe into the IV port and left the room.

I reached for Simone. Her fingers laced through mine. When I tugged her hand, she got up from the chair and slid beside me on the bed.

"I was so scared," she whispered.

"I know."

"Don't you die on me, Chene."

"I already promised Pappy to stay alive. Otherwise, it would spoil his vacation and he wouldn't like that."

Her face was pressed against my neck. My right arm was around her shoulders, holding her close. I should know better than to joke about dying. After all, it was death that brought us together. Simone reached across me and found the controls for the bed. Slowly it tilted down to a sleeping position.

"I'm not going anywhere," she whispered.

"Good to know." That was the last thing I remember before the drugs kicked in and put me to sleep.

****

Daylight was peeking through the edges of the curtain. It was a struggle to get my eyes open. Simone was gone, but I could hear water running in the bathroom. The outer door swung open and a lanky nurse marched in. Even though I was still hooked up to the monitors, she did a quick check on my vitals, raised the back of the bed into a sitting position and looked at my bandaged shoulder. Satisfied, she rearranged the gown to cover me and stepped back.

"How are you feeling?"

"Not bad. But it tastes like you fed me a fuzzy caterpillar."

She grinned. "That's the meds. Breakfast will be here shortly."

Simone came back into the room as the nurse left. As she was settling in the chair, the door opened again. A head of thick blonde hair peeked inside.

"I leave you alone for three months, three short months, and you go and get shot," she said. "If you wanted to see me, all you had to do was call. This is a lame cry for attention, Chene."

Detective Megan McDonald, my former partner, came all the way into the room. She was carrying a cardboard tray with four cups of coffee and a large bakery bag. Megan smiled as she placed everything on the tray beside the bed. She reintroduced herself to Simone. Megan had worked the serial killer case with me. That's when we'd met Simone.

"Pappy reach out last night?"

She nodded. "He's calling in a few favors. I offered to help out for a couple of days."

"Help out how?"

149

Megan shook her head. "Pappy will tell you. He should be here any time now. Raspberry or blueberry?"

Simone perked up. "Are you talking coffee or pastries?"

"Muffins. And black coffee, but I did bring cream and sugar if you like." She handed the bag of pastries to Simone. I watched as she withdrew a large raspberry muffin. My stomach growled loudly enough for everyone to hear it. With a smile, she passed it over. Megan pulled the lid from a coffee cup and set it on the table before me.

"Breakfast, cop style," she said with a grin.

"Who's outside?" I asked.

"Donna. They split it up into two-hour shifts. Kozlowski took the first one. Probably ended up with a date by the time Laura came back."

"That wouldn't surprise me a bit."

There was a thump on the door as Cantrell entered. He nodded to Simone and accepted a quick hug from Megan. "Y'all start without me?"

"Only the coffee. Apparently Chene missed the in-flight movie and the gourmet dinner that was served last night."

He accepted the coffee and dug into a blueberry muffin. Pappy waited until everyone finished eating before sketching out his plan.

"Y'all oughta be gettin' cut loose this morning. Doc be in shortly. McDonald will be keepin' an eye on Miz Bettencourt."

"I don't need a babysitter," Simone said defensively.

"We aren't taking any chances," Megan said.

Simone cut her eyes to me. I nodded in agreement.

"You should take a couple of days off. I'd rather have Megan with you."

"More'n just her. Ah'm pulling Naughton and his crew in too," Pappy said. "Ah take it serious when someone starts gunnin' for my team."

Megan turned to Simone. "We'll swing by your apartment, so you can pick up enough clothes for a couple of days. Then we can go to a safe hotel that will be well guarded."

"What about you?" Simone asked me.

"I'll be fine. Pappy and the squad will take good care of me."

She moved over and stood in front of Cantrell. This time Simone placed her hands on her hips defiantly and stared at him for a couple of beats. Then she said, "You'd better."

Cantrell made no response. At length, he nodded. Megan grabbed Simone's purse from where it dangled off the back of a chair. With a gentle touch, she turned her toward the door. Simone hesitated. Ignoring both of them, she walked over and took my face in her hands. Then she leaned down, resting her forehead on mine. With a serious look on her face, she kissed me softly on the lips.

"I expect to see you tonight." She pulled away.

"Yes, ma'am."

She hooked the strap of her purse over her shoulder. With Megan leading the way, she left the room. Pappy waited until the door closed.

"That un's got some fire in her."

"Yeah, she does."

"McDonald will take good care of her."

The door opened again. A hospital staff member

brought in a breakfast tray. She looked cautiously at Cantrell, then dropped the meal on the table and hurried out of the room. He took a tentative step forward, peering at the food. Runny scrambled eggs, bread lightly toasted and coated with two inches of margarine and what may have been hash browns adorned the plate. To the side was a container of red gelatin. Pappy snagged it from the tray and grabbed the spoon.

"Seriously? You're swiping my Jello?"

He shrugged. "Y'all can have the eggs. It's protein."

****

Kozlowski stopped by my place and grabbed some clothes. Once the doctor cleared me, I started to get dressed. The nurse, who was a curvaceous brunette with very dark eyes, insisted on assisting. She gave me a frown reminiscent of the nuns from the elementary school when I tried to pull on my shirt. Deftly she guided my left arm into the sleeve, then moved in front of me to do up the buttons.

"Be careful with that shoulder. If you rip those stitches out, it will set back your recovery. And Dr. Carmichael gets grumpy when his stubborn patients don't follow his orders."

"I'll keep that in mind."

She slipped my arm into a sling and ran the strap behind my neck. Before I could comment, she amped up the frown. "Do *not* screw with me. You damn cops are the worst patients when it comes to your own well-being."

"Might have something to do with our efforts at trying to protect innocent people," I said.

"Can't protect them much if you can't take care of

yourself."

She was still glaring when I stepped into my boots. Then she thrust the discharge papers and a bag with a couple of prescription bottles into my free hand. There was a knock at the door and Koz came back in, pushing an empty wheelchair. The nurse looked at him briefly, then nodded.

"I appreciate your help," I said.

"I had the pharmacy here fill those scripts. The antibiotic will keep you from getting any more messed up than you already are. At least, physically messed up. The other one is for pain. Take it at night. And be careful out there. Sometimes I think the world is going bat-shit crazy." She glared at Kozlowski. "If he gets busted up and comes back in here, I'm holding you personally accountable."

He grinned and winked at her. With a shake of her head, she roughly pushed past him and out the door.

"Let's go for a ride."

"Where's my creds?" I asked.

"Pappy's got them. He'll have the squad together when we get to the post."

I moved from the bed to the wheelchair.

"You didn't stick around all night?"

"Left when Laura came back."

"McDonald figured you might have hooked up with someone from your distant checkered past."

"That's cold," he said.

"Yeah, but was it accurate?"

Koz chuckled. "Not very distant past. And don't complain. She just got done taking care of you."

"Is there anywhere you've ever been when you couldn't pick up a woman?"

He considered it. "Haven't scored at a funeral. Yet."

"It's important to have goals in life."

"Copy that."

It occurred to me that I hadn't seen him since Monday when I got involved in this case. "By the way, I bumped into one of your old flings recently. Angela Durfee, one of the Ah Girls."

A devilish smile lit up his face. "Oh baby!"

"Funny, she had a similar reaction."

Koz hit the button for the elevator. "She's got a great…voice."

"You are an evil rat bastard."

"I can't help it if women find me charming and irresistible."

"Don't forget modest."

****

I stopped at my desk. After all these years, it felt odd not to have a weapon on me. From the locked drawer, I withdrew the 9mm Beretta that Ted had given me when I made sergeant. I did a quick check of the magazine and spare, then tucked the gun into a holster on my right hip. The spare magazine clip went into a pouch that clipped to my belt. My regular gun had been taken at last night's crime scene.

Koz watched, holding two cups of coffee in his massive hands. He passed one over as we walked to the conference room. Everyone was gathered in their usual spots. Cantrell smirked when he saw the sling on my arm but refrained from commenting. He waited until I sank into my chair at the other end of the table. My badge and ID were there. The badge got hooked on my belt. I slipped the ID into my back pocket on the right side.

"As of right now, y'all on board with this un. We got until six p.m. Friday to figger it out." He let his eyes flick around the table. "All other assignments is otherwise on hold."

"You must be getting close," Laura said, "otherwise, why would they start shooting at Chene and Banks?"

"Maybe they didn't like his taste in cars," Suarez said.

I scowled at him. "That Pontiac is a classic. Solid, fast, dependable."

"Sounds like a description for Kozlowski," Donna chimed in.

He winked at her. "Only fast when I need to be."

Cantrell wearily raised a hand, and the bantering faded. "Yer wheels is good as dead. Ain't enough insurance money in the world to resurrect that." With a flick of his wrist, he sent a keyring sliding down the table. It skidded to a stop in front of my coffee cup.

"What's this?"

Pappy gave me a sly wink. "They some wheels impounded off a drug boss last year. State gets to keep the property for costs. Was gonna be auctioned next month. Figgered y'all could use 'em for a while."

"Where's my ride?"

"Towed to the evidence lot. What's left of it, anyway. Y'all might get a few things outta the glove box or trunk that ain't full of bullet holes."

"So, what's the plan?" Suarez asked.

Cantrell dipped his head in my direction. I took the cue. "Laura is right. We must have been getting close to someone to trigger the action last night. We start there.

155

Koz, you and Laura check with the medical examiner. They should have identified those mutts from the shooting."

"Got it. And then?"

"Run them down. Find out who they worked for. See if they were local or brought in. While you're at it, see if you can connect with Max and pass the details along." I expected a growl of protest from Cantrell, but he let it pass. "Max would know if these guys were tied to any particular arm of organized crime."

Laura held up a thin sheaf of papers. "That broadcast on Channel Four yesterday turned up a few leads. People who claimed to know Charity when she was in school."

Pappy gave me a nod. That was more than we expected when I'd met with Olivia Sholtis yesterday. The story had been run again on the six o'clock broadcast and featured on the station's website.

"How many hits?" I asked Laura.

"Seven. All in the general area of that school. Want to see them?"

I shook my head. "Nah, you keep them. Start working those after the medical examiner."

"Will do." She tucked the pages in her notebook.

"Whatcha gonna do?" Cantrell asked.

"I'm going downtown to talk with MacGregor."

"Y'all take Spears with ya. Nobody runs alone on this un no more."

"Then you can take Suarez and go back to that neighborhood. We were going to interview a possible witness from the disappearance. Name is Griffith. Maybe that crew was trying to keep us away from them."

Pappy nodded. "We'll find 'em."

We all stood up. Everyone except Pappy. He didn't say a word, just let his eyes flick around the room. He drained the last of his coffee and banged the mug sharply on the conference table. "Y'all watch yer asses. An yer partner's too."

"Copy that," Koz said.

Donna followed me outside. Parked near the main door was a bright red Jaguar sedan. Its lights blinked when I pressed the button on the key fob. The leather seats were cool. Pushing a button on the dash brought the powerful engine to life. Donna buckled in beside me.

"Do you get to keep this?" she asked, with an edge of wonder in her voice.

"Get real. You heard Pappy. It's a loaner." I goosed the gas pedal and felt the powerful engine rumble.

"When I get a loaner, it's got as much power as a golf cart."

She watched closely as I familiarized myself with the controls. "Sure you're okay to drive?"

"Only one way to find out." I shifted it into gear and headed out for Gratiot Avenue. The car was a dream. It was almost as if it anticipated my movements. We rolled south, heading through traffic for downtown.

Donna settled back in the seat and slipped her sunglasses on. "I could get used to this."

"You ain't the only one."

****

MacGregor was scowling as we exited the elevator. I introduced Spears. He jerked a thumb toward the conference room. It was the same one Diana Trevino had been in Monday night. A lot had happened since then. We sat at one end of the table near the door.

"How's Banks doing?" I asked.

"Feisty."

"She did well last night."

He nodded once. "I know. Told her the same thing. Banks is a good agent. I hate having her on the sidelines."

"Sidelines is a hell of a lot better than the morgue."

MacGregor started to respond, then cast his eyes toward Donna. She tilted her head slightly to the side, as if expecting him to do something unpredictable. He looked back at me.

"You got a problem?" I asked.

"What the fuck, Chene! You almost got her killed. You and this bullshit investigation! You're too close to these gangsters!"

My blood pressure bounced. "It was your half-assed case that started this!"

"That's a crock of shit! We've got that old mobster dead to rights!"

"If that case is so solid, who the hell was shooting at us?"

Somewhere along the line, we'd both gotten to our feet. MacGregor looked ready to come across the table at me. Donna stepped in front of him, placed both hands on his chest and shoved him back to the wall. He started to grab her wrists, but she slapped them aside. Hard. I reached up and undid the Velcro strap on the sling, pulling my arm free. MacGregor drew a deep breath and forced it out. I threw the sling on the table.

"You want to fight me, jackass? Let's go," I growled. "Right here. Right now. C'mon, jackass!"

He shook his head in disgust. "Like I couldn't win against the weary one-armed man?"

"That's the only way you're ever going to beat me." My voice was a snarl I barely recognized.

We glared at each other, anticipating who would make the first move. There was no way to know how much strength I had after just getting out of the hospital, but I was about to find out.

Donna thumped MacGregor's chest with the palm of her hand. "You boys done with this macho bullshit display or are you going to whip out your dicks so I can measure them?"

Nobody moved for a spell. Then he coughed out a laugh and raised his palms in surrender. Donna took a step back but didn't seem to relax. I realized my right hand was clenched into a fist. With an effort, I released it and shook out my fingers, getting the blood flowing.

"You're an asshole," MacGregor said.

"Right back at you. Are we going to talk now?"

MacGregor looked at Donna. "Measure our dicks! You really said that!"

"Seemed like the next logical step in that display of testosterone."

There was a small refrigerator in the corner of the room, built into a cabinet. He moved to it, yanked open the door and lifted three cans of an energy drink. MacGregor glanced over his shoulder. I shook my head. Donna took one. We tried sitting at the table again. She passed me the sling. It took a couple of tries, but I managed to slide it back in place.

"What the hell was all that about?" I asked.

MacGregor didn't immediately respond. He snapped the cap on the drink and took a pull. Donna placed hers on the table without opening it.

"How long have you been dating her?" she asked him.

MacGregor set the can down and slowly turned it with his fingertips. "About ten months now. We're both single. Working long hours. Had a few assignments together. A couple of stakeouts. An undercover job where we posed as a couple. That kind of thing."

How did I miss that?

"She's going to be all right," I said.

He nodded. "I know. This fucked me up. Guess I'm still freaked by it."

I shifted my eyes toward the door. "You two dating common knowledge?"

"Oh hell no. They got rules against that. If it goes much longer, we'll have to come forward. One of us might get transferred to a different field office."

Donna winked at him. "We aren't telling anybody. If you promise that you won't try to fight Chene again. Cantrell expects me to bring him back in one piece."

"It's not you," MacGregor said to me. "It's the situation."

The three of us sat quietly and considered the case. There were still too many loose ends to satisfy me. Or Cantrell.

"Beyond Banks getting shot, how do you see this?" I asked.

"The search for Agonasti is still part of our investigation."

I nodded. That was about what I expected from him. "You think this case is rock solid?"

"Don't you?" MacGregor asked.

I scoffed at that. "It was never that good. Right

now, it's looking about as strong as the Lions defense in the fourth quarter."

That got a laugh out of him. "Well, it doesn't have as many holes in it as your Pontiac does."

"Yet another guy without taste in quality automobiles."

We all took another couple of minutes to slow it down. MacGregor drained the rest of his energy drink in several swallows. I wondered if he'd slept since the shooting or if he'd been at the hospital all night.

"What are you guys doing?" he asked.

"Chasing leads. You?"

"SAC is going to shut down your efforts to further investigate this case. He still believes we have enough on Agonasti to push for a conviction."

"You gotta find him first," I said.

MacGregor shrugged. "We will."

"You've been looking for seventy-two hours now and haven't found him yet. He will turn up when he's good and ready. Leo Agonasti was never involved in violent crimes. He was in the background. Cleaning money from illegal enterprises, investing it in legitimate businesses. He started several companies to spread the cash around."

MacGregor shrugged again. "Still illegal."

"Statute of limitations has passed."

"What the hell do you want from me, Chene?"

"Time. Keep the SAC out of the way and let us do the job."

MacGregor didn't respond. Donna got to her feet. "Go home, Mac. Take a scalding hot shower and a four-hour power nap. Then go to the hospital. You can entertain Banks with stories of how you wanted to whip

Chene's ass."

"Wanted to try," I muttered.

MacGregor slowly shook his head. "You're really a stubborn asshole."

"Seems to me that's what you two have in common," Donna said.

Chapter Fourteen

We were headed out of downtown when my phone chirped. I was struggling to pull it out of my shirt pocket while driving. Donna grinned, shook her head, reached across the dashboard, and pushed a button on the display. The phone stopped ringing. Kozlowski's voice came through the stereo speakers.

"Got the ID on two of those jokers from last night. Tall one was named Croyton, Michael Raymond. Recently did four years in Jackson on felonious assault charges, which was his second trip on the merry-go-round. Not exactly a student of quantum physics. Lots of stupid shit in his record. Bounced around from one fun bunch to another."

"Sounds like muscle for hire," I said.

"Yeah. Only thing out of the ordinary was the body armor. All three were wearing tactical vests of some sort."

"Military or police versions?" Donna asked.

"Nah. Looks like something you'd get from the internet or maybe one of those extreme sporting goods stores."

"What about the other guy?" I asked.

"Bertenelli, Francisco. Another clown with a penchant for violence. Had more arrests than you've had girlfriends. Lots of assault charges, mostly with his hands and feet, some with a weapon. Favored using a baseball bat in several cases. New to the area. Came up from Cleveland about two months ago."

"Cleveland?" Donna said. "You're talking Cleveland, Ohio?"

"What, you're thinking Cleveland is nothing but the Indians, Browns and the Rock and Roll Hall of Fame?" Kozlowski said.

From my peripheral vision I could see her shrug. "Never really thought about it much."

"Sounds like the two gunners on the flanks. What kind of details on the third guy?" I asked.

"This is where it gets interesting. No records on him yet. Prints aren't in the system, so no military or criminal history."

Something tickled the back of my memory. Short in stature, favoring the two-gun approach with heavy revolvers. That limited him to twelve shots, but he had the other two blasting away with the machine pistols. Maybe he had extra rounds in his jacket.

"Any identification on them? Paperwork, keys, anything at all?" I asked.

Koz chuckled. "The two mutts had full wallets. Fake driver's licenses, a couple of bogus credit cards and almost a thousand dollars cash in each one. No keys. Like they didn't expect anyone would be around to identify them. Nothing on the mystery man."

We were stuck at a light on Jefferson and Woodward downtown. I hadn't planned on it but decided we were going to run up the shoreline.

"What about a vehicle? These guys didn't take a cab or an Uber to that site. Did the city cops pick up a car?"

He covered the mouthpiece on his phone and

relayed the question. "Atwater is checking with the locals. In all the excitement, it may have been overlooked."

"Send me a picture of the unknown guy. Hell, send me all three."

"On it. What else?"

"Find that car. What about Max?"

"There's been no answer to the number you gave me and no access to voice mail. Makes me think it's a burner. Is it possible he'll be more forthright with you than me?"

"I'm counting on it. While you're there, check the weapons these morons used. See what you can find out about those revolvers. Then you and Laura can take a look at those calls from the newscast. It's a long shot, but at this stage, it's worth a try."

"On it, boss."

He clicked off the call. I merged with traffic and headed east on Jefferson Avenue. "So, the car can answer my phone?"

Donna laughed. "How old was that Pontiac?"

"Old enough."

"You got a plan for finding this Maximo character?"

"I'm going to send up a smoke signal."

****

The look on Donna's face was a mixture of amazement and confusion, with a dash of trepidation. She was perched on the passenger seat of the speedboat, one hand resting on her holstered weapon, the other lightly grasping the railing in front of her.

"You sure this will work?" she yelled to be heard over the wind. The boat was running at about thirty miles an hour.

"Gotta have a little faith. Ted says the message was delivered."

I swung toward the marina where Sharky's was located and cut the throttle. At the entrance to the canal was a gas dock, suitable for boats of all sizes to stop in and fill their tanks. I aimed for the last pump and slowed it even more. A couple of teens in shorts and T-shirts were on the dock, moving between boats with long fuel hoses. There was a group of people milling about, enjoying the weather and the perfect conditions of the lake. Several men and kids were on the edge of the pier, fishing poles extended into the water. There was a shack set back a bit, where the cash register, snack bar and coolers filled with beer and pop were.

As I eased up to the last spot, a guy moved forward to get the bowline. Behind him, an old man wearing shabby jeans, a worn denim shirt and a large straw hat dropped his pole on the dock and briskly walked behind the deckhand. From the shack on the pier, another old man dressed in the same type of clothes emerged. He ambled over to the edge and scooped up the pole, focused on the fishing. As soon as the side of the boat touched the dock bumpers, the first old-timer stepped from the pier and dropped onto the deck. I nudged the throttle and spun the wheel. We raced out onto the lake.

"Hell of a way to make an entrance, Max."

He clamped a hand to the crown of the hat and moved forward. Without hesitation, he settled onto the bench beside Donna.

"I'm getting too old for this shit," he yelled in my direction.

Donna maintained her position beside him. They

didn't bother with introductions. No one spoke again until we were in the middle of Lake St. Clair. I aimed the speedboat on the far side of an ocean-going cargo freighter and cut the power until we were just matching their slow pace on the water. Together we watched the ship trudge north.

"If it's your intention to stay out of sight during this shit storm, you're doing a damn fine job of it," I said.

"Not that I've got much choice. Feds are looking for me too."

"Got a feeling the feds ain't the only ones," I said. This far from shore no one could listen in on our conversation unless they had planted a bug on one of us or the boat. Before leaving the dock, I'd swept the craft, using a little handheld device Kozlowski loaned me. Satisfied that there was no electronic surveillance, I dug out my phone and passed it to Donna. She brought up the mystery shooter's photo and showed Max.

"This one of the idiots from last night?" he asked.

I nodded. "Yeah. He was with two guys named Croyton and Bertenelli. They looked like hired muscle."

"I heard of them. Not enough brains between the two of them to make an egg salad sandwich."

Donna wiggled the phone back and forth. "And this guy?"

"Dude was about five foot six. Thin. Wore a suit and tie. Used two revolvers," I said. "Made me think of a cowboy from a bad Western movie."

Max pulled off the straw hat and ran his fingers through his hair. He shifted on the bench seat and glanced at Donna out of the corner of his eye. I was standing by the hatch that led to the cabin below. He hesitated, fiddling with the hat's brim.

"No time to be cute, Max. Donna works with me. Pappy pulled the whole team in this morning after that execution went sour. Who is this chump?"

"Name's Tancredi. Something flowery, like Armando or Alberto or some shit like that. He's been trying to make his bones for a few months now."

"He's not in the system."

Max shrugged. "Not surprised. I think he's a distant relative of the Vitale family. Always trying to show people how smart he is, how tough he is."

"He's not that tough anymore," Donna said quietly.

"Was there a connection with the Vitale family and the Giacalone or Tocco crews?" I asked.

Max waved his hands in the air like a magician. "There are all kinds of connections if you go back far enough. You want, I can tie them all to the Purple Gang for ya."

That was a reference to the notorious organized crime syndicate from the 1920s that ruled Detroit. They covered everything from murder to extortion to bootlegging, kidnapping and much, much more. "I'm not looking for a history lesson. Let's keep the focus on current events. Why would this Tancredi guy start a shootout with cops? What is his connection with Leo Agonasti?"

"I don't know," Max said sullenly.

I took a couple of beats to reflect on that. Max should know everything that went on in this city when it came to organized crime. It was difficult to believe that he wouldn't know what the connections were and the reasons behind it.

"That girl was killed fifteen years ago," I said. "Was there anyone around back then who had a grudge against Leo? Someone who wanted to keep a hammer over him? Maybe to use him to get to Giacalone?"

"What are you getting at?" Donna asked.

"The evidence that ties Agonasti to the body of Charity Gray had to be buried with her at the time she was killed. Somebody went to a lot of trouble to set that up. And they must have been very patient to wait all this time."

"Then the house demolition…"

"Was unexpected. Whoever put her body there never anticipated that the place would be torn down. Somebody wanted that skeleton available and ready to be recovered," I said. "The mayor of Detroit's rejuvenation plan just stepped up the timetable."

Max shook his head slowly. "I've been wracking my brain, Chene. There ain't a damn thing that comes to mind."

I reclaimed my phone and scrolled through the list of contacts. Surprisingly, there was a strong signal out here on the lake. She answered on the second ring. I made the request and set an appointment.

"What should I do now?" Max asked.

"You keep playing hide-and-seek. See what you can find out about this Tancredi character."

"You remember where Leo keeps his yacht?" he asked.

"Sure."

"Drop me over there. But not too close. Just in case the feds are watching. I've got a car stashed. And I'll start digging." From his jeans, Max dug out a cheap cell phone and handed it to Donna. "Programmed with my

169

latest number."

She tucked it in a pocket. "You buy a lot of these?"

He grinned. "I can get you a couple of dozen if you're interested. Volume discounts and all."

****

"Where are we headed?" Donna asked. We were back in the Jag, traveling west on I-696. She reached up and pressed a button near the ceiling. A smoky glass panel rolled back, letting fresh air into the cabin. I could get used to this kind of ride very quickly.

"I need someone who is good with research. Somebody accustomed to digging deep. We've got about thirty hours left on Pappy's deadline."

Donna tilted her head back, feeling the breeze on her face. "Something tells me you're not headed to see a librarian."

"Not exactly. But she does have a knack for gathering information. And she could crush the image of a librarian to little pieces."

"So, a naughty librarian."

"Don't go there."

I rolled to a stop in front of the small ranch house. Movement inside the window caught my attention. The door opened before we were halfway up the walk, and a slender redhead emerged. There was concern in her green eyes. She skipped down from the stoop and covered the distance between us quickly.

"Hey, Jamie," I said.

"Hello, cowboy. You don't need to get shot to come and visit." Avoiding my wounded arm, she moved to the other side and gave me a gentle hug.

I'm still awkward around most women. There was a slight hesitation before my right arm circled her waist for a brief squeeze. "You remember Donna?"

Jamie let me go and stepped back. "Sure. We met during the Morrissey case. Let's go inside and you can explain."

We settled around the kitchen table. There were tall glasses filled with ice and a pitcher of lemonade in the center. Jamie served us and settled on the edge of her chair to my right, a legal pad and pen within easy reach.

"How's Malone doing?" Donna asked. Jamie lived with another cop, a sergeant with the MSP. Malone worked at a post nearby that managed the highway patrols for part of the Motown area.

"He's good. Had to be in court this morning."

On the phone earlier, I'd been reluctant to say much. It was entirely possible the feds or someone else was tapping my line. Now I spelled it out for her. I needed whatever information she could uncover about organized crime, particularly the families that were involved forty years ago. While I talked, Jamie scribbled notes in her own style of shorthand.

"You mentioned a deadline?" she asked while I sipped the lemonade.

"I hate to impose, but we've got maybe twenty-four hours before things get even crazier. The feds are trying to make a statement, with a bust related to one syndicate or another. Right now, it's all about politics, bullshit and headlines."

Jamie smiled and batted her lashes at me. "C'mon, Chene, you know that's what makes the world go 'round."

"Which is what brought you to mind. You were extremely helpful with the Morrissey case, and you certainly know how to dig. My only concern is that you might get someone's attention who doesn't want you poking around."

She waved her hands apart as if chasing a pesky fly. "I've got enough contacts who are still working that know how to bury any connection with me. I should get some information by early evening. And a lot may be available on the internet. Besides, I'm just a harmless little old lady writing mystery novels."

"Old doesn't come close to you," Donna said with a laugh. "And Chene told me about some of your previous escapades. I'm not buying the 'harmless' image."

Jamie shrugged away the compliment. I doubted she was even in her midthirties. I waited until her gaze shifted back to me. "Is there any way you can dig without leaving a trail? Whoever is really behind this didn't hesitate to bring out the guns last night. And despite your past, I'm disinclined to let your stubbornness get in the way of your health and safety."

"That's sweet. I can use some back-channel approaches. There are a couple of academics I know who've done papers on Detroit's organized crime dynasties," Jamie said. She tapped a polished fingernail on the legal pad. "Besides, it's just research for a book. My focus is on fiction now."

Donna glanced at me. "Sometimes truth is stranger than fiction."

"Sounds like something from *Mark Twain*," Jamie said.

"Yeah, but there's no arguing it," I said.

"You didn't want to talk about this on the phone. How do I get you the details on whatever I find out?"

I'd been considering that for a while. "Let's go old

school. Nothing digital, just print whatever you can find."

"Then what?"

"Is Malone working tonight?"

She nodded. "Three to eleven."

"Well, if you put whatever you find in an envelope, it would be easy to deliver to the post, along with a burger or two. Or maybe some sushi."

That earned me a grin. "That's a pretty smooth plan, cowboy. And once Malone has the details, he can pass them on to you."

"One brother cop to another. That also keeps you in the shadows."

Jamie pushed back from the table and stood. "Then I'd better get started."

"You don't sit still long enough to get dusty," Donna said.

She walked us back outside. As was her custom, Jamie looped her arms around my neck and gave me a tender kiss on the lips. Donna just stood there with a sloppy grin on her face.

"Give Simone a hug for me," she whispered as she pulled away.

"Will do. And thanks, Jamie."

"Go to work, Chene. There are bad guys that need catching."

****

It was early afternoon when we stopped by Sharkey's. Ted was behind the bar, flirting with three older women at the counter. Donna ducked into the restroom. I slid onto a stool and waited, my mind going back over the earlier conversations with MacGregor, Max, and Jamie. Ted leaned forward, a puzzled expression on his face as he spoke with the woman in the middle. He twisted his head to the left and right and received nods of confirmation from her two friends.

Ted turned to the service area and filled a blender with ice. He poured in several generous shots of tequila then grabbed a bottle from one of the coolers and filled the container. Ted was at an angle to me and when he looked up, I could see the grin on his face. Covering the blender, he powered it up. While it churned away, he pulled three large glasses from the overhead rack and coated the rims with sugar. Switching the machine off, he filled each glass, garnished them with a lime wheel and served the trio. The one in the center tasted it, beamed a smile, and blew him a kiss. He was laughing as he joined me.

"What the hell was that?"

"Tequila and prune juice."

I stared in disbelief. "Prune juice?"

Ted explained that the woman in the middle was an afternoon regular. She usually came in for lunch and a drink or two a couple of times every week. At her insistence, he began keeping a bottle of prune juice behind the bar. Claimed she made up the concoction. The doctor encouraged her to drink a few ounces daily, to keep her body functions operating smoothly. The tequila made it tolerable. The sugar and the lime were just Ted's finishing touches.

"You wanna know what she calls it?" he asked.

"Do I have a choice?"

"Nope. Ready?"

"Sure."

"A seniorita. You know, like a margarita for senior citizens. Says she's starting a movement." He hesitated, struggling to hold back the grin. "Get it? Prune juice. Starting a movement?"

The trio were laughing and toasting each other. Then they all raised their glasses to Ted.

"You are a warped and depraved old man."

"That's nothing new." He went behind the counter to whip up another batch. One of the waitresses brought me a mug of coffee. I ordered two grilled chicken sandwiches and moved to a table by the windows. Donna joined me, throwing a quick wave to Ted.

"How's the shoulder?" she asked. I'd pulled the sling off earlier and tossed it in the back of the Jag.

"Only hurts when I bang it against something."

She nodded. "So, what do you think of Max's story?"

"He may be holding something back. Max is no angel. But we need to figure out who this guy Tancredi was working for."

Lunch arrived. We stopped talking about the case and worked on the mountain of seasoned fries and the sandwiches. As we were finishing up, my phone chimed with Megan's number. Donna wandered over to the bar as I answered the call.

"Still alive, I see," she said.

"So nice to know you worry about me. How's Simone?"

"Nervous and anxious to talk to you. Got a minute?"

"Sure." There was a brief, muffled conversation before Simone's voice warmed my ear. "How's the shoulder?"

"Doing fine. Are they taking good care of you?"

"Yes. I almost expect Megan to follow me into the

bathroom."

I told her it was a necessary precaution. Simone didn't sound very enthusiastic about the situation. I needed something to loosen her up a bit. Reluctantly she passed the phone back to Megan.

"Who's with you?"

"Two of the bomb guys. Naughton and Giles. Why?"

"She needs to do something normal. Even if it's just for a couple of hours. It will help keep her calm."

"You got something in mind, Chene?"

"A shopping trip. I'm going to send Donna to meet you at Somerset. Use your cash or plastic, and I'll pay you back."

"What are we shopping for?"

"Whatever she wants. Tell her it's for Paris. We were talking about going in September. Have Donna and Giles do the couple thing and shadow you."

Megan hesitated. "Anything she wants at The Somerset Collection is going to be costly. We're talking Gucci and Louis Vuitton here. And my credit cards don't have much room to spare."

I gazed across the room to the bar where Ted and Donna were talking. He was watching the trio of older women head for the door, slowly shaking his head.

"Forget the credit cards. Donna will bring cash."

"Better make it worthwhile. Even the Godiva store will be costly. And I'm getting a craving for dark chocolate truffles."

"Tell Naughton to meet me at the post in half an hour. Stay at the hotel until Donna gets to the mall. Let me talk to Simone."

We had a brief conversation. She perked up with

the idea of the shopping excursion and the mention of the trip to Paris. I ended the call then joined Donna and Ted at the bar.

"How much cash you got in the safe?" I asked him.

He shrugged. "Couple of grand, maybe more."

"I'll take it."

"The hell you mean, 'I'll take it'? Do I look like a bank to you?"

I explained the situation and the need to keep the activity off the credit cards in case they were being tracked. Donna watched the exchange with wide eyes. Ted walked into the office and came back a minute later with a thick envelope wrapped with a rubber band.

"Three thousand. You wanna count it?"

"Nah. I trust you. Mostly."

That earned me another shrug. "Better than I usually get."

Chapter Fifteen

Nothing against Donna, but I wanted someone intimidating to back me up on my next stop. In truth, I wanted two guys whose size alone could make someone hesitate. That's where Naughton would come into play. His physical appearance could make people think twice before acting. While not as large as Kozlowski, Naughton didn't look like the kind of person most people would screw with. Maybe his abilities at defusing bombs would also extend into tense situations. He got to the bullpen about five minutes after me.

"What's the plan, Chene?" His voice was coarse and scratchy. Cantrell swore it was the result of swallowing bullets during a firefight in Afghanistan.

"Need your eyes and ears, along with your muscles. Kozlowski and Atwater are going to join us as well."

He wiggled his eyebrows up and down. "We having a party?"

"Starting one. C'mon, I'll fill you in on the way."

Naughton gave me a wicked grin, then turned and swept his hand down the aisle, like somebody on a game show. "After you, boss."

We ended up not far from Agonasti's Grosse Pointe home. Donna had obtained the details during her research. Koz and Laura were waiting just down the block as I rounded the corner. We stopped alongside.

"You must be out of your fucking mind," Koz snarled.

"Nothing new there. I just want to have a quiet conversation with a certain homeowner. Maybe he can shed a little light on these recent events."

Laura leaned forward, so I could see her past Kozlowski's bulk. "Where do you want me?"

"Across the street. There's good elevation." I pointed to what I had in mind.

She nodded and slid back.

"Locals on this?" Naughton asked.

"Yeah. They got the perimeter." I glanced at Koz. "You in?"

"Out of your fucking mind," he muttered. "Of course, I'm in. Your lady friend would kick my ass twice if I don't cover yours."

"Let's roll."

I waited until he had turned around and pulled in behind me. Laura jumped out with what looked like a gunny sack and trotted across the street. We each tucked an earbud in place. Within ninety seconds, her voice confirmed she was in position. I rolled up the driveway. Koz followed.

The front door of the old Grosse Pointe home opened as we approached. A stocky man wearing a lightweight charcoal suit and an open-collared white shirt greeted us. A thin panatela was balanced between the first two fingers of his right hand. "Afternoon, officers. What can I do for you?"

"Like a few minutes of your time, Mr. Tocco," I said.

"You got a warrant?"

"Don't need a warrant just to talk."

Movement behind him caught my eye. Koz was on my left flank, Naughton on the right. A slender man in his thirties appeared alongside Tocco. He extended a smartphone in my direction. His other hand was empty.

"My youngest son," Giovanni Tocco growled. "Lorenzo, say hello."

"Hello, police officers. I'm recording this conversation at the advice of the family's counselors. Would you mind stating your names?" Lorenzo's voice was that of an educated man. His posh suit couldn't be found in a local department store. Neither would the shoes. It was extremely doubtful he went to one of those sports bars that doubled as a barbershop for the haircut. I couldn't swear to it from the distance, but I was willing to bet his nails were manicured.

"Sure, I'm Brady. These are my associates, Gronkowski and Edelman."

Tocco barked a laugh. "Well, you sure as hell don't play for the Lions."

"Their names are unnecessary, Mr. Tocco. You already know mine. That should be sufficient."

"Well, it is true that you're a smartass. What is it you want, Chene? My secret cannoli recipe?" The laughter was gone. We were back to serious family business now.

"There was a shooting last night. You may know about it. Three men assaulted two law enforcement officers."

Tocco nodded sagely. "Saw it on the eleven o'clock news. But what's that got to do with me? I'm just a quiet businessman, enjoying a summer's day."

Koz shifted behind me. I knew he was having difficulty staying quiet. "Two of the gunners were dumb-shits. Meat for hire. But the third has me curious. Kind of a pretty boy. Last name was Tancredi. Word is he might be a shirttail relative to the Vitale family." I took one step closer and showed him the picture on my phone.

"That stupid fuck," Giovanni Tocco muttered. "Matteo Tancredi. Thought he was a goddamn cowboy, just like his *il nonnino*. Matteo Tancredi is one of Luca Vitale's punk grandsons."

"Was," I said, tucking the phone back in my pocket. "I was under the impression that Vitale has been out of the business for quite a while now. Any truth to that rumor?"

Tocco gave me another sage nod. "Stroke left him paralyzed. Luca's older than dirt. But he has been taken care of. His interests were…equally divided."

"Any idea who Matteo was working for?"

I waited while Tocco thought it over. Kozlowski shifted his bulk. Naughton seemed to be made of stone. Both men were studying the front of the house, checking the windows and the roof. But a shootout on Tocco's front lawn seemed unlikely. Which is why I'd called and requested the conversation to take place here. My gaze flicked to Lorenzo. He was still holding the phone out. I doubted he was going for video. It didn't matter.

Giovanni Tocco rolled the panatela between his fingers thoughtfully. "I don't want to be in the middle of a family battle. We have a, what do you call it…" He turned his head for a quick glance at his son.

"An accord," Lorenzo piped in.

The old man acknowledged this with a raise of his hand, bringing his eyes back to me. "Yeah, an accord.

There's enough action and territory here, no reason for anybody to go pissing on the other guy's petunias." He brought the cigar up horizontally and ran it under his nose. "Matteo thought he could reclaim his grandfather's action."

"How long has it been since Luca Vitale's...interests were divided?"

"Two, maybe three years." Tocco shrugged. "There were no hard feelings. Luca had no sons alive, and the girls weren't active in the business. Bianchi made a very generous offer." Another wave of the hand. "We all discussed it. It was clean. Logical. Like I said, there were no hard feelings."

"Nicola Bianchi ended up with the operation. Wasn't he one of Vitale's lieutenants? Did a few years in Jackson State Prison on the road construction bribery scandal."

"That's the guy. But there have been no disruptions. We all...get along."

"You're telling me Matteo Tancredi was working for Bianchi?"

Tocco slowly wagged his head back and forth. "Doubtful. That was one of Vitale's demands. Separate the business from every member of his immediate family. Leave them in peace," Tocco said. "But if you like, I'll make a call, tell him to expect you. Bianchi's got nothing to hide. He's in the wholesale produce business, down at the terminal below the bridge."

I considered that. It was obvious that Giovanni Tocco wasn't going to give me anything else. He was still rolling that cigar between his fingers.

"Appreciate your time, Mr. Tocco."

"You got brass balls, Chene, meeting me like this.

I've got three men guarding me at all times."

"Yeah, I know. But any sense of trouble, and you would be down before any of us could even bother to pull a weapon. You know what they say. If you cut off the head of the snake, the rest of the body dies."

He scowled. "Think you're that fast?"

"I don't have to be. Watch." I raised my hand and extended it palm up toward the center of his chest. Just above my fingers, a red dot appeared on the fabric of his white shirt. Tocco lowered his chin, letting his eyes take it in. I withdrew my hand. The dot vanished.

"You didn't get where you are by having a gun battle with state police detectives. All I wanted was a few minutes of your time and some information. I appreciate that. And your assistance." I moved back and gave him a nod as a sign of respect.

Tocco slowly shook his head. He raised the cigar again and studied it for a moment. Naughton moved forward and snapped open an old Zippo lighter that bore the USMC logo. With the flick of his thumb, he sparked it to life and extended the fire toward Tocco. They locked eyes briefly. Tocco popped the panatela in his mouth and bent forward, drawing in the flame.

"Pop! You know what the doctor said."

Tocco leaned back and puffed a cloud of smoke into the air. Without looking at Lorenzo, he muttered, "Fuck the doctor. I haven't enjoyed one of these in two weeks. Guys are going to wonder why I still carry it."

Naughton cracked a grin as he returned alongside me. "Sometimes a cigar is just a cigar."

"Damn right." Tocco smiled at him, then turned and went inside.

We headed down the driveway. Kozlowski shook

his head in disgust. "You're still out of your fucking mind. And now your antics are corrupting Naughton too!"

Naughton laughed. "It's a little late for that."

****

Nicola Bianchi's business was down at the Detroit Produce Terminal, right near I-75 on the southern edge of the city, not far from the Ambassador Bridge that connected Detroit to Windsor, Canada. We took both cars and made the run in twenty minutes. The clock was ticking on Cantrell's deadline. Bianchi portrayed himself as a regular working guy. His office was set back from the truck wells. We climbed a rusty flight of iron stairs to get to his domain. At this time of the afternoon, the terminal was relatively quiet. Laura led the way with Koz at her shoulder. There was a middle-aged Hispanic woman working on the computer inside the office. She didn't even blink when Laura flashed her badge.

"He's expecting you." She hooked a thumb at the wooden door behind her. It was an antique one, with a frosted glass panel making up the top half of it.

Naughton moved beside me. "*Gracias, Consuela.*"

"*De nada, hombre.*"

"You know her?" I asked as we went by.

"Nah. But her nameplate is on the back of the cubicle wall."

Kozlowski rapped a monstrous knuckle on the glass as a courtesy, then swung the door open. Bianchi was sitting at an old wooden desk, running his finger down a computer screen. He glanced up at the four of us, rolled back and halfheartedly raised his hands as he got to his feet.

"I didn't do it. Whatever it was, I didn't do it," he said with a grin.

Koz shook his head. "Typical mobster. Totally innocent."

Bianchi was a thin guy, about five foot six. He was dressed in black slacks and a white golf shirt. There was some muscle tone to the arms. Dark brown hair with a little curl to it covered his head. Bianchi had a trace of beard stubble, but I got the feeling it was a week's worth of whiskers. He wore gold rings on the first two fingers of his right hand. Nicola Bianchi kept turning them, using just his right thumb. Nerves?

"I take it you spoke with Giovanni Tocco," I said.

"GT called about half an hour ago. Said you'd probably be dropping by. Does this have anything to do with the bird dogs across the street?"

Bianchi was referring to the state police cruiser. Before visiting Tocco, I borrowed a page from Pappy's playbook. "*Steal help iffun ya need it.*" That's when I'd called the downtown post and requested a cruiser park out front. There was also an unmarked car on the side street as well. Just in case Tocco's call was a reason for Bianchi or his men to have a sudden change in their afternoon plans, I wanted surveillance on hand.

"I heard they have great donuts at that coffee shop," Laura chimed in.

"What can I do for the state police?" Bianchi remarked. His eyes were on me. Koz and Naughton had taken up stations beside me, exactly how they stood at Tocco's house. Laura was further to my left.

"Let's get down to it. Shooting last night out in Oakland County. Three gunners against two cops."

He nodded. "Heard about it on the late news. Every

185

station had coverage. It's a testament to the violent, challenging times we live in."

"Cut the crap. I want to know who sent them."

Bianchi turned his palms up. "I had nothing to do with that. What reason would I have for getting into a gunfight with law enforcement?"

"Matteo Tancredi thought it was a good idea," Koz said quietly.

Bianchi jumped as if Kozlowski had punched him. "You're shitting me."

"Was he working for you?" I asked.

"No way! No way in hell! I swore on my daughters' lives that I would not let any of Luca Vitale's relatives work for me. I swore! Luca lives in Phoenix. He's at a top-of-the-line assisted care facility. And I'm the one who pays for it! There is no way I'd bring that punk in to work for me. He's a pain in the ass with an irritating sense of entitlement attitude to match." Bianchi took a breath and went to the desk. He bent over and braced both hands against the top. "That goddamn kid."

"Well, if he wasn't working for you, who would have brought him into the trade?" Kozlowski asked.

Bianchi took a few minutes to gather his thoughts, head down, clutching the desk. Then he drew a deep breath and stood upright. "You know Giovanni wouldn't. Neither would I. Giacalone would never touch him. He has too much respect for Luca. That leaves just one."

"Which is?" I had a hunch but wanted Bianchi to confirm it.

"Daniel Spadafore. Fifth or sixth generation; family goes back to the 1910s and the mob wars. Mean bastards. Back in the day, rumor had it that his family was tight with Detroit's mayor. You know, the one who ruled for twenty years or so."

"You're talking Coleman Young?" Kozlowski asked.

"That's the one. All kinds of rumors about his dynasty in office and the generosity of the Spadafore family," Bianchi said.

"Let's stay focused on today," I said. "Tell us about Daniel Spadafore."

Bianchi gave his head a shake as if to clear his thoughts. "Spadafore's always been number four in the food chain. It's been that way forever and a day. Giacalone, Tocco, Vitale and then Spadafore. Four families or divisions or territories or whatever the hell you want to call it. But with an understanding. An agreement."

"An accord," I said.

Bianchi ran a hand through his hair. "Yeah, that. When Luca was stepping away, there was a little give and take, but not much. Things remained status quo. Pretty much the way they had been for twenty years or more."

"Except Spadafore didn't want to honor Luca Vitale's request," Koz said.

"Yeah. I heard that Matteo approached him when he came back in town. His family moved out to the desert somewhere in Arizona about fifteen years ago. They wanted to put some distance between them and the old man's turf. Then when Luca took ill, that is where he wanted to be. Close to his daughter and the grandkids. Family." Bianchi shrugged. "There were some mumblings. Some whispers. Who knows if there was any truth there?"

"Tell us about the rumors," I said.

Bianchi thought about it. "Luca liked to brag, tell a few stories about some of the capers he pulled or orchestrated. He enjoyed being the center of attention. Probably half the shit he claimed to have done was made up or really done by someone else. I don't know for sure."

"You think Matteo was impressed by the old man's antics? His trip down memory lane?" Laura asked.

"No doubt. That's why he showed up here, about six months ago. Wanted to make his mark in the business. Thought he was hot shit."

Koz slowly shook his head. "He's dead shit now."

Bianchi let his eyes go around the room, staring at each one of us. When he came back to me, I nodded. There was no need to show him the morgue photograph. He got the idea.

"So why would Spadafore come after the cops?"

"Beats the hell out of me. We're not exactly drinking buddies."

Naughton surprised me again. "So where do we find him? Aren't his interests primarily in gambling?"

"Yeah. He lives out in Bloomfield Hills. Likes the Oakland County crowd, playing with big money. Got a little bar not far from where the dome used to be in Pontiac. Still draws some people in. And I think he got a microscopic slice of one of the casinos. Heard he paid big money just to get close to the slot machines."

My eyes flicked to the crew. Koz caught the signal and moved forward. Bianchi seemed to shrink when standing next to him.

"You holding anything back on us, Nic? Anything

that might prove your hands were just a little bit dirty in all this shit?"

Bianchi was rapidly shaking his head. "Oh hell no! There's no reason for me to be tangling with you guys. I have no idea what led to that shooting."

"We're going to pay your buddy Spadafore a visit. If he tries to disappear or play cute, we'll know you tipped him off." Koz's voice sounded even lower than normal. "And you would not like it if that happened." He reached out and squeezed Bianchi's shoulder. "Not at all."

"I'm not calling him. He's a pissant. I don't even like to eat dinner with the bastard," Bianchi assured us. "If he's stupid enough to have been behind that shooting, let him answer for it."

Chapter Sixteen

We assembled back at the squad for a briefing. One of the other guys from Naughton's crew had run out to cover for Donna. I waved Naughton into the conference room with us. Pappy raised an eyebrow but didn't say anything. We all dropped into chairs. Laura started with a summary of the identities of the three shooters. Then she pointed at Kozlowski.

"We found the vehicle back at the scene. It was parked just around the corner, on the opposite side of the street, where they could watch the house that you parked in front of," Koz said quietly, speaking in a matter-of-fact tone.

"Anything of value?" I asked.

"It was a Chevy SUV, full size. Reported stolen earlier this week. Vehicle identification number didn't match the plates. Inside was filled with fast-food wrappers, empty bottles and a cooler. Also looked like a sleeping bag was spread out in back, in case someone wanted a catnap. We had it towed to the impound yard. The lab rats will be cataloging everything. Fingerprints galore."

"Sounds like a stakeout," Naughton said. "Wonder how long they'd been watching that area?"

Koz agreed. "Royal Oak PD is doing a canvass of the residents now. Trying to see if anyone remembers anything about those wheels or those guys hanging around. Chances are one or more of them would walk down to the main road for food and supplies. Someone may have seen them."

I gave an update about our meetings with Tocco and Bianchi. Then it was Pappy's turn. He hooked a thumb at Suarez.

"Pappy and I found the Griffiths. They moved from the neighborhood where last night's shooting was. Now they're living in a nice condominium place out in Farmington Hills," Suarez said.

"Anything worthwhile?" Kozlowski asked.

Suarez cut his eyes to Pappy, then over to me. It was obvious that something was up. Cantrell was in the process of firing up another cigarette, blowing smoke out of his nostrils like a wayward dragon. Pappy tipped his head at the kid. "Y'all set it up."

"We found the wife, Rachel, working at a church's food pantry out there. She's a volunteer with a few other women. Her husband, Frank, still works at Quality Meats down in Eastern Market. She was a little reluctant to discuss anything from so long ago. Pappy sort of persuaded her to talk with us in the privacy of her home," Suarez said.

Pappy shrugged as another plume of smoke drifted to the ceiling. "Was either that or the Oak Park Post. Got a nice interrogation room innit. Might as well let 'em hear it."

Suarez placed his digital recorder on the table and turned it on. His voice filled the room, stating the date, time, location, and the people present. Once the preliminaries were set, Pappy took over.

Cantrell: You used to live on Normandy, at the time Charity Gray went missing. Tell us about your life back then.

Rachel Griffith: We had a nice little house. It was in the middle of a small subdivision. Our place was on a corner, so we didn't have neighbors on one side. Frank and I had been together about four years then. He worked days at the meat plant. I worked evenings at Surfside. It was a gentleman's club, out near Orchard Lake, on the water.

Cantrell: Everything good 'tween you and Frank?

Griffith: Um, yeah, it was like most married couples. We did okay.

Cantrell: Neither of us is married. Why don't y'all spell it out?

Griffith: Well, Frank's a lot older than me. Almost twelve years. And by then, he wasn't showing a lot of interest, you know?

Cantrell: Meanin' yer sex life?

Griffith: Yes, it wasn't something that happened often.

Cantrell: So, what about that date? Y'all remember anything unusual during then? Or around that time?

Griffith: Just this one day. I don't think it's related.

Cantrell: Better let us decide if it is.

Griffith: (huffs out a breath) Like I said, I worked at Surfside. They did a lot of drinks and dinners for businessmen. It was kind of like a private club. All the waitresses wore these little uniforms. A tight blouse with a scooped neckline, showing a little cleavage. Well, a lot of cleavage. And these real short skirts.

Cantrell: Uh-huh.

Griffith: But we made good money. The tips could be great on a busy night. A lot of cash made up for getting my ass pinched. All the waitresses knew the score. We'd play along. The boss even let us have one free drink with customers at the end of the night. But only one.

Cantrell: Customers was mostly businessmen. Drinks and dinner?

Griffith: Yes. I'd been there almost six years. It was about this time that one of the guys took a shine to me.

Cantrell: What can y'all tell us about him?

Griffith: (hesitates) The only name I knew was Joe. He was probably in his mid to late twenties. Kind of olive skin, with this head of thick black hair. He was a little taller than me, with big shoulders and arms. I got the sense he was a tagalong.

Cantrell: How's that?

Griffith: He was always with this other couple of guys. He never paid the bill, only had two drinks and dinner, even if the others drank for hours. Joe was a background guy, kind of tagging along.

Cantrell: All right. Joe do more than give you a grab or a pinch?

Griffith: (sighs) Well, he did brush his hand on my leg a couple of times, being really sneaky yet shy about it. Almost like it was an accident. We couldn't wear tights or stockings. The girls were showing a lot of leg, and they had to be bare and smooth. Shaved them every day. It was required.

There was a long pause in the conversation, as if Griffith were lost in the memory of the job and her interactions with customers. Pappy gave her some time, then prompted her.

Cantrell: And one day with Joe?

Griffith: His friends were leaving as I finished my shift. I had a drink with them as I was cashing out.

Chatting a little bit. Just being friendly. But my car wouldn't start. Joe offered to give me a ride home.

Cantrell: Joe bein' nice, savin' y'all cab fare.

Griffith: Exactly. There was no Uber or things like that back then. Frank would be asleep since he worked early. I thought he was just being friendly.

Cantrell: He wanted more?

Griffith: Yes. He waited until we were about halfway to my place. Then he pulled over and we started necking.

Cantrell: Y'all try an' stop him or was it...consensual?

Griffith: I liked it. His first kiss was kind of awkward and shy. But when I started kissing him back, he really got going. Joe was grabbing my boobs. And my legs. He would have taken me right there if I let him.

Cantrell: But y'all stopped him?

Griffith: Yes. Frank and I weren't the greatest, but we were married. I had just turned forty, so a little flirting with him really boosted my ego. It was fun making out with a cute younger guy, but that was as far as I wanted to go.

Cantrell: He okay with that?

Griffith: Yeah. He was a little disappointed at first. Then he was kind of embarrassed. Joe got himself squared away and drove me home.

Cantrell: Y'all remember exactly when this was?

Griffith: No.

Cantrell: This the only time Joe made a pass?

Griffith: Do I have to tell you?

There was a tapping noise.

Suarez: This is Detective Suarez speaking. I'm advising you that this is a homicide investigation. If you have additional information that may be pertinent to this case, and you withhold it, you can be charged with obstruction of justice. That's a felony in Michigan. You could be looking at twenty years in prison.

Griffith: (gasps) Will you tell Frank?

Suarez: What you tell us will become part of our investigative files. If it leads to an arrest, your statements and testimony may be needed in court.

Griffith: Oh God!

Cantrell: Tell us!

There was another pause. I could imagine Cantrell's steely gaze boring right through her. I have been the focal point of that look before. It is not pleasant.

Griffith: It was a couple of days later, middle of the afternoon, probably around three thirty. I had just taken a shower, getting ready for work. Someone rang the bell. I only had my robe on. It was Joe. He wouldn't leave. Kept telling me he wanted me. Had to have me. That he was in love with me.

Cantrell: What happened?

Griffith: I got him out back. We had a little patio there, with an old wooden picnic table. You couldn't see it from the house next door. And there were some bushes, you know, like a hedge that Frank had planted by the sidewalk. So, it was private, you know. And Joe just kept grabbing me.

Suarez: How was he grabbing you?

Griffith: First, my arms, so he could pull me close. Kissing me. I struggled a little, but not much. (pause) I kind of liked the attention. He got me excited.

Cantrell: Go on.

Griffith: Joe got my robe undone. He started

getting a little rough. Kept begging me to take him inside. I wouldn't. I couldn't. We had been sitting together at the picnic table. He stood up and pulled me up with him.

Cantrell: And?

Griffith: Joe turned me around, bent me over the end of the table. And he took me from behind. I must have cried out when he started. It was so unexpected. I was surprised how much it turned me on. Joe didn't last very long. But he let out a little yell when he finished.

Suarez: What happened after that?

Griffith: (pause) We heard a noise from the hedge by the sidewalk. I could just make out a face, peeking through. It looked like a girl. She must have watched the whole thing. Joe yanked up his pants and ran after her. He just pushed through the shrubs. I went back inside, locked the door, and went to shower again.

Cantrell: Joe come back?

Griffith: No. He had parked on that side street, so nobody would see his car in my driveway or out in front. I figured he talked to the girl if he caught up to her, then drove away. I never saw him again. He never came back to the Surfside.

Suarez: Did you get a good look at the girl?

Griffith: No. It was just a face. Just a glimpse. I was too busy trying to cover up and get away from Joe.

Cantrell: Y'all never thought about this when it was on the news? 'Bout a girl disappearing?

Griffith: I worked nights. Never paid any attention to the news. Didn't read the paper back then. I still don't. It's depressing. Nothing but bad news.

Suarez: We're going to have a sketch artist come out here. You can describe Joe, give us a few more details.

Griffith: It was fifteen years ago! I can't remember much.

Cantrell: (loudly) Y'all telling me ya can't remember what the guy looked like? You do this kind of thing often? Sex on the picnic table?

Griffith: No! It was the only time!

Cantrell: Then start remembering.

Suarez reached over and switched off the recorder. Everyone was staring at the little device. It was Donna Spears who voiced what we were all thinking. "Fuck me hard!"

"Damn right," Pappy said.

Suarez passed out copies of the sketch. It was a good, clear drawing. On the bottom right corner were basic details as to approximate height and weight. We all studied it for a while, letting the image sink in. Then all eyes came up and looked to Cantrell. He laced his fingers together, stretched his arms out, cracking the knuckles loudly. There was a satisfied smirk on his face.

"Whatcha think, Chene?"

"We've got more questions than answers, but this is a hell of a lead. Great work, Pappy. You too, Ramon." Cantrell waved a hand as if batting away the compliment. Suarez simply nodded. "Okay, let's kick this around. Did Rachel Griffith tell you anything else worthwhile?"

"She showed us some pictures from back in the day," Suarez said. "She was pretty, nice figure, long dark hair. Turns out she worked there for another couple of years, then it started going downhill.

"She added a few pounds, stopped taking care of

herself. The clientele preferred the younger waitresses, so her shifts were getting cut. The less she worked, the heavier she got. Finally, they fired her. She found another waitress job, working days. Gave her a chance to spend more time with her husband."

"Did she remember anything about the car Joe drove?" Kozlowski asked.

"Yeah," Suarez replied. "She said it was blue. Didn't know the make, model or even how many doors it had."

"Shit," Koz muttered.

Donna was slowly turning the sketch back and forth in front of her. That caught Pappy's attention. "Whatcha got, girlie?"

"There are some facial recognition programs out there. Homeland Security and INS have a good one. Plus, there are some that could take this sketch and age it fifteen years, so we'd get a sense as to what this guy looks like now," Donna said.

"You know anybody at Homeland?" I asked Pappy.

He nodded and pointed a gnarled finger at Donna. "Git with me when we done. We'll make a call."

"What about this club, this Surfside? Any idea if it's still around or who owns it?" Naughton asked.

"A lot could have happened in fifteen years," Laura said. "Do you know something about it?"

Naughton laughed. "Fifteen years ago, I was in the sandbox, trying not to blow myself up disarming IEDs. I don't know shit happening around here from back then. And I'm from Livonia. Never been to Oakland County until I started on the job."

We were all quiet for a couple of minutes, trying to

look at different angles. "What are you thinking, Chene?" Koz asked.

"Let's throw out a theory or two and see what sticks. For the sake of discussion, let's say that to an innocent bystander, or a fifteen-year-old Catholic school girl, it looked like he just raped the Griffith woman on the patio. This Joe guy grabs the girl and whether accidentally or by design, he kills her. Then he panics and throws her in his car. And either he knows how, or he knows someone who knows how to dispose of her body," I said. "And they just so happen to know about this old house in a rundown neighborhood in Detroit."

Pappy was nodding slowly. "Keep it goin'."

"Somehow, there's a connection with Agonasti. But we don't know what that is yet. That's where a part of a business card and hanky are left with the body. This Surfside place may have been run by the Mob. Laura, start digging on that angle. Is it still in business? If so, who owns it? Pull tax records, financials, any information you can find. See who owns the land this place is built on too. Same idea if it's changed hands or names."

"Got it, boss." Laura Atwater made a note.

"Donna, work with Pappy on the sketch. Try your luck there. And make sure you reach out to Yekovich over at the Cyber Squad. He may have some tricks up his sleeve. We need a modern version of this mug to start circulating."

"Right away," she said.

I turned my attention down the table. "Suarez, you got any contacts in the Organized Crime Unit with Detroit PD?"

He didn't hesitate. "Yeah, I know a couple of guys. But what about the FBI? Shouldn't we talk to them?"

"Fuck them assholes," Pappy growled. "They done screwed this case sideways inna first place. We gonna solve it." He glanced around the table and received a nod of agreement from each of us. "Then we gonna rub their federal government noses innit!"

This was met by a round of chuckles and grins, but nobody argued.

"Pappy, why don't you stick with Suarez. See what the DPD has on file. Maybe this Joe guy was in the game somehow. But I do have one other suggestion."

Cantrell narrowed his eyes at me. "Yeah?"

"Everyone get out of here. Get some food and some rest. You all pulled extra duty last night. I don't want us stumbling over something tomorrow because we're burnt-out."

"This from a man who rarely sleeps," Koz muttered.

"Fuck you very much," I said.

"What about me?" Naughton asked.

"Same idea. Just make sure your team is covering their assignment. I may have a need for your services tomorrow."

"Copy that."

The others began to gather their notebooks and depart. Cantrell and Donna headed down to his office to make a few calls.

"You're actually headed home?" Kozlowski asked.

"Not directly. Wanna tag along?"

He flashed a wicked grin. "Oh, yeah!"

It was time to make a run at Spadafore. But I had a slight detour in mind.

Chapter Seventeen

Megan McDonald had selected the Townsend Hotel in downtown Birmingham as a safe location. This chic, upscale facility was probably the last place anyone would think of looking for someone under police protection. She had booked an executive suite with an adjoining room. The hotel was only two blocks away from the city's police station. Patrols went by frequently. I told Donna to go home after she finished with Pappy, since Kozlowski would be going with me.

"You staying the night?" he asked as we parked on the street.

"Not a chance. But I promised to see her today."

He chuckled. "Better be careful. This could get serious."

"More serious than staring down a bunch of gangsters?"

We crossed the lobby and stepped into the elevator. Koz mashed a thumb against the button. "Serious relationships in our line of work could be trouble."

"Atwater's married. Doesn't seem to be a problem for her."

He chuckled, then shook his head in disgust. "I'll bring McDonald down for some dinner. I get the impression she's staying until this is over."

"Smooth way to change the subject. But yeah, that's a good idea."

I'd called as we arrived, so McDonald was expecting us. She opened the door to the plush suite and led us in. Simone was sitting on a sofa. There were half a dozen shopping bags at her feet. Some of the store labels were recognizable. I could feel the credit card melting in my wallet. She jumped up and wrapped her arms around my neck.

"Hey," I said as she kissed my cheek.

"Hey yourself. Where's your sling?"

"Left it in the car. I didn't want to attract attention."

She giggled. "Oh, and walking alongside Kozlowski doesn't do that?"

"I am the very soul of discretion," Koz called out. "Nobody notices me that I don't want them to."

"Yeah," Megan said, "he's so dainty. C'mon, giant, I heard you're buying dinner. I've worked up quite an appetite today. The shrimp scampi with a side order of sirloin steak is calling me."

Kozlowski rolled his eyes. "I was thinking cheeseburgers. Maybe if you're nice, a side of fries."

"Dream on." Megan threw me a wave and led him out. The door slammed and I heard her make sure it was secured.

"Who else is here?" I asked Simone, guiding her back to the sofa.

"A guy called Giles. He's been with me all day. And a female officer named Lucy O'Connell. She just came on duty about an hour ago. They're in the next room. Megan wanted to give us some time alone." Simone lowered her eyes. "But I'm guessing this isn't a booty call."

That got a laugh out of me. "Not sure I could

handle that kind of activity just yet. And I wouldn't want to disappoint you."

She flashed a smile that reached all the way to her eyes, making them sparkle. "I'm a little shy about performing in front of an audience. Or knowing the people in the next room are supposed to be keeping a watch over me."

"Show me what you bought." I dropped onto the sofa and pulled her down beside me.

"I am *not* giving you a fashion show!"

It was refreshing to see her sense of humor was intact. Simone showed me a little black dress, a pair of heels that were mostly straps of leather crisscrossing her foot, a couple pairs of linen slacks, jeans and two tops. There was a bag from a lingerie store that she refused to open or discuss. Perhaps a surprise for a later date. Simone pushed the bags to the opposite end of the sofa, covering up the mystery package. She snuggled alongside me, finding a comfortable position.

"How is it that Donna shows up with $3,217 *in cash*? Do you have a printing press stashed somewhere?"

I winked at her. "I've got my resources."

"Chene…" She tried to give me a stern look but was unable to hold it.

"Relax. It's not illegal gains. I borrowed it from Ted. He knows I'm good for it. And this way, you're not flashing credit cards, which can be traced."

Simone had not met him yet, but she knew all about my relationship with the old saloonkeeper. That seemed to satisfy her. I figured either she or Megan were keeping the receipts from today's spending. For a while we talked about the investigation. I looked at my watch. Koz should be back shortly.

"Did you want to order dinner?" she asked.

"No, I'm good. Late lunch. But what about you? I understand shopping can work up an appetite."

"Megan's going to bring up a Michigan salad for me. Dried cherries, walnuts, bleu cheese, all that good stuff. We peeked at the menu when you were on the way. That's how she knew about the shrimp scampi. Giles and O'Connell are going to wait a while and get something to eat."

"That's a good plan."

"How long will I have to stay here?" Simone asked quietly.

"Pappy gave me a deadline of six p.m. tomorrow to solve this case or step away. We're putting it together. With the whole squad working on it, we've got a good chance. Made a lot of progress today."

Simone leaned against my right side. "Are we really going to Paris?"

"You said September, after the tourists are gone and kids are back in school. Or am I confused on the date?"

"That's when my mom and I were talking about going. Would you really go with us?"

It was a comment she made in passing a while ago. With everything that had happened lately, it was a surprise that I was seriously considering it.

"My passport is current. But I've never been to Paris. I would need someone who knows their way around, someone fluent in the language. Preferably someone to keep me out of those churches and art museums, tourist traps and other scary places. Could you recommend anyone like that?"

Gently she picked up my left hand. She turned it horizontally, so the palm was facing me. With a forefinger she drew a wobbly circle around my palm.

"When it comes to Paris, you will need an experienced guide. You'd probably irritate a true Parisian, so it would be best if you were with someone who is familiar with the area." She continued to slowly draw on my hand. "Because unlike Michigan, France looks nothing like the mitten."

Simone let go of my hand, leaned closer and kissed me. My right hand tangled in her hair, holding her close.

The door to the connecting room opened. A slim, dark-haired woman wearing jeans and a polo shirt appeared. There was a 9mm Glock strapped to her right hip. Lucy O'Connell. She cleared her throat, which was enough of a courtesy for us to break the kiss.

"McDonald and Kozlowski are on their way up."

"Thanks for the warning," I said.

She nodded and stepped back into the other room.

Simone gazed at me with wide eyes. "Do you know her background? She was telling me about it before you got here."

"She works with Naughton in Squad Five. That means weapons and explosives. I would imagine she's got the training to do the work."

"Lucy was in the marines. She was assigned to EOD. That's Explosive Ordinance Disposal." Simone lowered her voice to a whisper. "She's quite the badass. She's also a sharpshooter. Giles said she's won several competitions."

"I'll keep that in mind."

We got up from the couch. Simone carefully

wrapped her arms around me, avoiding my left shoulder. "Be careful. But go get the bad guys."

"We will. Let's talk with your mom when all this is over and pick a date. See if she's comfortable having me go along."

"Can we get a suite like this?"

"Probably not. Ted's gonna want his money back."

****

Daniel Spadafore had fingers in several pies. That wasn't uncommon in the organized crime world. Some "families" owned related businesses. Others were so widespread you couldn't connect the dots. And maybe that was the point. Nicola Bianchi told us that in addition to the saloon, Spadafore had a residential construction business, a dry-cleaner, a party store and a banquet hall. There was also a rumor about a couple of used car lots. Spadafore liked to hang out and run his show from the saloon. The place was called The Speakeasy and was decked out like a 1920s Prohibition-era bar. The waitresses dressed like flappers from that period. The bartenders were decked out with slicked-back hair, bow ties and sleeve garters.

Apparently, this venue appealed to the crowd who liked to attend sporting events, back when the Pontiac Silverdome and the Palace of Auburn Hills were in their heyday. Both stadiums had outlived their usefulness and were since demolished. The professional teams, the Lions and Pistons, had relocated to new upscale venues in the downtown Detroit area. While the teams were no longer in the vicinity, patrons still visited frequently. Even out in the parking lot, you could hear the ragtime music blaring from speakers within.

"You got a plan?" Koz asked as we pulled in

beside the saloon. "I'm only asking since it's just the two of us."

"Not exactly." I pointed to the lot next door. Parked in the shadows was a dark blue state police cruiser with the lights off. As we stepped from the car, both front doors opened. Two uniformed troopers headed our way. One was carrying a thick envelope. They moved into the glow of the overhead lights behind the Jaguar.

"You look like hell, Chene." Malone reached out to shake hands. He passed over the envelope. I tossed it on the front seat of the Jag.

"Feel about the same," I said. "You know Kozlowski?"

"Sure. Been a while."

"Saw you at the Tigers game last month. You were with a hot-looking redhead with a great set of—"

"Hey!" Malone protested, but there was no hiding that grin.

"Legs! I was going to say legs. She had on these white shorts…"

"We get the idea," I said.

Malone hooked a thumb over his shoulder at the other trooper. He was a stocky black man with an impressive set of shoulders. "This is Bigelow. Chene and Kozlowski."

"Sarge was just telling me about you guys. True that you sometimes break the rules to make your cases?"

Kozlowski and I shared a quick glance. The giant shook his head and chuckled. "You've been misinformed, little brother. We don't break the rules. Sometimes…we bend them a little."

"A little misdirection never really hurt anyone," I said.

"Malone said you loaded a joker onto a skydiving plane and everyone else was wearing parachutes, except this guy and…"

I raised my hand, fighting off a laugh. Malone was grinning. "Can't believe you dug that one up. That was what, three years ago?"

"Almost four. Just before Labor Day. Didn't you actually take off and fly over Canada?"

I shrugged. "Dumb shit believed we were going to get to altitude above Lake Erie and 'accidentally' run out of fuel. Found out he couldn't swim."

"But is that legal?" Bigelow asked, his eyes wide in the parking lot lights.

"We never violated his rights," Koz said. "We didn't throw him out of the plane. Just made him think we might do it."

Bigelow was shaking his head. "Nobody better fuck with you guys."

"That's always a prudent approach," Koz replied. "Except for some assholes last night who crossed paths with Chene."

"That shooting in Oakland County, was you?" Bigelow asked. There was something that could have been admiration in his voice.

"Obviously, they didn't get the memo about Squad Six," Malone said. "How do you want to play this?"

"Koz and I are going in to have a little conversation with Daniel Spadafore. Supposedly he's the owner of this fine establishment. And he may have been behind last night's fireworks."

"Think the kid and I will go grab a cup of coffee,"

Malone said.

"Appreciate that. My crew's been stretched pretty thin."

Malone nodded and slapped Kozlowski on the shoulder. "C'mon, rookie, let's go in."

Koz and I gave them a few minutes to get situated in the bar. "What's in the envelope? I'm guessing it's not barbecue recipes."

I explained about my earlier visit to Jamie and the request for some research. Koz picked up right away about the idea of staying off the grid. "Kind of smooth, having Malone pull double duty as a messenger and backup."

"Seemed like a golden opportunity. Let's go meet the mobster."

Kozlowski stretched his arms high. "It's your party. I'm just along for the ride. And to make sure nobody else tries to kill you."

We entered the saloon. It was five times noisier inside. A young woman wearing a dress that may have been spray-painted on greeted us with a dazzling smile. She didn't hesitate when we asked about Spadafore. Koz was right behind her, analyzing her wiggle as she guided him up a short flight of stairs to an office.

"Down, boy," I muttered as she left us in front of a door.

"She might have been armed. That's why I was watching her so closely."

"Uh-huh."

He scowled. "Hey, I'm not dead. Or involved."

"Get the door. Spadafore's waiting."

We walked in. The room was maybe a nine by twelve-foot space, with faded white paint on all the walls. The floor had commercial carpet in an ugly shade of gray. Probably the cheapest he could get. There was a simple counter-style desk without drawers. A phone, a cell phone and a laptop computer were on the top. No papers or files. An old wooden chair with casters was behind it. And sitting there was Daniel Spadafore. Two guys who probably played football in college flanked the inside of the door. Although both were solid-looking, neither one came up to Kozlowski's shoulders. They were wearing jeans, sneakers, and nylon windbreakers as if they were expecting rain.

"Evening officers," Spadafore said. He had a voice that was more of a croak than anything else. It could have been the result of an old throat injury. Or too many cigarettes and too much scotch.

Spadafore was short and flabby. Even his fat had fat. What little hair he had was a rim around the skull that reminded me of a monk in an old movie. He was dressed casually. Both his slacks and sport shirt were frayed and faded.

Koz stayed by the door where he could watch the two bodyguards. "It's detectives. But I'm thinking you already knew that. Maybe through the mob grapevine." His eyes flicked to the guards. "If you're smarter than you look, you two cupcakes will step outside."

The guy on the left rolled his shoulders. Spadafore saw it and jerked a hand up to stop him.

Koz raised his eyebrows. "You gonna prove how dumb you really are?"

"You ain't so tough," the guy muttered, ignoring the signal from his boss.

It always surprises me how quickly the big man can move. Before the bodyguard got the last word out,

Kozlowski spun. He jammed the heel of his right hand into the guy's nose. His left hand flashed inside the guard's jacket and pulled out a gun that had been hanging in a shoulder holster. The injured man slid down to the floor, both hands cradling his broken nose. Koz pressed the weapon against the other guy's chest. My own gun was out, aimed at Spadafore's heart.

"What the fuck!" Spadafore shouted.

"You want to dance, Danny boy?" I yelled. "I don't take it lightly when assholes start shooting at me!"

Spadafore had both empty hands in the air. "Calm down. Everybody! Just calm the *fuck* down!"

"I only popped the one," Koz growled. "What do you want me to do with this piece of shit?"

Somehow Spadafore was able to stand up. I was less than six feet from him. He kept his hands in the air. "Jerry! Take Tom out of here. Go get him fixed up!"

Jerry was playing statue with his partner's gun jammed against his chest. He didn't dare move.

With his free hand, Koz reached in and yanked a gun from Jerry's waist. He shoved it in the pocket of his jacket. "Any more toys?" Koz grunted.

Jerry managed a minute negative shake of his head. "No, sir."

"Nice to see respect for authority," Koz said. He took a step back and lowered the gun. Jerry reached down and dragged Tom to his feet. Once they were out the door, Spadafore dropped back into his chair.

"Sweet Jesus Christ," he muttered.

"Any other playmates we need to take care of?" Koz growled, slamming the door shut and blocking it with his bulk.

"Nah. We're alone now." He gazed up at

Kozlowski. "You probably broke that idiot's nose. You didn't have to do that."

Koz shrugged. "It will give him character. Maybe the incentive to find honest work."

Spadafore dug a pack of cigarettes from his shirt pocket and shook one free. He fired it up with a flashy gold lighter. I noticed a significant tremor in his hand as he snapped the lighter shut.

"Rumors around town that you guys are visiting all the families. Figured it was only a matter of time before you called on me. Thought having Tom and Jerry here would balance the scales."

"Scales look balanced to you now?" I asked. The gun was still in my hand. Koz had tucked the one he'd pulled off Tom into his jacket with the other one.

"Not really," Spadafore said.

"You got that right," Koz muttered.

"Do you know why we're here?" I asked.

"May have something to do with that shooting that was on the news." Spadafore shifted in the chair, which creaked in protest. "Or maybe not."

Kozlowski had turned on his digital recorder before we entered the building. It would not be admissible in court, but I wanted a transcript to fall back on if we ever needed it.

"Are you going to tell us those mutts last night didn't work for you?"

"Which mutts might that be?" Spadafore tried to sound vague and uncertain.

"Croyton, Bertenelli and Tancredi." I threw copies of the morgue photos on the table in front of him. "They may have looked a bit livelier the last time you saw them."

Spadafore flinched and pushed his chair back a little. For a mob guy, you would think seeing dead bodies wouldn't be new for him. Maybe it had been a while since he'd gotten blood on his hands.

"That asshole Tancredi. He started believing his grandfather's fucking glory days and war stories. Thought he was invincible."

"What about these other two jokers?" Koz growled.

Spadafore lifted his chubby arms in a helpless gesture. "Muscle comes and goes. I probably saw these guys hanging around but never really knew them."

"You telling us that Tancredi acted on his own?" I asked incredulously. "Because I don't see some third-generation jackass wannabe making that kind of call. This punk thought he was a damn cowboy with a pair of six-shooters."

"And since he was working for you, stands to reason you ordered the hit," Koz said, looming over the desk at Spadafore.

"No! I didn't order a hit or any action. I don't even know whatever the fuck he was doing lately."

"How many idiots you have working for you, across all your operations?" I asked. There was an undercurrent of fear running through Spadafore. I knew this meeting wasn't going as he'd hoped.

Spadafore let his gaze flick between us. He sucked a deep draw on the cigarette, pulling the ember all the way to the filter. Blowing out a cloud of smoke, he pinched the coal between his thumb and forefinger. When it was out, he flicked the butt in the general direction of the garbage can. Missed.

"I've got businesses scattered across the territory.

213

You know that. Most of Oakland County is mine and a small slice of western Macomb. I'm talking three to four hundred guys. I can't keep track of them all."

"But you know Tancredi." It was a statement, not a question.

Spadafore shrugged. "Yeah, I know him."

"Then you should be able to tell us what part of your empire he was involved with?" I asked. My energy level was bottoming out. I leaned on the edge of his desk. Kozlowski hovered on the other side.

Spadafore didn't respond. He looked like he was debating how much information, if any, he was willing to share.

"I'm getting bored with this," Koz said. "This dumb piece of meat either doesn't know shit or isn't going to cooperate. That's bad for our rep."

"True," I said. "You want to take care of it?"

He flashed an evil smile and pulled a pair of latex gloves from his inside jacket pocket. "This," he said quietly, "will be a pleasure. One less pissant mobster to darken our day."

Spadafore stared in disbelief as Kozlowski tugged the gloves on. Then he withdrew the pistol he'd taken off the guard with the broken nose.

"You can't shoot me! There are laws against that kind of thing."

I waved a finger back and forth. "Laws are for law-abiding citizens. You are not one. Therefore, they don't apply to you."

Koz took a step back. "Don't want to get that arterial spray on my clothes. This is a new jacket." He extended the gun toward Spadafore.

"You can't just shoot me!"

"Wanna bet?" Koz thumbed back the hammer and squeezed the trigger.

For the second night in a row, there was a blast of gunfire in my vicinity. Spadafore screamed as the bullet ripped into the ceiling. At the last moment, Koz had tipped the barrel up, sending the slug through the roof of the saloon. Spadafore was clutching his chest, breathing hard, eyes wide in disbelief.

"The next one will be the last thing you ever hear," Kozlowski said. "Unless you start talking."

"*Sweet Jesus Christ.* You guys are crazy."

I waved two fingers at Koz. "Finish this. Either he doesn't know jack-shit or he's too fucking stupid to save his own life."

Koz grunted. "Head or chest?"

"Your choice. But I'm not sure any bullet will penetrate that much fat."

"Good point." Koz tipped his hand back slightly.

"Wait! Wait! Wait!"

Koz glanced back at me. I raised one finger then pointed it at Spadafore. "Start talking. Now. One hesitation, one word of bullshit and he finishes this."

"Tancredi was working for Reggio. He runs the construction angle. Underbids contractors, skims a bit on the materials and the labor. He is old school as hell. Tancredi was supposed to be learning the business."

Koz and I exchanged a glance. "Is it possible Reggio sent him after me?"

"How the fuck would I know that?" Spadafore's face was the color of pickled beets. I wondered if he had high blood pressure.

"You don't know what your captains and crews are doing?" I asked.

He shrugged his flabby shoulders. "I can't know everything."

"Sounds like you don't know anything," Koz said.

"Tell us about this guy Reggio." It was all I could do to smother a yawn.

Spadafore drew in a deep breath. "Word gets out I blabbed to you guys…"

"Your reputation isn't that great among the families from what we hear anyway," I said. "But it's not going to matter in fifteen seconds if you don't tell us what you know about Reggio."

For some reason, Spadafore decided to talk as if his life depended on it. He gave us details about Reggio and the construction business. Some of it was bullshit, but there was enough substance to give me direction. When he ran out of steam, Koz lowered the gun and glanced at me. I nodded and made the call. Malone answered on the first ring.

"There's an office upstairs. We have a gentleman you need to escort out. Find him a nice quiet spot where he can relax and perhaps consider his sins."

Malone chuckled. "I know just a place. Think he's got a reservation for forty-eight hours or so."

"Sounds like a plan."

Spadafore slumped back in his chair. Putting him in a cell would buy me a couple of days before we would have to press charges. That would be beyond Pappy's deadline. It would also keep him from notifying Reggio that we were looking at him closely.

"I won't talk to anyone. Swear to God I won't," Spadafore pleaded.

"Not sure how close you are to the Lord," Koz said, "but you'll have plenty of time to chat with him.

Who knows, you might even find religion while you're on the inside and be born again."

Chapter Eighteen

Stale air filled the house. It was warm and stuffy. I opened a couple of windows for cross ventilation and flopped onto the sofa. Koz had followed me home like a gigantic puppy dog. Out front was an unmarked patrol car with a trooper in plain clothes, guarding the property. Cantrell wasn't taking any chances. I knew better than to argue with him. The envelope from Jamie was on the counter. My plan was to start reading it after taking the meds. That was, until my phone buzzed with a blocked number.

"Chene."

The voice was garbled but the message was clear enough. "Coast Guard marker seventeen. One hour. Alone."

Switching off the lights, as if going to bed, I slipped out through the door from the Florida room that faced the canal. Undoing the canvas, I climbed aboard the speedboat. I switched the blower on, cleaning any fumes from the engine compartment. A minute later I had the lines off the cleats and was pulling the boat by hand up to the neighbor's dock. Only then did I key the ignition and ease out onto the lake. I didn't even turn on the marker lights until I was a hundred yards from shore.

Using the marine radio, I contacted the Coast Guard Station in St. Clair Shores and got the location for marker seventeen. I already had a hunch, but this confirmed it.

"Oh, I never learned how to run a boat," I muttered, recalling a conversation from earlier this summer. "What a crock of shit!"

I jammed the throttle wide open. The fiberglass craft leaped to life, heading out across Lake St. Clair.

It was about a forty-five-minute ride to the Harsens Island area. The marker was in front of what might have been a fishing shack sixty years ago but now looked like a five-bedroom colonial on an acre of property. I cut the throttle and let my following wake carry the boat forward. There was a long pier running from the seawall toward the channel marker. No one was visible. I shifted the motor into neutral and scanned the area. On my left, a set of navigation lights blinked on. I waited. It goes with the job.

An old Boston Whaler, one of those tri-hulled fiberglass skiffs with a big outboard engine, puttered out of a canal just beyond the coast guard marker. The boat moved slowly until it came alongside me. There was one person on board. He grabbed the chrome railing next to me.

"Hello, Jeff. My apologies for the clandestine meeting."

"What happened to 'never learned how to run a boat,' Leo?"

Agonasti threw back his head and roared with laughter. "Got me there. Don't suppose you believe I recently took lessons?"

"Hell no. You realize the feds are tearing up Motown looking for you?"

"Max has been keeping me informed. I'm glad to

see you survived the shootout last night."

There was enough ambient light from the channel marker and from our boats that I could see him clearly. Concern was etched across his face. "How's the shoulder? Any permanent damage?"

"It would probably be doing better if I took the meds and wore the fucking sling. But that's not going to happen right away. I'm too busy trying to solve this old homicide and keep your ass out of federal custody."

Agonasti wasn't a fan of vulgarities but right now, I didn't care. I was too damn tired and too damn sore to be pleasant and considerate.

"I have never killed anyone, let alone a child," he said quietly. "I hope you know me well enough to believe that."

"I do believe it, Leo. But proving it may be a bitch. We've got a lead on a guy, but it's thin." I pulled my phone and scrolled to the sketch of Joe. Agonasti leaned across the railing and gazed at the picture. He studied it for a minute, then withdrew, shaking his head. The current was dragging both boats downstream. Lights were on at several of the cottages there. Leo climbed aboard and tied a line from the skiff to one of my stern cleats. I put the boat in gear and headed across the channel at a slow pace.

"I've got less than twenty-four hours to wrap this up. Otherwise, Captain Cantrell will put his boot in my ass and hand over everything we've learned to the FBI. It may be enough to pull them off you. But I'm not getting my hopes up."

Leo scrubbed his face with both hands. "They must have some evidence that would tie me to this crime."

"DNA. According to the report, they found a cloth

with yours on it. And there was part of one of your business cards." I hesitated, finally grabbing the one point that had been nagging me. "How in the world would they get your DNA to compare a sample to in the first place?"

Leo climbed onto the passenger seat. "Diana mentioned this too. I have been wracking my brain. My doctor would never divulge such information."

"They'd need a warrant. No judge is going to sign off without probable cause. Been in the hospital recently?"

Agonasti sat up straighter. "My granddaughter was. About three years ago. Mikahla had kidney problems. She needed a transplant. They tested the whole family to see if anyone was a suitable donor."

"How did that turn out?"

Leo's face softened, and he favored me with a proud smile. "It worked out just fine. She got a new kidney. Life for her is good."

"One of yours?"

He nodded. "Want to see my scar?"

"Pass," I said with a laugh. "Somehow, they got a report with your numbers. Or they were able to pull from someone in your family and get close to a match. The feds probably have a warrant to get a DNA sample in addition to your arrest. Just to finalize their case."

"But how would they get a cloth at the scene?"

"That's another part of the puzzle. Especially when we're going back fifteen years. It's not likely you can remember everywhere you were every day.

"You said you were a background guy. Not exactly involved in the day-to-day operations. Was there anybody from Giacalone's operation, or one of the other families, that you didn't get along with? Anybody you ever tangled with? Any disagreements or feuds?"

Leo ran his hand over his face again. "No. Giacalone held me in high regard based on all the work I'd done for him. Many of the businesses I recommended turned out to be very profitable. It was a lucrative way to move funds between operations. Even when I made suggestions for the other families, they were satisfied with my input. On occasion, I was ahead of the curve, spotting a type of business that the police wouldn't think had anything to do with organized crime."

We motored on for a while in silence. Fatigue was getting to me. I was thinking about finding a marina to tie up at and crawling into the cabin below for a nap. But if I really fell asleep, there was no telling when I might wake up. And Cantrell's deadline was inching closer.

Agonasti jumped from his chair and marched over to me. "Stop the boat. I've figured it out!"

Leo Agonasti explained that fifteen years ago, he was just entertaining the idea of retiring. He had worked for organized crime in one form or another since his teens, but after college, his role was always behind the scenes. Leo would study financial trends and markets. He would analyze businesses that would be suitable for laundering money. Originally he worked solely for the Giacalone operation. But as his success grew, other divisions of the Mob would come to him for advice, with Tony Giacalone's approval, of course. And then a modest surcharge for his advice would be paid.

Over time, Leo would be invited to meetings with

the other families. There he would make a presentation about potential operations to invest in or those that had attracted the attention of law enforcement. With a proven track record, the Giacalone, Tocco, Vitale, and Spadafore family leaders would take his suggestions seriously. It wasn't uncommon for them to meet at a restaurant and have a late lunch or early dinner. Family time was sacrosanct. Being home with the wife and children was something to be honored at this level of the organization. Leo would dine with them, make his report, answer any questions and leave. Then other non-financial topics would be discussed.

"Giacalone kept me out of any other conversations. They wanted me distant. If I knew nothing about gang wars, violence, truck hijacking or controlling unions, I could never answer questions about them if the FBI ever discovered my role."

"That makes sense," I said. Despite Leo's request to stop the boat, I kept it going slowly forward.

"Sometimes, families would bring in lieutenants, guys who they wanted to run some of their sidelines. Giacalone was the person everyone else looked up to. He encouraged the others to pitch an idea. That would give everyone an opportunity to consider it. While it wasn't like they voted on moving forward, the families could bounce ideas back and forth."

"Brainstorming," I said.

"Precisely."

"You were present for this part of the meeting?"

Leo Agonasti nodded. "Giacalone wanted me there. I was an objective party, listening to their pitches, trying to spot any potential problems or flaws with the ideas. He would always defer any comments until after my response.

"Around this time, Daniel Spadafore was coming up the ranks. His uncle Carmine ran the family operations but was supposed to be grooming him. Daniel was coarse. Rough around the edges. Carmine was polished. But he wanted to encourage him." Leo paused and looked at the stars above us. "It was at one of those meetings when Daniel brought an associate, Nick or something, who had an idea for a new business. Something both he and Daniel felt could easily launder funds. It was so unusual they felt certain law enforcement would never take a second look at it. The others were less than receptive."

"Do you remember what the business was?"

Leo nodded wisely. "Yes, it was a company that would specialize in fireworks. Not manufacturing them but selling them locally. Multiple stores around the area. Selling firecrackers and bottle rockets and such to the public. Daniel felt it couldn't miss."

I was skeptical. "Around here, people use fireworks for the summer holidays and maybe New Year's Eve. That doesn't sound like a steady business to use as a front. What would they do the rest of the year?"

"That was the reaction from the other families. Yet in deference to Carmine, they all looked at me for advice."

"What did you say?"

"About what I told you now. It was never my intention to insult anyone or show disrespect. Giacalone had taught me that long ago. So, I told them it would be my pleasure to review a business plan and make a recommendation."

"Where was this meeting?"

"Mario's down on Second Avenue. We had a private dining room. Why?"

I waved the question aside. "Go back to the discussion."

"Young Spadafore wasn't pleased that they all didn't jump on his associate's idea. He was grumbling, made some comments about how he was a relative and I was just hired help. A flunky. I remember Carmine putting a hand on his forearm and Daniel yanking his arm free. His friend wasn't at the table. He was relegated to standing behind Carmine, like a bodyguard. I recall he didn't look particularly comfortable in that setting."

Leo described the tension in the room. Giacalone signaled that it was time for him to go. Agonasti offered one of his business cards to Spadafore, sort of a peace offering and encouraged him to send the proposal and the business plan over so he could review it. Daniel Spadafore refused to take it. Agonasti just set it on the table by his place. At that point, Leo Agonasti left the restaurant.

"I never gave it another thought until just now."

I was grinning at him. "You may have just solved two parts of the puzzle."

"How?"

"I've got a hundred bucks says Mario's uses white linen napkins. Or they did fifteen years ago."

"But what's the motive?"

"I didn't say the case was solved. But you've given me another idea."

****

Jamie's research proved enlightening. She had

225

assembled enough information on organized criminal activity in Detroit that would easily fill two volumes of a book. There were print copies of newspaper and magazine articles. She included pages of notes, typed up quickly in a scattershot way. I had neglected to narrow down the subject. Which meant Jamie had expanded her search to topics on the fringe of the organized crime families.

In addition to the Giacalone, Tocco, Vitale, and Spadafore families, Jamie included articles about Young Boys Inc. This was a notorious drug gang from the late 1970s who specialized in using juveniles to distribute heroin throughout Detroit. Since they operated like a business, the name stuck. The idea was that young teens could not be charged as adults if they were caught. That also made it difficult for police to infiltrate the gang. Young Boys Inc. even started franchising their operations, extending the heroin trade into Boston and other areas. When the gang leaders began to argue, murders quickly followed.

Next up was information about Richard Wershe Jr., known as White Boy Rick, who became involved in the crack cocaine trade at the tender age of fourteen in the early 1980s. Wershe became an informant with the FBI, identifying higher-ups within the drug business. In the late 80s, he was busted with at least 9,000 grams of cocaine and $30,000 in cash in his possession. White Boy Rick was convicted and served more than thirty years in federal prison.

Reading about these old familiar cases stirred up a few memories. It wouldn't be difficult to jump on the internet and search for more updates, but I didn't have the time. What I needed was more of a focus on the family operations. Jamie's documents included extensions of the various operations, either real or assumed, for the Giacalone, Tocco, Vitale, and Spadafore crime families. As it was, I could barely keep my eyes open. In the morning I planned to have Laura review it as well.

****

Pappy was at his corner table at Lil Nino's at six thirty, Friday morning. He had just settled in with his first cup of coffee and a copy of the *Detroit Free Press* when I approached. To say I was expected would have been an understatement. I slid into a chair across from him. There was a steaming mug of black coffee already waiting for me.

"Y'all look like hell. Damn doctor gonna kick your ass, iffen your girlie don't beat 'em to it."

"Morning to you too."

The waitress appeared beside me. Knowing it would be a long time before my next meal, I ordered a stuffed French toast with a side of bacon and crispy hash browns. Pappy nodded his approval.

I filled him in on my meetings with Spadafore and Agonasti. By now I wasn't expecting an outburst about meeting with the guy who was the subject of the manhunt. We kicked around ideas for the investigation until our food arrived. Neither of us spoke while we dug in. Pappy made a couple of notes on the edge of his paper. He would tell me when he was ready. With the food gone and coffee refilled, he leaned back and checked his watch.

"Y'all got eleven hours to figger this out. The others got some work to do this morning. Whatcha gonna do?"

Before I could answer, my phone buzzed. It was Donna Spears. No one was close to our table, so I put it on speaker.

"Pappy's with me. What's up?"

"I've got a name," she said quietly. "With about an eighty percent certainty. But we need to run to the Cyber Unit."

"Where are you?"

"I'm at the post."

"On my way." I stood up and threw some cash on the table. "You're going to the DPD with Suarez this morning?"

He nodded and pulled a cigarette from the pack. "Yep. Got a meeting at nine. Y'all call me with details. Then I've got a regional conference at noon. State, city, counties and even the feds. We all gonna talk 'bout the issues, mebbe plan a task force or two. It be downtown, so Suarez be free iffen you need him."

I started to turn for the door, but his voice stopped me cold.

"None of this goddam Lone Ranger bullshit. Y'all got somethin' worthwhile; I want more'n just Spears with ya."

"You got it. Anything else?"

"Don't fuck up my vacation."

That got a laugh out of me as I trotted out to the Jag. Five minutes later, Donna jumped in as I pulled into the lot at the post. I caught a trooper headed into the building and gave him the files from Jamie, asking him to deliver those immediately to Laura Atwater. She knew they were coming.

"You got an early start," I said.

She shrugged. "Clock's ticking, boss. I'm not the

only one."

I noticed the personal vehicles for the others were already in the lot. Laura was researching the background on the Surfside property. Kozlowski was going to dig into anything he could think of to find out about Reggio. I'd tried the name on Agonasti last night, but he didn't know it. He was going to speak with Max. With any luck, the name would mean something to him.

On the way to the Cyber Unit building, Naughton checked in. Everything at the hotel was in good standings. He had rotated two of his team during the night and had Lucy O'Connell there with him now.

"Simone may feel more comfortable with another female around," he said. "I got the sense Giles was getting on her nerves."

"That unusual?"

"Guy's comfortable with bombs and weapons. He's a klutz around women. Whenever he meets a beautiful woman, he starts hearing bells. Makes him skittish as hell."

The call was coming through the car's speakers, so Donna could hear everything as well. "He starts hearing bells. Like alarms?" she asked.

"Naw. Wedding bells! Dumb shit's been married and divorced four times."

"Idiot," Donna responded with a laugh.

"Call if you need me, Chene. I enjoyed yesterday's diversion. A nice change of pace from the routine."

"I'll keep it in mind."

Ending the call, I swung into the lot at the Cyber Unit. Yekovich was standing beside a restored Pontiac Firebird convertible, admiring the candy-apple-red paint job. The personalized license plate identified it as a 1967 model. He nodded as we approached.

"You rebuilt this?" Donna asked.

"Everything but the paint. This has been a work in progress for years. Hey, Chene. Heard about you getting dinged the other night. Surprised to see you up and around with this."

"I'm not dead yet. Donna said you have something."

"Got it all cued up inside."

He buzzed us through security and led us back past his office to the large area where his team of technicians worked. There was a skinny young woman with short, jet-black hair whose fingers were flying over a computer keyboard. She glanced up as we entered the area and leaped from her chair.

"Hiya, Chene!"

It took me a moment to place the face. "Pinky, isn't it?"

"Yep. Good to see you, Sarge."

"You too. New hairdo?"

"I needed a change. Blonde with rainbow highlights gets old after a week or two. But I'll probably go with something blue or purple for the fall. Keeps the boys from getting bored."

Yekovich introduced Donna to his favorite tech. Pinky turned to a large monitor on the back wall. The sketch of 'Joe' was in the center of the screen. Pinky stood beside the monitor, as if lecturing to a class of students and tapped a wireless keyboard.

"When Detective Spears sent us this, I tried an age progression program. That gave me a couple of variations on what he would look like. One was if he stayed the same weight. One version added about fifty pounds and if his hair receded."

As Pinky spoke, the image changed, reflecting the options she described. These were possibilities we could use. I focused on the screen while she continued.

"I ran both versions through every database I could think of." Pinky cut her eyes at Yekovich. "And a couple I don't officially have access to."

The Cyber Unit boss shook his head in disgust but kept quiet.

"There were no hits. Nothing." Pinky clicked another button on the keyboard and brought up the original sketch.

"You didn't bring us in here because you came up empty." I stepped closer to the monitor and faced the others. "Are you waiting for the dramatic theme music to come up?"

Pinky flashed what Megan McDonald used to call 'the doe-eyed innocent look.' She fluttered her lashes and gave me a shy smile.

"You're trying to take away all my fun, Sarge."

"Hardly. But if you really have something, you win a steak dinner."

Her face lit up. "With a shrimp cocktail? For two?"

"Deal. Tell me."

"Let me introduce you to Joseph Goren." She hit another key, and the screen split, revealing a photo alongside the witness sketch. If they weren't the same guy, they were twin brothers.

"Fuck me hard," I muttered. "Details!"

"When I didn't get a hit anywhere else, I had two options. Cold cases or closed cases. He came up on the former."

A missing persons case on Joseph Goren had been

filed a week after Charity Gray disappeared. His parents had contacted the Hazel Park Police Department. There was a preliminary investigation, but for all intents and purposes, Joseph Goren disappeared without a trace. No activity on his bank account or credit cards. Pinky had even managed to get a file number.

She extended a note with two fingers. "Hazel Park PD is expecting you at eight. Detective Lou Magnus has the case and the file, for what it's worth."

Donna snagged the note. I pulled one of my business cards from my jacket pocket and handed it to Pinky. "You know where Sharkey's is, in St. Clair Shores?"

"Sure, it's down by the marina."

"You take that card there and ask for Ted. Dinner is on me."

Her face lit up again. "I was only kidding, Chene."

"I wasn't. Dinner for two. You earned it."

"We're not supposed to accept gifts, Pinky." Yekovich shook his head. "You know the rules."

Angrily, I spun to face him. "Fuck your rules," I snarled. "She just helped prevent an innocent man from going to prison. And where is it written that one employee of the state's law enforcement contingent can't buy dinner for another?"

Yekovich raised his palms in surrender. "But you're not paying. This Ted guy is."

"He'll put it on my tab. Satisfied?"

He considered it. Donna was hovering, anxious to get moving. So was I. "Go solve the case, Chene. You're spoiling my Friday."

"We're gone. Thanks again, Pinky."

"Any time, Sarge. You're my favorite cop!"

Donna and I headed down the hall. "Sounds like you got a groupie, boss."

"Just what the hell I need."

Chapter Nineteen

Hazel Park is a small city on the southern end of Oakland County. We pulled into the municipal lot and entered the building. The sergeant at the desk checked the log, buzzed a phone, and waved us through. There was a bullpen for detectives down the hall on the right.

Inside, three detectives were at work, typing on computers and talking on the phone. A bulky man in his late fifties glanced up and waved us forward with two fingers. I introduced us.

"Looking for Lou Magnus. Is that you?"

The guy snorted a laugh. "Nobody told you about Lou?"

"What's to tell?"

"Lou is short for Louise. She's due in about five minutes. Want some coffee? It ain't half bad."

Donna went with him to grab a cup. I wandered over to a vacant desk and studied a few pictures pinned to the cubicle walls. Young kids, maybe eight or ten, decked out in baseball uniforms. Looked like a boy and a girl. I leaned closer for a better look when someone cleared their throat behind me.

"Cute kids. Are you Detective Magnus?" I asked, turning around.

"That's me. You the state guy?" She may have been pushing forty, but it looked like she was winning. Her grip was strong. I put her about five foot six and a solid one-thirty. She had brown hair clipped short.

"I'm Chene. Spears is getting coffee."

"Let's use the meeting room. It's a tiny slice of privacy." Magnus picked up a file from beside her computer. We settled in across from each other in the little conference room. Donna came in right behind me, cradling a steaming porcelain mug. She introduced herself.

"How long have you worked the Goren case?" I asked.

Lou Magnus shrugged. "Inherited it about four years back, when I made the move to detective. We have a small squad. Two of us split the old open unsolved files. We read through them, see if there is anything that hasn't already been done. Or if the science changes and gives us a new avenue."

"That folder looks pretty thin," Donna said.

"I've had pizzas that are thicker, and I'm not talking Chicago style." Magnus flipped it open and spun it around to face me. "Original report was made fifteen years ago. Chased down a few friends and known associates. Guy just up and vanished. No action on his bank account. Cell phone showed no use except three days before the complaint. Nothing in his apartment to indicate where he might have gone or even who he was working for."

Reading over the report, I saw it was made by his parents. "They still around? No other contact with them?"

"When I got this file, the mother was in a memory care unit. Dementia. She passed away a couple of years ago. The father was long dead." She hesitated, then raised her eyebrows. "You gonna tell me you found him?"

Donna passed over a copy of the sketch. Lou Magnus looked at it closely, then turned the file back around. She flipped a couple of pages and compared it to a photo that was probably from a family vacation. It wasn't perfect, but it was damn close.

"Well, he didn't age much," Magnus said. "What's he involved with?"

I summarized the Charity Gray investigation without getting in too deep. Magnus passed the paperwork back so we could review it. She went to get her own mug of coffee as Donna and I worked through the pages. Near the back was a list of people his parents thought Joseph Goren might associate or hang out with. There were about a dozen names, addresses and phone numbers. All men. It also indicated how they knew Goren. Near the bottom was a name that practically jumped off the page. I had been skimming the list and almost missed it. Pulling the file close, I ran my finger down to the second from last name.

"Call Kozlowski!" I snapped.

Donna pulled her phone and had him on the other end in three seconds. She put it on speaker mode and set it on the table between us.

"Whatcha got, Chene?"

"We have a name to go with that sketch. Joseph Goren. He's been missing since the week after Charity disappeared."

"So much for that lead," Koz muttered.

"Yeah, but that just gave us a link. Joseph Goren's family provided the cops with a list of people he was friendly with before he vanished. Names, addresses, phone number and how he knew them."

"Standard stuff," Koz said.

"List includes his cousin. Anthony Reggio."

There was five seconds of silence. Then Kozlowski erupted. "YES!"

"Tell me you've got something on this name."

"I've got a bit and still digging. Where you at?"

"Hazel Park. We'll be back at the post in twenty minutes," I said. "What about Laura? She having any luck?"

"She's been jumping between the computer and that stack of files you dropped off. You gonna call Pappy?"

"Not yet," I said. "Let's make sure we've got something first."

"Copy that."

****

On our way back to the post, a phone started ringing. It wasn't mine. Donna jumped and pulled the burner that Max had given her yesterday from a pocket. She took the call, and his raspy voice filled the car.

"Leo told me you're looking for a guy named Reggio. This be a worthless piece of crap known as Anthony Reggio?"

"Could be. What do you know about him?"

"Egotistical jackass. Knows everyone and everything. That's according to him anyway. He's been working for Spadafore around twenty years now."

"Anything else you can share?"

"Likes to play the role. Has a guy who shadows him. Tall, scrawny dude named Lionel or something like that. Supposed to be a ninja wizard or some shit."

"Good to know," I said.

"If you're going after this jackass, I want in."

I pulled up to a red light and hit the brakes a little harder than necessary. "Do *not* go near him! If this fits together like I think it will, Leo needs him alive in order to clear his name!"

"I'm not going to kill him…"

"Bet your ass you're not. Stay the fuck out, Max."

There was silence for almost a minute. I stomped on the gas and we raced up Gratiot toward the post. My eyes were on the road, not the phone, so I didn't know if he'd hung up or not. As I turned into the lot, Max said, "Call me when you can."

"I will."

****

Laura got to us first. She was waving a stack of paper back and forth, as if trying to create a cool breeze. Her eyes had a hint of satisfaction, as if she were the bearer of good news. Lord knows we could use some.

"You look like a leprechaun with a pot of gold," Donna said.

"Think of it as a version of the winning lottery ticket. And I'm the only one holding the right combination of numbers." Laura extended the printed stack to me. "Koz heard this already. He's still digging on that name you called in."

"Do I need to read through this, or you gonna fill us in?" I asked.

Laura boosted herself up onto her desk and swung her legs back and forth like a schoolgirl. Donna dropped into a chair.

"The Surfside was a private gentleman's club originally opened in 1962 on the shores of Orchard Lake. This was a spacious facility and between '62 and

2014, when it was sold, the place went through periodic renovations. We're talking major work. New HVAC, flooring, kitchen, expanded the dining room twice, triple-paned thermal windows to enhance the view of the lake. They also acquired the adjacent properties on both sides. Being private meant there was only a discreet sign out front." Laura pointed at the stack of paper I was holding. "Page three has some old photos. Apparently, they did some charity work, brought presents for underprivileged kids at Christmas, donated substantial money to a few organizations. Otherwise, they kept a low profile."

"Was it the same ownership from '62 until '14?" I asked.

Laura tipped me a wink. "There were five different corporations, all privately held, during that timeframe. Most of the shareholders' names changed, but one was constant all the way through."

"And who might that be?" Donna asked.

"Carmine Spadafore. Which ties in with the information from that research file you gave me earlier," Laura said.

Jamie's files had been bursting with details. I knew Laura would speed-read through it all and comprehend it much faster than my blurry mind could last night.

"Do you think this was a front for his organized crime operations?" Donna asked. "A place where he could run dirty cash through and make it legit?"

"It wouldn't surprise me a bit," I said. It was entirely possible that Agonasti either knew about it or could have set it up for Spadafore with the Giacalone family approval.

"Carmine Spadafore died in 2014. Stomach cancer.

A year later the business was sold to a developer. The Surfside was torn down. Several expensive condominiums were built on the land, taking advantage of being waterfront properties with access to the lake." Laura pointed again at the stack of papers. "There were a few articles in the Oakland Press about that place. Some issues about excluding women and minorities from being members. Times have changed since the sixties. But being a private facility let them do what they wanted to."

"Was Daniel Spadafore a shareholder in the last corporation?" I asked.

Laura checked her notes. "No. From the names listed with the state, they were all senior citizens, probably people who worked with Carmine in one capacity or another. There was a doctor, an attorney, an accountant and one longtime councilman from Orchard Lake."

"So why would they sell after all that time?" Donna asked.

I'd been wondering the same thing. "Could be a number of reasons. Spadafore may have had it in the corporate bylaws that upon his death, the property was to be sold and the proceeds split, in accordance with the number of shares they all held. Or it could have been an opportune time, what with the price of waterfront real estate, to make a hefty profit and walk away."

"One way or another, it looks like during its run, The Surfside was a mob hangout. Chances are young Daniel liked to strut his stuff there, as if he owned the place," Laura said.

If Carmine Spadafore used this as his clubhouse for his operations, chances are good that Daniel and his minions were there too. From what Rachel Griffith described, this was a place where they could drink and party without any concerns about being observed by law enforcement. Joseph Goren was a shirttail relative to Anthony Reggio. Rachel placed him on the scene. Somehow Goren caught Charity Gray and killed her. Maybe he turned to his cousin Anthony Reggio to help take care of the problem.

Kozlowski joined the party. "I'm waiting for a few calls back. What did I miss?"

"Apparently, these organized crime families have been working together for years," Laura said. "It's like we heard yesterday, they formed some type of agreement. Made me think they all had certain territories, and everyone honored the boundaries."

"Seems odd to me that these mobsters would just get along with each other," Donna said, "and not see it as some kind of competition."

Laura pointed at the files from Jamie. "The tri-county area is huge. It makes perfect sense to divide it up into segments. Some of these historians indicate that certain families, back in the '30s and '40s, agreed to such an arrangement. After World War II, with the suburban sprawl underway, they just moved the boundaries a little. It's also possible they all put a percentage of their…revenue into a pot for some of the standard expenses they'd all share."

Kozlowski slowly shook his head back and forth, a surprised look on his face. "Like a freaking franchise. You chip in for the advertisement and promotions. But these guys weren't advertising in the *Freep*."

"No, but back in the day, there would have been a fair amount of corruption. City councilmen, union leaders, even the mayor back then could have been influenced by the Mob. Cops too," I said.

"Wait a minute," Donna said in surprise, "you're telling me these mobsters actually collaborated on bribes and manipulations? Wouldn't everyone know about this? Other officials, the people in general?"

"That was a different world back then," I said. "Cell phones didn't become popular until the 1990s. Social media didn't exist. There was no such thing as a twenty-four-hour news cycle. Publishers had more control on the newspapers; producers did the same with the local and national television broadcasts. They decided what stories the public would hear about and what spin they wanted on it. Corruption was a great deal easier back then."

"The good old days may not have been so good," Koz said.

"Most people were content with what they were told. What they needed to know. When it came to underhanded activities, murder, drugs, scandals, and corruption, they didn't want to know," I said.

Laura pointed at the papers from Jamie. "Certainly seems that way."

****

Pappy and Suarez returned half an hour later. Their conversation with the Detroit Police had been positive. They had a little additional information about Reggio and his activities with Spadafore's enterprises. Since they stayed out of the city limits, there wasn't a lot of detail. But at this stage, every little bit helped. We moved into the conference room. Cantrell fired up a cigarette.

"Gimme whatcha got," he grumbled through a haze

of smoke.

"We've got a full name on Joe and a connection to Anthony Reggio. They're cousins. Joe is Joseph Goren. He's been missing for fifteen years," I said.

Cantrell squinted at me. "Coincidence?"

"No such thing," Laura said with a grin. "You've taught all of us that."

"Then fill me in, girlie."

Laura preened a little in her chair and gave him the report. She covered the connection with Reggio, the idea that Goren had turned to his cousin with the problem of being discovered by the young girl and the possibility of Reggio wanting to get some payback from Agonasti for rejecting his business idea.

"Y'all doing the whatyacallit, the hypothetical," Pappy said.

"It's conjecture. But it fits with the facts that we do have," I said. "Reggio has been running Spadafore's construction outfit for twenty years. He would know about areas where work was being done. If we had time, there might be a trail of building permits going back that far. Maybe even for the house where Charity's remains were found."

Kozlowski joined in. "Take the testimony from that waitress, Griffith. She does the bone dance on the patio table. The girl sees the action. Maybe the noise was enough to attract her, to get her attention. Goren finishes and goes after her. Autopsy report lists cause of death as strangulation. Her hyoid bone was fractured. Charity was a small girl. In the heat of the moment, Goren could have grabbed her neck. It's possible he panicked."

"Then he puts the girl in his car, or maybe in the

trunk." Donna picked up the narrative. "He calls his cousin, who has probably bragged about his success with the occasional rough stuff for Spadafore. Reggio helps him dispose of the body. He probably planted the business card at that time."

Cantrell was nodding calmly. "Y'all make sense. It's a good theory. Ya got any proof to back it up?"

"We've got a lot of missing pieces. All we need is a search warrant. With that we can go after his records, both at his home and office. Laura's got a list of all his vehicles and properties. Even a vacation spot by Lake Huron," I said.

He let his gaze go around the table slowly. He came back to me. "Speakin' of vacation, y'all got about seven hours left. Them mountains is calling me."

"We're right on this, Pappy," Laura said. "We can solve a cold case homicide and bust a member of organized crime. Not to mention proving that the feds were wrong."

"Ah do like that idea," Cantrell said with a wink and a grin.

I nodded at him. "We all do. Say the word, and I'll call the judge for search warrants. But we need to move fast."

Cantrell stubbed out his cigarette. "Make it happen. Y'all can borrow Squad Five to help ya out. I gotta run back downtown for dat meeting." Before any of us could move, he bounced to his feet and waved a gnarled finger at us. "Watch yer asses. And your partner's too. Now go git this sumbitch."

Chapter Twenty

With Cantrell's approval, I called Judge Kevin Larabee. Normally I'd go to the courthouse and meet with him in chambers. But time was against me. After hearing me out, he asked half a dozen questions, as if checking the boxes on the search warrant request. Before placing the call, I sent them via email.

"You want to search his business, vehicles, home, garage, computers, phone records and financials. There is a vacation property up north too, near Tawas City. Damn, Chene, what about the guy's dental records?"

"I doubt he's got anything stashed in his molars, Your Honor."

"You're citing conspiracy to commit murder, conspiracy to kidnap, conspiracy to assassinate two law enforcement officers and the criminal use of firearms. The reports provided are substantial," Larabee said thoughtfully. "And you're searching for records and materials that would support these charges."

"That's correct, Your Honor. My apologies for the short notice and the unorthodox process, but we're tight on time."

The judge chuckled. "Captain Cantrell is well known for his unorthodox efforts, Sergeant. Apparently, that's starting to rub off on you."

"Can't argue with that, Judge."

There was a brief silence. "I'll sign and you'll have

the approved copy in your email in five minutes."

"Thank you, sir."

"You're welcome, Chene. Weren't you one of the officers involved in that shooting Wednesday night?"

"Yeah, that's right."

"Then go get this son of a bitch."

"Roger that."

True to his word, the warrants appeared in my mailbox. Showtime.

Suarez was standing at his desk, an anxious look on his face. I printed out copies of the search warrant, folded one set and handed it over.

"Get Giles from Squad Five. He's already waiting for you, and he knows the routine. Patrol has two uniformed troopers ready to go."

"Are we being cordial or kicking ass?" Suarez asked. He had read over the search warrant paperwork while I was on the phone with the judge.

"However it rolls. I want you knocking down the front door of his residence at the same moment we brace Reggio at his office. Grab any computers, files, paperwork, bank records."

"Guy like this is liable to have a safe," he said thoughtfully.

"Ask the wife to open it. If she won't, Giles can probably break it with a little C-4," Kozlowski said. "But that could get messy."

Suarez blanched. Koz burst out laughing. "Dude, that was a joke."

"The way you guys play, nothing would surprise me." Suarez shook his head in wonder.

"One more thing. Any room that's got a dropped ceiling, pop the tiles and check it out." I pointed to the door. "Be ready for the call. We're heading out."

Suarez nodded. "Time to kick some ass."

Laura took a burner phone, left the number open and dialed the Premiere Construction office. She asked for Reggio, pretending to be a representative from a staffing company. Her voice dropped an octave. She gushed on, saying she was in the area calling on businesses and was oh, so hopeful that he might have a few minutes for her. Reggio didn't hesitate.

We had enough. Before we started out, I remembered Pappy's warning at breakfast. I called Megan's cell. Time to bring in the marines.

"How's it going?"

"Simone's getting a little antsy. She's not the only one," Megan said quietly. "She's in the next room, kicking Naughton's ass at gin rummy."

"You feel safe on your own if I pull him and O'Connell?"

Megan picked up on my vibe. "Something going down?"

"Didn't the nuns ever tell you that it's rude to answer a question with a question? And if I tell you, Simone will drag it out of you. I don't want her worried, but there's no time to scramble somebody else over there."

There was no hesitation. "I can take care of her. And there's a Birmingham cop I know who owes me a favor or two."

"Make it happen. I'll call Naughton next."

"Go nail the bastards." She clicked off.

I gave it a minute as we got in the car, then called Naughton. He answered before it finished the first ring.

"When and where?" he said.

"Right now. Sterling Heights. Donna will text you the address. Is O'Connell as good with a weapon as I've been hearing? We're talking firing, not disarming?"

"Damn near better than me."

"Bring her. You got vests and gear with you?" I asked.

"Don't leave home without it."

"Twenty minutes. Get close and call me. We'll meet up before approaching."

"On it, boss."

I stomped on the pedal and the Jag zipped north on Gratiot. Kozlowski and Laura were right behind me.

"Do you think Pappy is pissed that he's not at the party?" Donna asked.

"He'll be more pissed if we screw up his vacation."

Premiere Construction's main office was in the northwest quadrant of Sterling Heights, just off Ryan Road near the M-59 highway. There was a strip mall about a mile from the place. We gathered in the parking lot. Laura had called the local cops and apprised them of the situation. There were two patrol cars in the lot. The intent was that they would monitor the perimeter. Pappy had supplied my temporary wheels with all the necessary equipment. Maybe he'd been a Boy Scout.

Naughton and O'Connell arrived within three minutes of the rest of us. We all geared up with vests and windbreakers that had Police in yellow foot-high letters across the back.

"How do you want to play this?" Naughton asked.

"Squad cars will block the driveway when we are about to enter the building. This is part of a small industrial complex. There is a pole barn in the back of the property for supplies, trucks, and equipment. Reggio drives a Caddy, bright blue. We saw it in a designated spot driving by. I'm just hoping for a quiet conversation."

"I'm just hoping to go scuba diving on the Great Barrier Reef," O'Connell said, adjusting her vest.

Koz raised his eyebrows. "Damn, baby, you and I gotta talk."

I jumped in before she could respond. "Stow it. From the blueprints we studied, there are three exits. Front, back and middle of the building. I'll take Koz and Atwater inside with me. Naughton, you take the center, Spears on the front, O'Connell on the rear. That work?"

Everyone nodded. Donna grabbed a shotgun from the Jag's trunk and filled the pockets of her jacket with shells. O'Connell and Naughton each pulled an M1 automatic rifle from the back of his SUV. Kozlowski thought for a moment, then lifted an M4 from his trunk. Laura and I kept our automatic pistols.

"There may be innocents inside. I do not want a bloodbath. I want Reggio alive, in cuffs and talking his ass off." My eyes flicked to the group. "We good?"

I received grunts of consent all the way around. The four uniformed officers watched from the background. I reminded them of their roles.

Kozlowski lifted his phone. "Suarez is in position at the house."

"Let's go ruin Reggio's day," Naughton muttered.

"At least he had time for lunch," Donna grumbled.

It looked like a parade, with four cars driving quickly up the road. We left the Jaguar in the strip mall lot. The patrol units held back. I was in Kozlowski's car and Donna was with Naughton. There was a spot for visitors by the front door. Koz parked there and we climbed out. Naughton angled his vehicle in such a way that the Caddy was blocked in. Everyone had earbuds and a radio set to a clear frequency. In fifteen seconds, we were all in position. I led the others inside.

A slender black man, wearing slacks and a long sleeve dress shirt, rose from behind a desk as we entered. Koz was on my left hip, Laura on the right. He took a second to register the hardware. Then he raised his hands just a little.

"You the ninja?" I asked.

"I'm Luther, Mr. Reggio's assistant."

"You can make it easy or hard." Koz gestured with the rifle. "Easy, you get face down on the floor with your hands behind your back. Hard, I do it for you."

"That may be more difficult than you think," Luther said, focusing his attention on Kozlowski. "I may not look—"

The boom of a handgun filled the room. Laura's hands were extended. A vapor of smoke poured from the barrel of her gun. Blood flowed from Luther's right wrist. He clutched it with his left hand, staring at her in disbelief. Koz moved forward and threw him face down on the floor.

"What the hell?" he asked.

"Check his sleeves. He's wearing some kind of spring-loaded blade. You can see the edge of it," Laura said. "Chances are he would have thrown that at your eye, not your vest."

Kozlowski put a knee in Luther's back. He ripped up the sleeves, revealing the sheath strapped to each forearm. Koz yanked those free and jammed the blades in his back pocket. He snapped handcuffs on him.

"I need a doctor. She shot me!"

"Fucking ninja bullshit. You're lucky she's a sharpshooter. I would've put a round through your head!" Koz yanked an extension cord out of the wall socket and quickly tied it around Luther's ankles.

The door behind Kozlowski opened. A heavyset man in his fifties appeared, took one look, jumped back, and slammed the door. Anthony Reggio was in the house. An alarm blared.

I charged through the door. Laura and Koz were right behind me. Outside, gunfire erupted. Reggio was digging through his desk. The three of us rapidly spread out, facing him.

"What the hell is going on?" he screamed.

"State police," I shouted over the blare of the alarm. "Hands up! And they'd better be empty!"

"I didn't do nothing! This is all a mistake!"

Koz raised the M4. "Can't miss from here. You wanna live? Raise your goddamn hands!"

Reggio knew he didn't stand a chance. He dropped an old revolver on the desk, then lifted his hands. Laura started to move forward but I waved her back.

"If he twitches, shoot him in the balls."

"Got it, boss."

I spun him around to face the wall, quickly patted him down then put the cuffs on him.

"How do you turn off the alarm?" I asked.

"Punch 666 on the keypad," he grumbled, jerking his head toward the control panel.

"That's cute," Laura said, silencing the noise. Outside we could still hear sporadic gunfire.

I pulled Reggio from the wall and shoved him into

a chair. "Spears! Gimme an update!"

Her voice crackled in my ear. "Six gunmen came out of the barn. Bunch of ugly ones. O'Connell took out two. Somebody else took out two more."

"Naughton!" I yelled.

"Not me, boss. We've got them pinned behind a panel truck. But somebody else has an advantage."

Kozlowski spun on his heel and headed out the rear door to join the fray. I notified the others. In the distance, sirens wailed. I looked down at Reggio. He was fidgeting, trying to get comfortable with his arms cuffed behind him. Laura moved to the wall and peeked out the window. She glanced back at me.

"Anthony Reggio, you are under arrest for conspiracy to commit murder, kidnapping, assault with a deadly weapon, the assault on two law enforcement officers. You've probably heard all this before, but Detective Atwater is going to read you your rights."

Laura pulled out her phone, switched it to record mode and informed Reggio of his Miranda rights. She got him to confirm that he understood them. Laura clicked off the recording, touched a couple of buttons on the screen, then tucked it back in her pocket.

Outside there was another volley of gunfire. Then everything went quiet. The silence was deafening. Donna appeared in the office doorway. Kozlowski's voice came over the earbuds.

"Step outside, Chene. Donna will help keep that jackass in line."

"On my way." I turned to Donna and Laura. "If he tries anything, shoot him wherever you want. Just don't kill him."

"My pleasure," Donna said.

Walking out of the office, I paused next to Luther. Donna had quickly fashioned a bandage on his wound. "Medics on the way. Should be here in an hour or two."

"This really sucks, man."

"Next time, pick better clients."

In the parking lot, two other patrol cars had joined the party. Uniformed cops were checking the pole barn, confirming that no one else was hiding in the rafters or inside any of the equipment. Naughton and O'Connell were gathered by the front bumper of a battered Chevy pickup truck. Kozlowski joined us.

"Update," I said.

Naughton gave his head a little shake. "Craziest thing I've ever seen. Lucy took out the first two guys when they refused to stand down."

"I identified us as police officers and instructed them to surrender their weapons," O'Connell said. "The dumbass on the left said something like 'I'm not afraid of a little girl,' and he started to raise his piece. So, I shot him. Twice."

Kozlowski nodded. "Double tap. The way you're trained. And the second guy wasn't any smarter."

"He got a shot off, but I was already moving. I think he hit the side of the building, about ten feet off the ground," O'Connell said. "I defended myself."

"Glad you're on my side," I said, turning to Naughton. "What happened next? You said something about someone having an advantage."

Naughton nodded. "I ran back to join Lucy. Before I could get off a round, four shots were fired. High-powered rifle from the sound of it. Elevated position, guessing by the angle. Two more bad guys went down." He pointed at the roof of a neighboring building.

253

"I heard there were six gunners. What happened to the other two?"

"Kozlowski took out one when he joined the party. The last guy's gun either jammed or he emptied his clip." Naughton led me to the back of the Chevy. There was an iron supply rack welded to the truck bed. A chubby guy with a torn shirt was slumped in the bed, one hand cuffed to the rack above his head. There was a smear of blood on his mouth.

I glanced at Koz. He shrugged his massive shoulders. "Guy made a derogatory comment about O'Connell. Thought he could use a lesson in manners. And he was still holding his weapon at the time."

Two of the uniformed cops approached. The pole barn had been cleared. Naughton looked at me. "I want to check out that building next door. I can take these guys with me. For cover."

"Go for it."

"Gonna update Pappy?" Koz asked.

"Let's see what Naughton finds out first. May as well give him as many details as possible. You should call the incident team. They'll need to get everything recorded and collect the evidence."

"Already on the way," O'Connell said. "I took the liberty after the fireworks was over."

Koz looked from O'Connell to me, then back to her. "You ever want to get out of messing with bombs, we'll make room for you in Squad Six."

Lucy gave him a dazzling smile. "Nah, I like blowing shit up too much to get stuck doing investigations."

That shut him up. At least for a moment. Naughton jogged over to join us.

"Pea gravel up there is a little scuffed up, but no brass. I did find a spot on the edge of the roof where someone could have rested a tripod for a rifle. That roof has the perfect angle to take out those guys from there. No footprints or gun. Nothing but bird shit. We're talking about a fucking ghost."

Kozlowski grunted and met my eyes. "I'm not surprised. Are you?"

"I'm surprised he didn't shoot them all."

"You have someone else from the squad up there?" Naughton asked.

I shook my head. "Let's say it was someone with a vested interest."

Chapter Twenty-One

My call to Cantrell with an update went quickly. He rattled off rapid instructions, then disconnected. Pappy had his own arrangements to make. It's possible Special Agent Sedlak was at the same conference. I had no doubt Cantrell would find him soon. In addition to the crime scene unit and an ambulance, two MSP squad cars arrived. Three unmarked cars from the Metro North post were already there to execute the search warrant. Kozlowski brought Reggio out and jammed him into the backseat of one of the squad cars. Koz and Laura took his car and followed. The ambulance attendants had Luther cuffed and strapped to a gurney. The chubby guy from the pickup truck was chained to the jump seat.

Donna and Lucy were talking off to the side. I watched the crime scene crew for a moment as Naughton approached. We had all given preliminary statements individually. Paperwork by the pound would follow.

"You sure know how to party, Chene," Naughton said. "Want a lift back to your Jag?"

"I'd appreciate that."

The four of us rode to the strip mall parking lot. I popped the trunk. Donna and I threw our gear inside. Naughton appeared at my shoulder.

"Should we head back to the hotel? Give

McDonald a hand?" he asked.

In all the action and the aftermath, I'd momentarily forgotten about Simone. By rights, everything should be over. But I wanted to play it safe.

"I'll update McDonald. And I appreciate your help with this whole mess." I checked my watch. Two hours before Pappy's deadline. "McDonald will bring her to my place. You mind playing shadow for just a little longer?"

"Not a problem." He thumped a fist on my good shoulder.

I turned to O'Connell. "Glad you were with us."

"This was almost as much fun as blowing stuff up," Lucy said with a grin. "Almost. Count me in on an operation like this anytime. You know how to show a girl a good time."

"Think you're confusing me with Kozlowski."

"We'll tag them from the hotel to your place and hang out until it's all clear," Naughton said. He nodded at Donna and climbed into his truck.

In the Jaguar, I called Megan and relayed the details. As I was filling her in, Simone took the phone.

"Are you all right?" she asked.

"I'm fine. We're headed to the post to finish this. Pack your bags. Megan and the others will take you to my place. With any luck, I'll be home by seven."

"Thank God!" I could hear her breathe a sigh of relief.

"See you soon." I ended the call and glanced at Donna as we hit a red light.

"You did well today. Not just with the gunfight. Everything."

She nodded. "Only got off two shots. Think the

ricochet caught one guy at the same time the mystery shooter hit him. You figure Max was on that roof?"

"Makes sense. He knew we were going after Reggio. And even though he's a goddamn dinosaur, I'm willing to bet he can ping that phone you're carrying, so he knows exactly where we are."

Donna considered it, turning the burner over in her hand. "Anything we can do about that? Can we charge him?"

"Knowing it was Max is one thing. But proving it is another matter. No physical evidence at the scene and chances are pieces of the rifle he used will probably be in the middle of a landfill or the river before sunset. He's been in the game a long time."

****

We were back at the post. Reggio had been fingerprinted and photographed. He was locked in an interrogation room with one of the uniformed troopers. The four of us were in the bullpen, trying to be patient. My eyes were glued on the clock. Ninety minutes. A flurry of footsteps sounded in the hall. Pappy came around the corner, looking like the pied piper, strutting into the room. MacGregor and Sedlak were right behind him.

Cantrell spun to face them and spread his arms wide. "Next time y'all need a case solved, ah expect a call. And a good bottle of bourbon."

Sedlak scowled. "Seeing is believing. Do you have any proof to back up this wild story?"

"Files, records, connections and more," Laura said, patting a stack of paper on her desk. "We also have teams conducting a search of his residence and business as we speak. Details will be coming in for a few days."

"Suppose he's lawyered up by now," MacGregor said.

I nodded. "Reggio's attorney arrived ten minutes ago. He's informed us that his client is willing to talk."

Sedlak squared his shoulders. "I'll be conducting the interview."

"Like hell!" Pappy growled. "My team got him. My team talks to him. Y'all can watch. This be a courtesy, nothin' more."

Cantrell curled a finger and led the two feds to the observation room. The others looked at me. "Atwater and I will go chat with Reggio. We've already established a little dialogue."

Koz and Donna scrambled to the conference room where they could watch on the video screen. Laura gathered up her file and led the way down the hall in the opposite direction. We entered the interrogation room. The uniformed trooper nodded and stepped outside.

Laura identified us to Reggio's attorney, a scrawny guy in his late thirties named Wallace Suskind. His suit looked cheap and rumpled. Something told me he wasn't one of the Mob's regular lawyers. Laura activated the microphone in the center of the table and identified everyone present, the date and time. She glanced at me.

"We already have it on record that you've been given the Miranda warning. No questions were asked on the way from your office to the post. We have the dashcam video that will substantiate that," I said. "You have legal counsel present. Be advised that at this moment, the property where the shootout took place has been sealed and will be thoroughly searched. Your residence is being searched too." I slid copies of the warrants to Suskind for his review. "Are you willing to answer questions?"

Reggio's wrists were still cuffed and chained to a metal ring in the center of the table. He shrugged. "Might as well. Maybe we can work out a deal."

"A deal?" I snapped. "You're involved in the death of a fifteen-year-old girl and the attempted murder of a law enforcement officer *and* a federal agent. That's just the tip of the freaking iceberg."

Suskind cleared his throat. "My client understands the precarious situation he's in. Mr. Reggio is hoping for some leniency. And it's a show of good faith that he's ready to answer your questions. Mr. Reggio wants to cooperate."

"Let's take the crimes one at a time then. Tell us about your involvement with the murder of Charity Gray."

Reggio's face revealed he had no idea who that was. I noticed a thick sheen of sweat on his forehead and cheeks. Laura opened a folder and withdrew two photos. One was the picture from the high school yearbook. The other was of her decayed remains on the autopsy table. She slapped them on the table and spun them around, so they were right side up in front of Reggio. His eyes locked on the remains for a second.

"Holy Mary, Mother of God," he muttered.

"Not even close," Laura said gruffly. "Start talking."

With the back of his fingers, Reggio flicked the gruesome photo back at her. "I never saw her alive. Never saw her like that. It was all Joey's fault. That dumb shit. He's the one who killed her."

"Who is Joey?" Laura said.

"Joey Goren."

She pulled a picture of Goren from the folder and flipped it over. "This guy? The one who's been missing for as long as Charity's been dead?"

Reggio nodded. Even though the session was being videotaped, I wanted verbal confirmation. With a nudge from the attorney, Reggio said, "Yes, that's Joseph Goren. My cousin."

"Tell us about Goren," I said. "Don't skimp on the details. We're certainly not in a hurry."

"Joey was a dumb shit. Didn't have the brains God gives a hamster. Couldn't keep a job. He was no good in school. I felt sorry for him. The relatives kept dropping hints. Like a putz, I hired him to do some basic run around stuff for me. This was after he bombed out of every job he ever had."

Reggio explained that in addition to his inability to maintain steady employment, Goren was inexperienced with women. He was too shy to date. Reggio even set him up with a hooker on more than one occasion. "Joey was a fumbler, a bumbler. But he was good at doing easy tasks, if I didn't give him more than one at a time. Like he could make a coffee run. Or go to the liquor store. But you couldn't give him a list. He'd never follow it."

"You're telling us he was a runner, a gopher," Laura said.

"Exactly. He'd do all right. And like I said, he was my cousin. I wanted to help him out. Then he started going with me to the Surfside. There was a babe there that got his attention. She liked shaking her goodies for him. Always treated him nice, flirted with him a bit. I don't remember her name, but she was a little older than him. He would fall all over himself when she was around. Joey gave her a ride home one night when her car broke down."

Reggio hesitated. He looked at a spot between his hands and slowly curled his fingers. It was like he was trying to physically touch the memory. His face was covered with sweat, and his shirt was stuck to his chest.

"What happened next?" I prompted.

"It was a day or two later. A Friday. Joey called me. All shook up. He wasn't making any sense. I told him to meet me at the construction site. He had this old Ford, a big sedan. It was quitting time when he got there. All the guys on the crew were heading out. Joey was a wreck. He was shaking all over."

"Where was the construction site?" I asked.

"Lower east side of Detroit. About halfway between the Renaissance Center and Grosse Pointe. One of those neighborhoods that was always being rebuilt. We had a couple of houses getting worked on."

"So once the crew was gone?" Laura asked.

Reggio explained that he managed to get his cousin calmed down. Then Joseph Goren told him the story about going to see the waitress, the sex on the patio and seeing the face watching through the shrubs. Goren ran out of words and led him to the trunk of the car. There was the young girl in the school uniform.

"She was dead. There was no pulse. She wasn't breathing."

"You just happened to have rolls of that heavy plastic laying around to wrap a body in," I said.

Anthony Reggio hunched his shoulders in an attempted shrug. "It was a construction site. I had that stuff all over the place. Kept some of it in my truck too. Tools of the trade."

"Keep talking," Laura said.

"We'd been hanging drywall that afternoon. There were a bunch of panels that the guys didn't get to. I'm no pro, but good enough to nail a section or two up. The crew would return on Monday and finish the room. They'd never notice if another couple a sheets was in place."

Reggio said they waited another hour until it was good and dark. Then he and Goren brought Charity's body inside. By then he had the plastic spread out on the floor, cut and ready to become her burial shroud. He gave another shoulder shrug, as if that was a common occurrence.

"So that's the whole story," he said. "Joey didn't mean to kill the girl. Just figured he'd get in trouble because of her seeing him having sex with the waitress. It being outside and all."

I scowled at him. "That's not it by a long shot. Tell us what else you put inside the plastic."

There was a layer of sweat on his forehead and cheeks. Reggio tried to raise his hands enough to rub his face, but the chain wasn't long enough. Instead, he turned his head and wiped his cheek on his shoulder, then repeated it with the other side. "I'd forgotten about that. Hiding that girl in the wall was just the capper for a really shitty day. There was a meeting with Dan Spadafore. All these big shot family guys, chowing down at that Italian place downtown. Mario's."

"Is this really relevant?" Suskind interrupted.

"It's pertinent to the case," I said. My eyes had never left Reggio. "Keep talking. You have lunch at this meeting?"

He nodded. "Yeah, a bunch of us. Dan and I were talking about starting a new business. The old man, Carmine, still ran the show back then. But he let us tell the others about it. There was some sharp guy the other bosses all looked to for advice. Dan Spadafore pitched the idea. Nobody liked it."

"What was the business?" Laura asked.

"Fireworks. We'd set up shops to sell them year round. Clean the money from some other operations."

"Hearing your idea get shot down must have made you angry. What happened next?" I asked.

Reggio brought his eyes up to meet mine. "I was nervous. Being around all those guys made me sweat like a firehose. I used my napkin several times to wipe my hands and face. This smart guy made some comments to Dan, offered him a business card. Dan wouldn't take it. Then the guy dropped the card on the table, got up and left. There was no telling if Carmine Spadafore was going to lose face with the others. He looked calm then, but we might catch hell later. So, I snatched the guy's card and shoved it in my pocket, along with that cloth napkin he was using. Mine was soaking wet by then."

That explained how Leo Agonasti's business card and his napkin were found on the scene. But I wanted a little more confirmation.

"So why put them with the girl's body?" I asked.

Reggio tried to shrug again. I glanced at Laura and nodded. She pulled her keys and unlocked the cuffs for a second. Then she fastened them back on his wrists, without the chain holding him to the table. Reggio nodded his thanks and wiped his face with both hands.

Suskind gave him a handkerchief.

"It was just a thing. We tucked the card in. The napkin was in my pocket. The card just kind of fell out when I stopped to wipe my brow. Doc says I got the disease that makes you sweat a lot. It gets worse when I'm nervous or stressed. There was some sweat that dripped off me onto her leg. I used the cloth to blot it, then left it in with her. But as the years went by, I kinda forgot about her."

That was enough to clear Leo Agonasti. Planting those two items on Charity Gray, whether accidental or deliberate, proved that he had never interacted with the dead girl.

"And you just put her behind the wall, then closed it up?" Laura asked.

"Yeah. Once we couldn't see her anymore, Joey settled down a little. At least, for a few minutes. Long enough to hold the drywall in place while I nailed it in. We picked up the tools and took everything back to my truck," Reggio said. His voice was quieter now, lost in the memory.

"What happened to your cousin? Joseph Goren hasn't been seen since that weekend," I said.

Reggio managed a full shrug now. "He's gone."

"No shit, Sherlock," Laura snarled. "Gone where?"

There was no response for a bit. Anthony Reggio's eyes were fixated on the heavy ring before him on the table. Suskind tapped him on the arm. Reggio looked at him briefly, nodded at some unspoken signal, then turned back to us.

"Gone. As in dead and gone."

"Tell us about it," I said.

Reggio explained that after they left the

construction site, he had Goren follow him. He was going to make sure Joey got home and stayed out of sight for a while. But by the time they reached Goren's apartment, his cousin was losing it all over again. Joey was having second thoughts now. He talked about calling the police, about explaining that it was just an accident. Reggio let him ramble for a few minutes. Then he had a better idea.

"I told him to pack some clothes for a day or two and we'd go up to my cottage. It's quiet and it was early in the season. We could stay up there and talk this over. Didn't want him to make a rash decision."

"This the place up in Tawas City?" I asked.

Reggio's eyes widened, then he chuckled weakly. "Shouldn't be surprised you know about that. Yeah, that's where we went. I was hoping that Joey would understand it was too late to go back. We had to forget about this girl. Forget it ever happened. Keep him away from the Surfside and that waitress. But the longer we were up there, the more stubborn he got. Joey kept saying he wanted to 'do the right thing,' both by this little girl and the waitress. Thought if he was honest about everything, she'd realize he loved her, and they could be together."

Laura shook her head. "He had sex with her one time and thought it was true love and they'd live happily ever after?"

"Yeah. I told you, he was a dumb shit," Reggio said.

"What happened next?" I prompted.

"It was getting late on Sunday. Cold and rainy. I knew no one in their right mind would be out. There's a big, wooded area at the edge of my property. Some nature preserve thing, ain't never gonna be developed. I got him to walk with me back a ways, told him I was sorry. Joey just nodded and turned around. Got on his knees with his back to me. I shot him. Buried him deep enough so the animals wouldn't find him."

"Jesus Christ," Wallace Suskind mumbled.

Chapter Twenty-Two

There was a rap at the door. It was ten minutes to six. Laura closed the files and we stood. Reggio looked relieved.

"We're not done. Not by a long shot," I said.

We exited the room. The trooper guarded the door. Cantrell stood at the end of the hallway. Special Agents Sedlak and MacGregor were behind him. As we approached, he led us into the bullpen. The others were waiting.

"Suarez called," Kozlowski said. "Found all kinds of financial records in the safe, along with a bill of sale for Joseph Goren's car and Goren's wallet. There was also some paperwork for a piece of undeveloped land out by Tawas City, not far from where Reggio has a cottage. He had several handguns in there, which may have been used in illegal activities."

"Puts it all in a neat little package," I said.

Pappy cleared his throat. "Ah believe Agent Sedlak's got sumthin' to say."

"Based on the evidence you've collected and the statement Mr. Reggio is making, we believe that he was involved in the conspiracy to cover up the death of Charity Gray and that his cousin was in fact guilty of her kidnapping and subsequent death. The attempt to frame Leo Agonasti for this crime has been explained. As a result, we are dismissing any charges against Mr.

Agonasti and closing the federal case files." Sedlak kept his face calm somehow, showing absolutely no trace of emotion.

"Will you be contacting Ms. Trevino with this news?" I asked.

"Agent MacGregor has already been in touch with her. He has relayed this same information. As a courtesy, I'd appreciate seeing the transcripts of the interrogation along with copies of any reports and files you've created."

Pappy chuckled. "We can be courteous. Y'all need anythin' else? Parkin' validation?"

Neither fed spoke. Cantrell stuck out his hand. Sedlak gave him a firm shake and left. Mac did the same, pausing to nod at me. We watched them exit the building. Pappy checked his watch and pulled a cigarette from his pack.

"Got her done with five minutes to spare. Y'all did good. Chene's got the lead. Finish up and get back on them other cases after the weekend. And iffen y'all run inna problem…"

"Don't call you," Koz said.

"Damn straight. Y'all got enough to keep yer asses busy for the next two weeks. Ah'll be back then."

He lit the cigarette, blew a plume of smoke toward the ceiling, nodded once, and headed out. Kozlowski and Spears walked down the hall to the observation room. Laura and I returned to the interrogation room. Reggio didn't look any better when we came back.

"Let's pick up where we left off," Laura said. "You just admitted to killing your cousin Joseph Goren and burying his body near your property in Tawas City. Any landmarks or ways to identify where his grave is?"

Reggio nodded. "There's a big cluster of birch trees back there. Three of them growing close together, like they split from the ground up. He's just left of that, about five or six yards."

Laura made a note on her pad and glanced at me.

"Let's flash forward to this week. When did you decide to start shooting at cops?" I asked.

"That was all on that jackass Tancredi. Spadafore should have never brought him into the game. He was even stupider than Joey. Made Joey look like a freaking genius."

"You're telling me the shootout was his idea?" I asked doubtfully.

"All that did was bring more attention on us!" Reggio rattled the handcuffs to emphasize the point.

"How did he know where to find us?"

Turns out that after they'd taken care of Charity's body, Joey Goren insisted they drive by the Griffith house, just in case Rachel was still there. So, Reggio knew exactly where Charity had been spotted and kidnapped. Once the news came out that her remains were discovered, he tried to keep an eye on the investigation. Then a rumor went around that the FBI was involved.

"I told Tancredi to just stakeout the house. Gave him something to do. First day or two, he got bored. That's when I said he could take a couple of guys to keep him company. Tancredi liked that. Made him feel like he was important. A man in charge of something. He was just supposed to watch and report if there was ever any cops looking at the house. I didn't even know if that waitress still lived there."

"What about the guns and the body armor?" I

asked.

Reggio wiped his face again. This guy needed a roll of paper towels. "He did that on his own. Had these two revolvers that belonged in a freaking museum. Between you and me, the kid couldn't shoot to save his ass. That's probably why he had Croyton and Bertenelli geared up. They were just knockaround guys. Made Tancredi feel like hot shit to boss a couple of men around."

"From hot shit to dead shit," Laura said. "You expect us to believe he was only going to watch that house in case the cops showed up?"

"Hand of God! I never told him to shoot anybody."

"You seemed ready to fight today when we showed up," I said.

Reggio raised his palms in a show of surrender. "Got a call from one of Spadafore's lieutenants. Told me that Dan had been taken by the cops. Everyone was on edge. Only a matter of time before it came around. They all knew Tancredi had been working for me. You just had to connect the dots."

Laura tapped her pen on the table. "We're pretty good at that."

****

Anthony Reggio would be spending the weekend in isolation at the Macomb County Jail. MacGregor had already contacted the US Attorney's office. In addition to the charges for the shooting and his role in Charity's homicide, Reggio would probably have a grocery list of charges coming from the feds for his involvement in organized crime. There was the possibility that he might make a deal and cooperate. His knowledge of Spadafore's criminal activities could lead to other investigations and arrests. But that was out of our concern. We had him cold on his complicity with Charity's case and the murder of his cousin.

It was a little after seven when I pulled into my driveway. Megan's ugly yellow Mustang was out front. Naughton's truck was two doors down across the street. The house was all lit up, as if there was a party going on. As I climbed out, I noticed something on the Jag's back seat. It was the sling I was supposed to be wearing. Maybe tomorrow.

Lucy O'Connell came out the front door. If it weren't for the weapon on her hip, she could be mistaken for a college coed on her way to a picnic. Or a hot date. She gave me a quick smile.

"Everything wrapped up?" she asked.

"Yeah, thanks again for the help. On all fronts."

"Anytime, Chene."

We went inside. Naughton was standing by the front window, keeping watch. Simone had cooked dinner for them all. It was a way for her to keep busy, keep her mind off things. Megan was at the dining table, finishing up a plate of pasta thick with a red sauce, meatballs, and chunks of sausage. There was a trace of wine in her glass. She gave me a big smile. "We saved you a plate."

"You're so kind."

Simone came around the corner. There was a nanosecond of hesitation before she embraced me. I wrapped my good arm around her.

"You look like hell," she whispered in my ear.

"Sounds about right."

"Think that's our cue," Naughton said. "Nice looking boat you got out back. Mind if I borrow it on my next day off?"

"As long as you're not going fishing. Hate to get worms and scales all over the deck. It's a bitch to clean."

"I'll call you," he said. Just like that, he and O'Connell drifted out the front door and were gone.

Simone stepped back but kept one hand on my good arm. She faced Megan. "You're probably anxious to get away from me, after these last couple of days."

"Hey, it was different. Think of all the fun background stories you heard about Chene." Megan carried her plate and glass to the sink, smirking a grin.

"That was educational." Simone giggled. "And now I have a whole list of questions for him."

Megan gave me a kiss on the cheek and headed out. I closed the door behind her and turned off a few lights. Simone was standing by the dining table, hands on her hips. There was a plate of steaming pasta waiting for me.

"Dinner, then a hot shower for you. No arguments, no delays, no bullshit. And if that damn phone rings, I'm throwing it in the canal."

I wanted to laugh but didn't have the energy. "Yes, ma'am."

****

By all outward appearances, Maximo Aurelio was just an ordinary, average kind of guy. While he enjoyed the occasional fancy meal and was seldom without female companionship, tonight he was ready for a quiet celebration. He cut through the crowd at The Octopus Beer Garden in Mt. Clemens and made his way to the patio that overlooked the Clinton River. At the far end, away from the patrons kick-starting their weekends, he saw a solitary figure raise a hand. Max joined him.

"Nice to see you, Leo."

"It's good to be seen. You've had a busy day."

Max flashed a grin and gave his shoulders a comical shrug. "Let's just say it was the perfect way to wrap up a strange week. Glad to get your call."

Agonasti motioned with two fingers at the young waitress who had been hovering nearby. She darted inside and returned a moment later with two steins of craft beer and a platter of food. Mahi Mahi tacos for Leo and a gigantic cheeseburger for Max. A platter of fries was set on the table between them. In between Leo's fingers was a folded fifty-dollar bill. The waitress favored him with a shy smile before making the bill disappear.

"I took the liberty of ordering," Leo said. "This seemed like the closest place to meet, after Diana called."

There was little conversation as they ate. It was a relaxed meal, surrounded by patrons out enjoying the pleasant evening. Both men took their time. At length, Leo pushed his plate to the side and studied his old friend.

"It should be safe to return to our normal routines, Max. I appreciate everything you've done on my behalf."

Max drained the last of his beer. Carefully he set the glass on the table before looking Agonasti in the eye. "You know someday the feds may actually have a case against us. I keep thinking this was like a pre-season game in football. Good practice for the big event."

"True enough. But I'm not suggesting we get lazy

in our precautions."

"Well, thank God for that. You probably used your one and only 'get out of jail free' card with Chene."

Agonasti nodded. "I do owe Jeff and his team my gratitude for their efforts. But this is also quite an accomplishment for them. Solving an old homicide and bringing down several members of an organized crime family will earn him some excellent media coverage. They may even get commendations."

"Not to mention there were several useless humans who won't be bothering anyone else again."

Leo let his gaze drift over to a sailboat making its way down the river. "Yes, Chene and that FBI agent took out three. And I'm aware of some type of action earlier today. Some clumsy degenerates tried to shoot it out with the state police. I understand they were dealt with severely. Don't suppose you heard anything about that activity?"

Max gave him a crooked grin. "Me? Nah, I was taking a leisurely ride along the lake. Didn't even have the radio on. It's kinda relaxing this time of year. I wouldn't want to be near any violence or gun battles. Chene seemed to have everything well in hand."

"Yes, he did. Diana was surprised to hear from that FBI agent. Apparently, she didn't have as much confidence in him as we do. Have you spoken with him this evening?"

"Nah. I pitched the burner phone that his bar buddy had the number for. Saw his car still at the post when driving past. Chene might be having a conversation with Reggio."

Agonasti finished his beer. "Perhaps we should keep a little distance. Give Jeff some time to finish up and focus on his recovery. Don't you have plans for a weekend getaway?"

"Going to a nice little cottage up in Lexington. Right on Lake Huron. Maureen likes the peace and quiet. It's a good place to relax."

Maureen was a commercial real estate agent Max had been seeing periodically. When it came to women, his friend had commitment issues. Leo signaled the waitress for the check. Max stood and shook hands with his old friend. Without another word, he disappeared through the crowd.

Twenty minutes later, Leo was in his Bentley, cruising down the road. Vivaldi oozed softly from the speakers, matching his relaxed mood. He cruised through St. Clair Shores and rolled into Grosse Pointe. Leo drove around the corner and stopped in front of his house. Lights were on and several cars were in the driveway. He parked but left the engine quietly running. Behind him, a car swung into the driveway. A young couple emerged and approached the house.

Leo stepped out of the Bentley but remained beside it. The front door of the house opened, and Diana Trevino welcomed her guests with hugs and kisses. Her eyes went to the street. Seeing him, Diana stepped aside so her guests could enter. She walked toward him. Leo gave his head a slow negative shake. Diana stopped, smiled, and raised her right hand, placing it over her heart. Leo touched two fingertips to his lips and blew her a kiss. He got back in the car and drove silently away.

Diana was visible in his rearview mirror until the road curved.

Chapter Twenty-Three

It was before the lunch rush Monday, so I managed to get a booth in a back corner. The place would be jumping within half an hour. Attorneys and office workers would begin crowding the tables, along with prospective jurors from both courthouses. The Pegasus Taverna is a mainstay in Greektown. Their menu offers some of the best fare in the city. I barely had a chance to glance at the options before Olivia Sholtis materialized. As I stood up in greeting, she leaned in and buzzed my cheek.

"Be prepared, Chene. I'm going to do some serious damage to your credit card. I haven't been here in ages. Saganaki, kabobs and a Greek salad are all calling my name." She flashed me the smile reserved for the camera and settled into the booth. "So, is this lunch *and* my exclusive?"

"That's right. Your broadcast about Charity was a big help."

"Should we talk on the record now or after lunch?"

"Let's relax and have some food," I said, knowing full well she would remember every part of the conversation.

The waiter appeared. He fawned over Olivia for a moment, then took the order and toddled off to the kitchen. He returned with beverages, a basket of thick-crusted bread, still warm from the oven and our salads.

A moment later he brought out the saganaki, a flaming dish of Kasseri cheese and brandy that he lit right beside the table. I kept the conversation on easy subjects until after the food was gone. Olivia dug out her notebook. She paused for a moment to sip the last of her Diet Coke.

"Ready!"

"When is this going to be broadcast?"

She gave me a comical eye roll. "You know damn well it's got to be verified and approved by my producer before it gets slotted. If this is juicy, it might be on the six o'clock broadcast tonight. Or maybe eleven. But that's a big if."

"I promised you the exclusive. You're getting the story a day before the official press conference."

"Are you doing that? The press briefing?" she asked.

"No. Captain Cantrell usually handles those, but he's on vacation. A public relations officer will make the formal statement. Probably have someone from the prosecutor's office as well. Maybe one or two people from Squad Six will be in the background. But not me."

Olivia squared her notebook on the table. "Start talking, Chene."

I gave her the rundown, starting with the investigation. She already knew about Charity's disappearance and the discovery of the remains. During the conversation, I made no mention of Leo Agonasti or the connections with organized crime families. I knew Olivia had one of Banks' business cards, so a follow-up phone call might earn her a vague statement from the feds.

"There were reports of two different violent

shootings last week," Olivia said. "One Wednesday night, the other Friday afternoon. I'm not talking about gangbangers and drive-by shootings. These had serious firepower. Shoot-outs."

"Is there a question in there somewhere?"

She flicked her nails at me. "Were either of these shootings pertinent to the case? And were you or your team involved in either one? Or both?"

"That's three questions. Yes, those events were tied to the case." I held up one finger. "This part here is off the record. Understood?"

Olivia flashed a brief pout. "Understood. Now tell me."

"Agent Banks and I were ambushed Wednesday night. We were injured during the event. Fortunately, a full recovery is expected for both of us. Three gunmen perished. You may be able to get a copy of the police report of that incident, but I'm not giving you any more details."

"Chene!" Olivia dropped her pen and grabbed my hand. "You idiot! You got shot? Why the hell didn't you tell me?"

"I'm fine. Just a ding to the shoulder. Probably end up with a scar."

She patted my hand. "Scars can be sexy. And they have better stories than any tattoos."

"I've heard that recently." The ambulance driver Wednesday night said it as well. The same comment from two different women must make it true.

Olivia was eager to get back to business. "What about that situation on Friday afternoon?"

"On the record, the investigation by the state police led to the site in Sterling Heights. When law enforcement officers arrived on the scene, with a warrant for the arrest of Anthony Reggio, and a search warrant for the property, several men began firing. Law enforcement officers defended themselves, subdued the hostile men and arrested Mr. Reggio. That's what the press conference tomorrow will confirm."

"Anyone ever tell you it's a turn on when you use official verbiage like that?" Olivia batted her lashes at me.

"That's cute. Do you want the rest or not? I need to get back to the office."

"Keep talking, Chene."

"Anthony Reggio will be arraigned tomorrow morning on charges that include being an accessory after the fact to the murder of Charity Gray. Reggio will also be charged with the attempted murder of two police officers and orchestrating the gunplay last Friday. There is an ongoing investigation which may lead to additional charges related to first-degree murder. I'm not at liberty to reveal anything else."

"So, he's an accessory to Charity's murder. But he didn't do it?"

I shook my head. "A man named Joseph Goren, who was Reggio's cousin, was the one who killed her."

"Is Goren in police custody too?"

I didn't answer. Olivia looked up from her notes. After a moment, I drained the last of my iced tea. "Off the record, we suspect that Goren was killed by Reggio. That's the ongoing investigation. Or at least a part of it. We've got an idea where his body is. Just trying to locate it."

Olivia sat back and absorbed it all. Her mind must have been spinning already writing up the story. I knew what was coming next. "Can I quote you?"

"I'm a confidential source within the Michigan State Police. You know the drill. Keep my name out of it."

"Chene, one of these days, I'm going to get you in the spotlight."

"Keep dreaming, kid. But I do have one more treat for you."

"What's that?" Olivia tucked her notebook and pen back in her bag.

"I'll buy you a goodie from the Astoria Bakery across the street."

She stood up and linked her arm in mine as we left the booth. "Chene, if Charlie ever leaves me, I'm coming after you."

****

Having lunch with Liv had been worthwhile. It's important to always keep your word, especially with a determined reporter. Now I was back at the post. I grabbed a fresh mug of coffee and dropped a dozen of the bakery's macaroons in the break room. It was time to review all the reports from the Charity Gray case. My shoulder felt remarkedly better. Having kept my arm in the sling for the last couple of days must have helped. The combination of the painkillers and some decent sleep probably didn't hurt either. My cell phone rang, indicating a video call with a familiar number. I had a moment's hesitation before accepting.

"Hello, Father Dovensky."

"I'm hoping you have a moment to talk, Jefferson."

The use of my full name had my attention. "Of course, Father. What's on your mind?"

"I just spoke with Sister Augusta. The medical

examiner is releasing Charity's remains today. You're aware, of course, that there's no family."

Sadly, I nodded. "What can I do?"

"St. Bartholomew's parish has an emergency fund. They will handle a cremation. Augusta has asked me to conduct a funeral Mass for the child. It will be Wednesday morning at ten. Beyond a few of the sisters and a teacher or two, I don't think there will be many people attending. Which troubles me. I wish there could be others in attendance to help celebrate this young girl's life."

"We'll be there."

"I appreciate it, Jeff."

"Tell Sister Augusta to contact me if she needs anything."

"Thank you. I'll see you Wednesday morning."

I switched off the phone. That sly dog. He knew damn well I could never refuse his request when those eyes of his were glaring at me. No wonder he used the video feature. It was the first time he'd ever done that. Probably wouldn't be the last. I had a few calls to make.

****

The parking lot at St. Bartholomew's Church had over fifty cars already there when I found a spot for the Jaguar. I walked around and opened Simone's door, extending a hand to help her out.

"Proof that chivalry is not dead," a playful voice behind me said.

I glanced over my shoulder. Jamie and Malone were approaching. She wore a demure black dress and small round sunglasses. With her high heels, Jamie was almost my height. Malone was in a black pinstripe suit with an arm around her waist. Simone and Jamie hugged briefly in the way women do.

"Really appreciate your help on this case and coming here today," I said.

"Glad to do it," Malone said.

Jamie giggled. "I think he was talking to me."

"It was meant for both of you."

We headed for the church entrance. On the steps, I could see the rest of the squad. Megan McDonald walked up and embraced Kozlowski. Everyone was in a somber mood. As a group, we entered the church and moved to pews on the left side near the altar. The first ten rows of seats on the right were filled. There was a mixture of people from different generations. Some former students gathered along with teachers, both current and retired. Word traveled fast.

Monday afternoon, I had pulled Donna and Laura aside and asked them to contact any of the faculty and the students who attended during the time Charity was there. Laura also had the list of calls that resulted from Olivia's feature story on the news last week. They worked their magic, tracking down people and explaining the situation. Many agreed to attend the service without hesitation.

Sister Augusta caught my eye as I escorted Simone to a seat in the second row. She gave me a deep nod, folded her hands over her heart and smiled her thanks. I nodded and settled in for the service. In front of the altar was a small stand with a blue-and-white marble urn. On an easel to the side was a picture of Charity, taken during a school event. It showed a wide smile, sparkling green eyes and shoulder-length black hair. Looking at that photo and the urn so close by was enough to break your heart. Simone clutched my hand. I noticed Jamie did the same thing with Malone.

There was time to take another glance across the aisle. I recognized several of the faculty members we spoke to last week. Alain Bisset tipped a wave in my direction. In the row behind him were Elizabeth Quick and Samantha Crosby. A young couple walked slowly up the center aisle and stopped beside me. Nancielle Chandler was in a black suit with a white blouse. The skirt was short enough that the nuns would have come running with a ruler in other circumstances. Her blonde hair was loose across her shoulders and draped down her back. She was clutching the arm of her husband, David. I managed to stand and shake his hand before Ellie started to crumble. She gave me a brief hug. He guided her into the pew behind us.

Angela Durfee, the English teacher, was next to Eric and Ruth Metcalfe. Sister Mary Margaret, looking official in a modern version of the old nun's habit, was on the far side of the aisle, quietly greeting some of the teachers and former students. Her voice was a low murmur. Our eyes met. She nodded once over clasped hands and moved along.

The music started, a traditional funeral hymn. Turning to watch the procession with an altar boy leading Father Dovensky up the aisle, I saw Naughton, Giles, O'Connell, and the rest of Squad Five, two rows behind me. They shared a pew with Yekovich and Pinky from the Cyber Unit. A solitary figure was further back on the right side of the church. There was also a couple one row closer who looked out of place but vaguely familiar.

Father Dovensky had never known Charity Gray.

Yet he did a masterful job, mixing anecdotes with prayers and passages from the Bible. Several people came forward and told brief stories about their experiences with Charity. Sister Mary Margaret spoke with tears flowing down her cheeks and a cracking voice, describing the young girl and her vitality. David Chandler spoke as well, commenting about Charity's energy, her sense of humor and the friends she had made during the freshman year.

After the service, people began slowly milling toward the exit. Dovensky had led the way, following the altar boy. The nuns streamed out behind him and an informal line formed. They began thanking everyone for taking the time to remember Charity Gray. The squad gathered by the altar, letting the others depart first. Laura, Donna and Megan stepped up and formed a loose semicircle around the urn. Megan bowed her head and said a quick prayer. Each woman gently touched the marble container before coming back. My attention shifted as someone approached us.

FBI Special Agents Banks and MacGregor came forward. "Thanks for letting me know about this. It was a nice way to remember who the real victim was in this whole mess," Mac said. He turned to chat with the rest of the squad.

I introduced Simone to Banks. "You look ten times better than the last time I saw you. How's the recovery?" I asked.

"I'm doing good. And it's given me some time to reflect."

"Any decisions come out of that?"

Banks smiled shyly. "I like my job. And I'm good at it. So is Mac. I'm requesting a transfer to the Ann

Arbor office. That should help eliminate any conflict with the two of us dating."

"Sounds like a good plan," I said.

"Yeah, we think so too. See you around, Chene."

"Take care, Robin."

Simone looked at me with big eyes. "Wait! Her name is Robin Banks. And she's an FBI agent. What the hell?"

"Don't swear. You're in a church."

"But Robin Banks!" Simone giggled.

"It's a long story." I leaned in and whispered in her ear. "I'll tell you later."

The solitary visitor came forward. Now that she was out of the shadows, I recognized Diana Trevino, Leo Agonasti's lawyer. Since arriving at the church, Simone had remained at my side. I introduced her. Diana gave her a friendly smile and a light handshake.

"I just wanted to express my thanks for all of your efforts on this case, Chene. It's nice to know that the federal government is no longer searching for one of my clients," she said quietly.

"Talked to Leo lately?"

She shook her head. "Not a peep. Nothing from Leo or Max. But then, that's not unusual. However, I've been asked to convey a message."

"If you haven't heard from Leo, how did you get a message?"

Diana's expression remained nonplussed. "The firm manages the legal affairs and concerns for many diverse aspects. One of my colleagues specializes in entertainment law. She has a client who is a very successful Hollywood actor and producer. He's interested in speaking with you about this and some of your other cases. He believes there could be sufficient material for a movie or perhaps a television series."

I was skeptical. "The state police has a public information office that takes care of such requests."

"This person is currently residing in France. They have a villa just outside of Paris. They will be there for the next three to four months. The ideal situation would be for you and Simone," Diana faced her and said, "may I call you Simone?"

"Of course."

Diana smiled again. "Thank you. As I was saying, the ideal situation would be for you and Simone to travel to France on vacation. You would be his guests at the villa. And he's willing to charter a private jet to bring you there and back."

"Agonasti has a long reach."

"I haven't spoken to Leo. This message was relayed through my associate." Diana had a business card pinched between the first two fingers of her right hand. She started to extend it, then rolled her wrist just enough so I could see something written on the back. "Thank you again for everything you've done."

"You're very welcome. Something tells me that our paths may cross again, Counselor."

"One never knows what the future may hold."

Diana gave us a small nod, turned, and left the church. The rest of the squad was outside now. Simone and I strolled toward the rear entrance. There was a cluster of people just off the marble steps. Kozlowski was in conversation with Angela Durfee, lightly holding her hand. She appeared to be clinging to every word. Father Dovensky was still in his vestments. He wrapped Megan McDonald in a bear hug. She'd known

287

him for more than twenty years. It had become their traditional way of greeting.

I stopped in front of the priest. "That was a beautiful service, Father."

"Considering how infrequently you attend Mass, I'm going to take that as quite a compliment, Jeff." He turned slightly, bringing his gaze to Simone.

"Father Dovensky, this is my lady. Simone Bettencourt."

The old guy took her hands in both of his. "So, Miss Bettencourt, I understand that you've been dating Jefferson for a little while now."

"Almost six months," she replied, giving the priest a timid look.

"We should have coffee some morning. I'm sure there are a few tales about his past that he has yet to share. They could be…enlightening."

Simone flashed a wide smile, her eyes twinkling. "Why do I get the feeling, Father, that you've been waiting a long time to tell these stories to someone?"

"My dear, you have no idea. He became very adroit at making excuses."

Before I could attempt to redirect the conversation, a firm hand gripped my arm. I turned and was confronted by Sister Augusta and Sister Mary Margaret. They guided me over to the side of the convent where the little garden was.

"We've received permission from the archdiocese to intern Charity's ashes here," Sister Augusta said solemnly. "It seems fitting. And we can always visit her as we go about our duties for the school, the church and the community."

"That's a great idea," I said.

"Tell him the best part," Mary Margaret urged.

The principal cleared her throat and smiled. "We've received an anonymous donation to the school, with the understanding that it establishes scholarships in Charity's name. There is enough money to cover tuition and fees for three students each year. An investment fund will be established, so the scholarships will be sustained in perpetuity."

"That's a very generous anonymous donor," I said.

"You wouldn't have any idea who that might be, would you?" Mary Margaret asked. She was giving me a glare that would have sent a teenager running. Or confessing to a truckload of sins they had never committed.

"Not a clue, Sister."

She scoffed. "Some detective you are."

"Mary Margaret! Sergeant Chene has done a great service for Charity and for us as well." Sister Augusta gave her a frustrated look.

The nun brought her hands together as if in prayer. "My apologies, Chene."

"No worries, Sister."

"Thank you for everything, Sergeant. And please, extend my thanks to your associates as well," Augusta said. She gently took my hand and gave me a warm smile. "Come along, Mary Margaret."

The second nun glared at me, then shook her head and chuckled. "Take care, Chene. Keep doing God's work."

"I think that's more in your purview than mine."

"Goes to show you never can tell."

I took a step back, unable to suppress a grin. "Are you quoting Chuck Berry, Sister?"

"Nah, he was quoting me," Mary Margaret said, with a wink and a smile.

Turning to head back to the church, I saw one more person waiting to talk to me. Olivia Sholtis was dressed in a black suit with a turquoise blouse. Her dark hair was brushed back. Thin gold earrings dangled from her lobes. She came up and took both of my hands in hers, just as Dovensky had done with Simone.

"Thanks for the exclusive. It's always a treat when I can scoop Channel Seven. It was sweet of you to let me know about the funeral service," she said.

"I appreciate your help."

"I snuck in the back of the church for the Mass. After everyone is gone, I'll do a quick wrap-up from the front steps. The last thing I wanted to do is invade someone's privacy as they remember this poor girl."

"That's a good idea. Very thoughtful of you."

Olivia released my left hand and brushed her hair back from her forehead. "I couldn't help but notice a lovely young lady at your side during the service."

"Don't start!"

"C'mon, Chene. It's the perfect opportunity. I'm here. You're here. She's here. We can have a little chat. Talk about that interview I've been pestering you about. I can do background now." Olivia laughed. "It doesn't have to be on camera. Just to help flesh out the story and…"

"Go away."

Chapter Twenty-Four

Coast guard marker seventeen was just up ahead. The speedboat had performed well, skimming across the lake. I was getting spoiled having it at my disposal. In another couple of months, it would be time to have it pulled and stored for the winter. I'd have to talk with Ted about that, since the owner was a lady friend of his. It was a perfect night for a cruise, with just a handful of thin clouds dotting the sky. I cut the throttle and angled toward the shoreline where the row of vacation cottages bordered the water. It was a few minutes before the appointed time, but I suspected Agonasti was already in the area. The note on Diana's business card wasn't much of a surprise.

The skiff he used Thursday night was not in sight. Scanning the horizon, I realized there was another channel off to my right, where the ore freighters ran between Lake St. Clair and Lake Huron. Other large vessels used this as well to bypass the cottages. A yacht exited that channel and made a wide sweeping turn in my direction. There was a pair of binoculars on the shelf beside the controls, but I didn't need them. I kicked the throttle up a notch and headed out to meet him.

The yacht slowed to an idle in the middle of the South Channel. I matched its speed and drew up alongside. No one was on the bridge in the open air above. Leo Agonasti stepped out of the port side door onto the walkway. He flashed a wide smile. Max appeared at his shoulder.

"I see you got my message," Leo said.

"Seems to me Diana was delivering more than one."

He showed no confusion at that. "I wanted to thank you in person for everything you did."

"All part of the job, Leo." I looked at Max. "Nice shooting on Friday. Obviously, you haven't lost your touch."

"I have no idea what you're referring to," Max said. The fact that he was able to say this while maintaining a straight face impressed me.

"Don't suppose you had anything to do with an anonymous scholarship donation to the school?"

Leo Agonasti shrugged. "School? What school?"

"You guys are something else. Remind me never to play poker with you two. Any other reason you wanted to meet out here on the water again, Leo?"

The two old men exchanged a glance. Leo nodded. Max pulled a phone from his pocket, hit a button, and waited all of ten seconds before it was answered. He muttered what sounded like 'go' into the phone, ended the call, and pulled the battery. Old habits do indeed die hard.

"I know you won't accept a gift from a grateful friend for what you did for me. Neither would your colleagues, especially Captain Cantrell. However, just saying thank you will never be enough," Agonasti said. He was leaning on the teak railing, looking at me with a devilish grin. "The next time you visit Sharkey's fine establishment, you'll learn that a special bottle of bourbon has been placed on reserve for you, the captain, and your associates to enjoy. This is a unique bottle."

Leo extended a promotional card about half the size of a sheet of paper. It announced the release of a special reserve brand of bourbon from Pappy Van Winkle. This stuff was expensive as hell.

"A delivery was just made to your friend Ted. The bottle will not be kept behind the bar but in a special locker. The distributor will check on the bottle periodically and replace it if it's running low." Agonasti threw me a salute and turned toward the cabin.

"So, what now, Leo? Business as usual for you and Max?"

That got me a laugh. "We're retired, Jeff. We're not in business anymore."

Max stood at the railing. I saw Leo appear on the upper bridge, settling in by the controls. The big diesel engines started pushing the yacht forward. Max sketched a wave as Agonasti executed another wide turn and headed in the general direction of Port Huron.

I waited until the yacht was out of sight. Then I gave the throttle a nudge and headed for home.

A word about the author…

Yes, my name really is Mark Love. I am a Michigan native who lived for years in the Metro Detroit area, where crime and corruption seem to be at the top of everyone's news. So there's always the chance to find something that can trigger a story idea and enough interesting characters to jump-start your imagination.

One of my passions has always been writing. I was even able to parlay that for a while, working as a freelance reporter for a couple of newspapers in the Detroit area. Writing features and hard news helped me hone my talents. But while newspaper work was interesting and paid a few bills, it was a far cry from the fiction writing that I truly enjoy the most.

I'm drawn to mysteries and thrillers, the kind of stories that have a fast pace, that keep you moving and keep you guessing as to what's going to take place next. Quirky or memorable characters are essential to a good tale. Mix those in with the elements of crime, perhaps a glimpse of the seedier side, and you've got me. So it's been one of my goals to write that type of story.

http://www.amazon.com/-/e/B009P7HVZQ
http://motownmysteries.blogspot.com
https://www.facebook.com/MarkLoveAuthor
https://twitter.com/motownmysteries
https://www.instagram.com/motownmysteries/